from GHOULS to GANGSTERS

THE CAREER OF ARTHUR B. REEVE
Volume 2

Edited by John Locke

Off-Trail Publications

Elkhorn, California

Vintage cover art by Howard V. Brown from
Electrical Experimenter, May 1919

FROM GHOULS TO GANGSTERS:
THE CAREER OF ARTHUR B. REEVE
VOLUME 2
Copyright © 2007, Off-Trail Publications
ISBN-10: 0-9786836-6-8
ISBN-13: 978-0-9786836-6-5

We are still collecting information on the career of Arthur B. Reeve. Anyone having
additional information, or corrections to the current volumes, is invited to respond
to the publisher at the below address.

OFF-TRAIL PUBLICATIONS
2036 Elkhorn Road
Castroville, CA 95012
offtrail@redshift.com

Printed in the United States of America
First printing: November 2007

Contents
Volume 2

I - NONFICTION

Preface

VOLUME 2 OF *From Ghouls to Gangsters: The Career of Arthur B. Reeve* consists of nonfiction materials by and about Reeve's writing career.

The main drawback in analyzing Reeve's career is the relative absence of Reeve's voice. If his estate papers survived—i.e. personal and business correspondence, financial records, diaries, etc.—their whereabouts are unknown. Thus his career must be reconstructed from external sources: his published works, film credits, newspaper articles, interviews, book introductions, correspondence in other estates, and so forth. We've collected all we could find and have been able to significantly boost the amount of information previously known about his life and works. However, precious little turned up from people who knew him personally. Consequently, there's not much insight into what he was really like; and what is known raises many interesting questions which can't be answered short of informed speculation.

Another problem is that Reeve had a vast and varied career, producing a great many works for all available media. **Section III – Reeve in Print and Performance** organizes this information as a readable reference. However, it's not obvious in perusing this material how it all fits together.

These problems are addressed, to the extent possible, in the chronological narrative, "The Career of Arthur B. Reeve," which attempts to reconcile his publishing and work record with events in his life, to both describe and understand his career. One tends to think of Reeve—at least from 1911 forward—as a magazine fiction writer who republished most of his work in book form, and that the rest of his work was a byproduct. Since the magazine appearances and books have been better documented, it's an easy conclusion to make—but it may introduce a bias to the narrative. We know all of Reeve's film credits, but because of the nature of the film business, we don't know how much writing he actually did, or what it might have paid. Of his newspaper work, we've documented a number of articles, but what percentage of the whole this represents is impossible to say. Reeve reported on many high-profile crime cases for New York and Philadelphia papers, but only a small amount of this reporting has been identified. On the fiction side, Reeve republished many magazine stories as syndicated newspaper features; some stories were published as newspaper originals before finding book publication; and some newspaper fiction was never reprinted. Some sections of his life may seem to exhibit reduced activity, but during these periods he may in fact have been producing work for which we have no record, or even work that didn't end up selling.

Reeve also appears to have made enough money off his work to support a reasonably well-off lifestyle: supporting his family, living where he chose, maintaining an office in Manhattan. Yet, there are enough clues to suggest numerous rises and falls in his fortunes, drastic enough to force lifestyle changes. But we don't have a complete enough picture, or the financial facts, to impose clarity on these impressions. When J. Randolph Cox first compiled a bibliography of Reeve's works for *The Armchair Detective* in the '70s, the information suggested that Reeve had a boom period of popularity between 1910 and 1920, after which his star faded, forcing him to make his living primarily from the pulps. Yet, with the addition of much new information, a sharp turning point in Reeve's career has not made itself apparent. A long, slow turn in fortunes seems more likely. Still, if we had perfect knowledge, perhaps Reeve's career fortunes would chart like a publicly-traded stock, zigging and zagging frequently with discernable trends emerging from the noise of detail. Regardless, we can conclude that Reeve was a remarkably successful writer who managed to reenergize his career at many points along the way.

Additionally, in Volume 2, **Section I – Nonfiction** includes a number of pieces by Reeve, including articles on crime, and every major piece he wrote about his own career or detective fiction. **Section II**, the Art Gallery, includes magazine cover reproductions, interior art, and other illustrative material from Reeve's career.

(Volume 1 includes a selection of short fiction highlighting all phases of Reeve's career.)

Acknowledgements

THIS WORK IS INDEBTED to researchers whose past works have explored the career of Arthur B. Reeve. Sam Moskowitz was first to write about Reeve in depth, in his book *Strange Horizons* (1975). In 1977, a pair of researchers, John Harwood and J. Randolph Cox, contributed separate articles about Reeve to *The Armchair Detective*. Randy Cox's article provided the first attempt at a bibliography of Reeve's work. In subsequent years, Randy's information was supplemented by Harwood, Victor Berch, and the late John Nieminski, who spent many (we hope, happy) hours at the Chicago Public Library extracting data from microfilm. Randy was very generous in contributing the accumulated information to this project, and obtaining additional materials.

Robert Sampson was the next person to cover Reeve in depth, reviewing much of his available work in a long section of *Yesterday's Faces: Volume 2: Strange Days* (1984). The most in-depth study of Reeve's work can be found in J.K. Van Dover's book, *You Know My Method: The Science of the Detective* (1994), which traces the use of science in detective fiction from Poe to Reeve. Ken's book is indispensable for evaluating the relationship of Reeve's science-based fiction to the actual science of Reeve's day. Ken also assisted this volume by sharing his research on Reeve's life.

Several people helped in further fleshing out Reeve's bibliography. Phil Stephensen-Payne searched his vast digital resources for Reeve citations. Gene Christie helped complete Reeve's listing from *The Scrap Book*. Ed Hulse contributed sage advice and information on the world of silent film serials, as well as a poster for *The Radio Detective*. Dennis Lien turned his library skills onto the Reeve hunt, discovered a number of obscure items, and significantly upgraded the listing of Reeve's British magazine appearances.

Institutions that provided valuable assistance include the University of Oregon, Special Collections; the Trenton Historical Society; the Syracuse University Library, Special Collections Research Center, Street & Smith Archives; and the Department of Rare Books and Special Collections, Princeton University Library, holder of the archives of the John Day Company, and the Arthur Bartlett Maurice correspondence collection.

Last, this work would not have been possible without the assistance and patience of Norm Davis, who allowed me repeated access to his collection of all-things-Reeve. The original magazines that Reeve appeared in are scarce at best and extremely rare at worst. Many of them, particularly the pulps, are not available in any library. Consequently, the reprinting of a number of stories herein make them freely available for the first time since original publication. Norm's contribution to the cause cannot be underestimated.

I thank all of these people for their generosity with time, resources, and encouragement.

John Locke
November 2007

ARTHUR B. REEVE
(1880 - 1936)

The Career of Arthur B. Reeve
By John Locke

ARTHUR B. REEVE dubbed his first detective story, "The Silent Bullet," a "commuter." It made the rounds of the publishing houses. It visited the desk of Robert H. "Bob" Davis, famed Munsey editor, and commuted onward from there. It was a decent story, well worth publishing. But perhaps Davis was swamped in inventory at the time. Perhaps he found the emphasis on the technology of crime detection a bit passive for his readers. At any rate, fate kept the story from the pulps and Reeve got "kicked upstairs" to *Cosmopolitan*.*

Cosmopolitan not only took the story but many more based on Reeve's detective, Craig Kennedy. The series was a quick hit in a magazine on the rise. Reeve eventually published eighty-two Craig Kennedy stories in *Cosmopolitan*, from October 1910 through August 1918. His neighbors in the pages of *Cosmopolitan* were writers the caliber of Booth Tarkington and Jack London. Reeve rivaled them in stature, becoming the most famous American detective story writer of the time; and Craig Kennedy was nicknamed "the American Sherlock Holmes."

It seemed *Cosmopolitan* couldn't contain Reeve; he expanded into other markets, pulp and slick. Starting in 1912, his stories were regularly collected in hard covers, with English editions following the American. He became as big a hit overseas. The timing of his success was propitious; it coincided with the meteoric rise of the film industry. And the movies came calling. Soon he was writing some of the most popular films of the day. Reeve's fortunes were like the title of one of his early novels: *The Gold of the Gods*.

Until the Gods withdrew their blessings . . .

Like many overnight sensations, Reeve's success took years in the making, which is readily apparent from the outline of his career. Information on his life comes from his record of publications, sporadic news reports, a handful of letters, and (usually brief) interviews. He never wrote of himself in depth, and no biographer stepped forward to fill in the blanks.

He was born in Patchogue, a Long Island town about 50 miles east of New York City, October 15, 1880, the son of Walter F. and Jennie Henderson Reeve.† He grew up in Brooklyn. His reading tastes leaned to the popular: "As a youngster I pored over Nick Carter and all the forbidden thrillers of youth. Later I graduated to Conan Doyle and spent hours with Sherlock Holmes."†† He tried to write his first detective story at the age of 12. He attended Brooklyn's exclusive Boys' High School, and immediately excelled academically. He persevered at writing, entering and winning prizes in essay contests. He made the staff of the school magazine, the *High School Recorder*, his senior year, editing "societies" with another student and contributing other content. He graduated, class of February '99, as valedictorian. His address, titled "American Characteristics," was filled with boilerplate sentiment, but included these comments, telling when considering the champion of science he was to become:

---

* Reeve, "How Writers Make Good," *Writer's Digest*, August 1930.
† "Arthur B. Reeve, Author, Dies at 55," *New York Times*, August 10, 1936.
†† *Trenton Sunday Times Advertiser*, May 22, 1932, in an interview following Reeve's move to Trenton.

> . . . all of us have spent these closing years of the most momentous century thus far in the advancement of the world, preparing to enter the twentieth century, a century which will require of us all those characteristics with which America and American life are so highly endowed; a century destined to eclipse even the previous one in the magnitude and value of its achievements; a century which promises to be just what we make it.*

Reeve spent four years at Princeton University (1899-1903), establishing himself as a polymath, studying "about everything with an 'ology or an 'onomy on the end of it," a standard quote from his brief biography.† He studied politics and jurisprudence with future President Woodrow Wilson, whom Reeve would later count as one of his readers. At Princeton, Reeve established a reputation as a great tutor, and took on other students, five to ten at a time. Some of these were athletes. Reeve facetiously shared credit for their successes on the playing field by keeping them in good standing academically. Reeve's four years were an "age of the gods" in Princeton athletics, and Reeve took keen interest, reflected in the sports articles he would later write.

Continuing his literary endeavors, he contributed to school publications—the *Princetonian* and *The Nassau Literary Magazine.* During his last two summers, he edited the Cape May (southern New Jersey) *Daily Star* with Henry Goddard Leach. One short story for *TNLM*, "The Golf Dream," featured a character named Craig Kennedy. "Craig" came from a cousin of Reeve's; "Kennedy" from a classmate, Charles Kennedy, later a faculty member in Princeton's English Department. Reeve claimed that the name, Craig Kennedy, always reminded him of his college years, "the greatest four years I have ever had." But it was just a name then; the detective came later.

Reeve graduated in June 1903, one of sixteen Princeton men elected Phi Beta Kappa. At the commencement exercises, he received $50 for winning The Lyman H. Atwater Prize in Political Economy.†† He went on to New York Law School. When he learned there were 16,000 lawyers in New York, he decided that writing made for a less crowded field. It's probably what he really wanted, anyway. He soon dropped out of law school and took a job as assistant editor at *Public Opinion* magazine, to which he also contributed articles on science and technology. The position lasted into 1906. He married that year, to Margaret Allen Wilson of Trenton, New Jersey. He met her when he was at Princeton and she was a teacher in the Trenton public schools. Their wedding, at Trenton's Third Presbyterian Church, was front-page news in the *Trenton Times* (January 31). They had a son, Arthur B., Jr., born about 1910, who earned the nickname "Junior" from his dad.††† A daughter, Peggy Jean, was born eight years later.

From 1906 to 1910, Reeve edited *Our Own Times*, an annual. In 1907, in addition

---

* Reeve's high school achievements and activities were obtained from *The Brooklyn Daily Eagle*. See the Bibliography for additional details.

† E.g. *Chronicle and Comment* (column), *The Bookman*, April 1913; "The Scientific Detective," *Dime Detective Magazine*, October 1, 1933.

†† "Commencement Day at Old Nassau," *NYT*, June 11, 1903.

††† A blurb in the *Pony Express* gossip column of *Writer's Review*, December 1934, had this item: "Arthur B. Reeve . . . always leaves his middle initial off his manuscripts because he claims he detests the name it stands for—Benjamin. Nevertheless it always pops up in print—for which he's very much B-Reeve-d!" That would seem to contradict his naming his son after himself. At any rate, we've not invited confusion by dropping Arthur Sr.'s "B.," since that's how the world knows him.

to a brief stint on the staff of *Survey*, he emerged as a freelance journalist, appearing in *Everybody's*, *World's Work Magazine*, *Outlook Magazine*, *The Independent*, and others. Also, in 1907, he started appearing regularly in Munsey's *The Scrap Book*, averaging a half-dozen contributions a year. He was apparently interested in everything and wrote on a wide variety of topics: science, farming, industry, sports, law, crime, fashion, social trends. Through the rest of the decade, his work continued to penetrate new markets: *Outing Magazine*, *Hampton's*, *Munsey's*, *The Live Wire*, *Railroad Man's Magazine*.* He even placed a humorous short story, "The Cat That Didn't Come Back," in the June 1907 *Argosy*, apparently his first published fiction as a professional.

Bob Davis recalled meeting Reeve that year:

> Enter Arthur Reeve, young, blond, blue eyed, full of youthful illusions and collegiate learning. . . .
>
> "I would like to submit a manuscript," said my young visitor.
>
> "Fact or fiction?" I asked.
>
> "Both, in a manner of speaking. It deals with certain established facts through which the reader finds himself led into the higher atmosphere of boundless imagination."
>
> I took the manuscript impatiently and turned to the first page. The title of that manuscript written by the then inconspicuous Arthur B. Reeve . . . was *Greatest of Mysteries—The Human Brain*.
>
> This isn't the time or place to quote any part of that essay except to record that it treated of the manifold complexities of the mind, the tricks of memory, its capacity for cataloguing the priceless and worthless reflections, to say nothing of its myriad ramifications, detections, conclusions, visions, and vagaries through a human lifetime, and last but not least the mystery of its illimitations.
>
> He had taken the thinking machine apart, examined it, put it together again, and offered it at the market rate. . . .
>
> At that time Craig Kennedy, scientific detective, had not been thought of, or else he was so far back in the dim recesses of the author's inner consciousness that articulation had not begun, and yet it was not improbable that the foundation was being laid subconsciously in that "greatest of mysteries," to which the young collegian had addressed himself.†

Reeve confirms that Craig Kennedy was long in gestation:

> Went to New York Law School and was fascinated by criminal law. Hence conceived the incongruity of combining science and law with a Nick Carter who should have both the University and Third Avenue Theatre melodrama in his make-up.††

Reeve's close friend, Dr. Otto Schultze, well-known Coroner's Physician for New York

---

* As described in Mort Weisinger's article, "Pseudonym Sidelights" (*The Author & Journalist*, August 1935), Reeve, upon running into Weisinger in the street, commented: "I used to write articles under a *nom-de-plume* years ago. . . . I did flocks of articles for newspapers under the name of T.D.M.—Too Damn Modest!" Most certainly, any such activity would have preceded his fame as a fiction writer.

† Introduction to Reeve's *The Fourteen Points* (Harper & Brothers, 1925), a collection of stories from *Flynn's* that Davis had instigated.

†† *Dime Detective Magazine*, October 1, 1933.

County, was Kennedy's prototype. Reeve confirmed the connection for a 1923 newspaper piece after reporters pointed out the parallels between Kennedy's fictional exploits and Schultze's real-life experiences. This all came as news to Schultze. Later he said, "I might have dropped the seed of fact, but Arthur made it flower into fiction."*

The "Scientific Detective" Hits the Slicks

The first *published* Craig Kennedy story, "The Case of Helen Bond," appeared in the December 1910 *Cosmopolitan* with a blurb under the title that read: "The First of a Series of Unusual Detective Stories in Which the Professor of Criminal Science Adopts the New Method of Making the Criminal Discover Himself." It was the first of 23 straight appearances and Kennedy was seldom absent from *Cosmopolitan* until the end of the run in 1918.

Cosmopolitan, despite the monthly Harrison Fisher glamour portrait on the cover, didn't remotely resemble the lifestyle and fashion magazine of today. Started in 1886, it had turned into a general literary magazine by the time William Randolph Hearst purchased it in 1905. In the pre-Hearst years, it had also established an identity as a promoter of technology, featuring articles on "horseless cars" and the future of the "aeroplane." It had published the occasional speculative serial, including H.G. Wells' *The War of the Worlds*. In fact, the magazine had been sold to Hearst when the previous owner, John Brisben Walker, became too involved with manufacturing an early automobile, the Stanley Steamer. Hearst turned the magazine toward muckraking journalism, a waning trend, and couldn't lift the circulation much. When Reeve entered the picture, the recipient of good timing, *Cosmopolitan* was making a marked transition to more fiction and regular writers, a period—the early teen years—when circulation about doubled, to a million.†

Following "Helen Bond" was an announcement for January's entry, "The Mystery of the Silent Bullet." It actually appeared as "The Silent Bullet," and that title-format became standard for most of Reeve's *Cosmopolitan* stories. When the first dozen were quickly collected in hard covers, "The Silent Bullet" was both the first story and the title of the book (Dodd, Mead, 1912).†† "The Case of Helen Bond" was split into two. The first 500 words became an introduction, "Craig Kennedy's Theories," wherein Kennedy spelled out his intentions: "I am going to apply science to the detection of crime, the same sort of methods by which you trace out the presence of a chemical or run an unknown germ to earth." A chemistry professor, Kennedy set his sights on becoming the country's first professor of criminal science. The remainder of the story became the second entry in *The Silent Bullet*, retitled "The Scientific Cracksman," which refers both to the method of the story's safecracker, and Kennedy, who deduces the method by duplicating it.

---

* "Craig Kennedy, Scientific Sleuth, Is Tracked Down," *The Olean Evening Times* (New York), April 20, 1923. Schultze's quote is from "Dr. Schultze Dead; Famed as Coroner," *NYT*, July 5, 1934.

† Frank Luther Mott, "Cosmopolitan; Hearst's International," *A History of American Magazines: Volume IV 1885-1905* (Harvard University Press, 1957).

†† The same collection appeared in the UK as *The Black Hand* (Nash, 1912). Reeve doesn't seem to have had the same immediate impact overseas as it is not until 1915-17 that Hodder issues ten Reeve collections in hard covers.

Professor Kennedy's academic work is offstage in the stories. Within the narratives, he functions as a detective. Thus, he has gone down in history as "Craig Kennedy, Scientific Detective," and not "Craig Kennedy, Professor of Criminal Science." It's unlikely, however, that "scientific detective" was Reeve's phrase. He never employs it in the text of the *Cosmopolitan* stories. However, *Cosmopolitan* did use it in *introducing* the stories, starting with the sixth in the May 1911 issue. Reeve must have quickly recognized its value. His first collection, *The Silent Bullet* (1912), bore the subtitle, *The Adventures of Craig Kennedy, Scientific Detective.** In his sales to other markets, e.g. *The Popular Magazine* and *Adventure*, "Craig Kennedy" and "scientific detective" became inseparable.

Even in that first story, the pattern of the series was laid down. The narrator would be Walter Jameson, Watson to Kennedy's Holmes. Jameson wrote for the generic-sounding newspaper, the *Star*. As a case proceeded, Kennedy kept Jameson in the dark. The suspense derived from Jameson's befuddlement in the face of Kennedy's mysterious behavior, which typically involved performing some sort of experiment, e.g.:

> Inside the mausoleum, Kennedy set up a peculiar machine which he attached to the electric-light circuit in the street by a long wire which he ran loosely over the ground. Part of the apparatus consisted of an elongated box lined with lead, to which were several other attachments, the nature of which I did not understand, and a crank-handle. ["The Ghouls," December 1913]

As would become apparent in the end, Kennedy had always had matters completely under control. With the culprit of the story captured or exposed, Kennedy would explain in great detail what he'd been up to, often with scant consideration to what the reader might realistically comprehend:

> "The applicability of the spectroscope to the differentiation of various substances is too well known to need explanation. Its value lies in the exact nature of the evidence furnished. Even the very dilute solution which I have been able to make of the material scraped from those spots gives characteristic absorption bands between the D and E lines, as they are called. Their wave-lengths are between 5774 and 5390. It is such a distinct absorption spectrum that it is possible to determine with certainty that the fluid actually contains a certain substance, even though the microscope might fail to give sure proof. Blood—human blood—that was what those stains were." ["The Ghouls"]

One might assume it was so much verbiage meant to cow the reader with trumped-up erudition, but Reeve knew his stuff. As summed up by J.K. Van Dover, whose book *You Know My Method* contains by far the most perceptive and in-depth analysis of Reeve's fiction:

> Reeve was careful in his research; Kennedy's machines (physical and intellectual) were often of quite recent design, and Kennedy's exposition of their mechanisms and

---

* Howard Haycraft, *Murder for Pleasure* (Biblio and Tannen, 1974), mentions that Reeve referred to *The Silent Bullet* in his *Who's Who* entry by its abbreviated subtitle, *The Adventures of Craig Kennedy*, causing headaches for bibliographers.

their powers was accurate.*

But Kennedy was not a research scientist, a creator of new knowledge. "He does not imagine or hypothesize or test."† Rather, he absorbed and regurgitated the popular science of the day:

> [Craig Kennedy] is the man . . who had the "hunch" . . . that the latest invention of an Edison, a Tesla, or any one of the big scientific sharps is just as important in nabbing a clever criminal as it is in running a trolley-car or adding a speaking part to the "movies." He is up-to-the-minute on every new invention. [Introduction to "The Green Curse," April 1913]

One imagines Reeve poring over issues of *Scientific American* or *Electrical Experimenter* for story ideas. *Cosmopolitan* prompted its readers to imagine scientists poring over issues of *Cosmopolitan*:

> Edison and Tesla have at various times complimented Mr. Reeve on his skilful use of the very latest scientific inventions in ferreting out puzzling crime-mysteries. [Introduction to "The Sybarite," May 1913]††

The inventions have mysteriously evocative names like the vocaphone, the sphygmograph, or the optophone which must have dazzled the readers of the day with a sense of possibilities made unlimited by technology.

Kennedy's deterministic application of science to crime detection reveals a strong attitude toward scientific potential:

> As Kennedy draws upon an apparently endless sequence of technological innovations, the reader obtains the impression that *all* technological innovations *always* work. There are no mechanical failures in the Kennedy stories, and no unintended side effects.†††

And no flawed or counterfeit data underlying the science. No provisional conclusions. No misunderstandings. Every serve results in game, set and match. Reeve's presentation of science comprises a *counter-faith*, especially apparent in stories like "The Devil-worshipers" (October 1914) and "The Voodoo Mystery" (December 1915), when Kennedy turns debunker, putting science face-to-face with the real enemy, superstition. As the magazine touted him, Kennedy was a "wizard of Truth" triumphing over "that other wizard of Sham and Falsehood."†††† Ironically, some of what Reeve presented as science—e.g.

---

* J.K. Van Dover, *You Know My Method* (Bowling Green State University Popular Press, 1994); 162. The book analyzes the use of the scientific method by early fictional detectives. Among others, Van Dover covers in detail Poe, Conan Doyle, and R. Austin Freeman. Reeve is the last and most recent subject.

† Van Dover; 161.

†† After writing a "biography" of Edison, Reeve sent the inventor a selection of his best stories and received a note of appreciation in return. The biography has not been identified, but was most likely a newspaper or magazine article.

††† Van Dover; 180.

†††† Introduction to "The Devil-worshipers," *Cosmopolitan*, October 1914

the lie detector—would eventually migrate into the pseudoscience category.

There's no requirement to hold Reeve up as the soothsayer of future-truth, though. The pressure to produce novel story ideas on a regular basis would have required him to cast a wide net among the theories of the day. In fact, he didn't restrict himself to the hard sciences. Psychological theories, particularly Freud's, turn up on occasion in stories like "The Dream Doctor" (August 1913), "The Soul-Analysis" (May 1916), and "The Psychic Scar" (April 1918). Freud's architectural view of the mind, with secret chambers to be unlocked, lends itself to the puzzle-solution structure of the detective story. It's a simple step to view the brain as a mind-machine to be disassembled and repaired with the right tools.

The Fictionist Broadens His Markets

As the Craig Kennedy stories poured forth, Reeve's journalistic career took a back seat. The regular appearances in *The Scrap Book* continued through 1911, but Reeve is primarily known as a fiction writer after that. He wrote occasional adjunctive material like his article for the July 10, 1913 *Independent*, "In Defense of the Detective Story." There are also scattered examples of crime articles he wrote, both for local newspapers and syndication. These examples suggest that his now-famous name allowed him to publish commentary on the most-publicized crimes of the day. But he's generally presented as the author of Craig Kennedy.

Following a trend, the second dozen Craig Kennedy stories were collected in hard covers as *The Poisoned Pen* (Dodd, 1913). The magazine rated Kennedy second only among readers to George Randolph Chester's conman, "Get-Rich-Quick" Wallingford.*

Reeve was rolling. In 1912, he broadened his scope with two 50-page Craig Kennedy stories, which appeared in *The Popular Magazine* (May 1 & July 1 issues). The first one, "The Green-goods King," sold to Street & Smith on December 15, 1911, which shows how quickly Reeve diversified his fiction markets. They sold (as did all his stories for *The Popular*) for a whopping $800 apiece, an indication of how hot a commodity he'd become. That May 1 issue ran ads for the top-of-the-line mahogany Victor-Victrola record player for $200, government jobs as railway mail clerks for $90 a month, an oak round-table with six matching chairs for $18.75, and Remington typewriters for $12.

Whether C.P. Narcross, *Cosmopolitan's* editor at the time, regretted losing the exclusive on the scientific detective isn't known. It could be that the stories for *The Popular* were inappropriate due to their length. The *Cosmopolitan* Craig Kennedys run around 7-8000 words, a fourth as long.

Meanwhile, the *Cosmopolitan* stories were syndicated and reprinted in newspapers, another avenue of income for the most successful authors, and one which would have built Reeve an even larger audience.

Later in 1912, Reeve put his detective credentials to good use, writing his first of four episodes of "Detective Burns' Great Cases," a series running in *McClure's* that William J. Burns co-wrote with a variety of authors. Burns was a former chief of the Secret Service who had established his own private-detective agency, calling himself "The Internationally

---

* Introduction to "The Steel Door," *Cosmopolitan*, November 1911.

Famous Sleuth."*

Reeve disappeared from *Cosmopolitan* briefly between November 1912 and April 1913. He turned up instead in *Hearst's Magazine*, formerly *The World To-Day*, acquired by Hearst in 1911 and renamed *Hearst's* with the issue of March 1912. Although the magazine published fiction, especially the work of English and European writers, its main emphasis was public affairs. The circulation stayed flat and, like *Cosmopolitan* before it, Hearst concluded it needed to become an entertainment magazine dominated by big-name fiction.† This shift roughly corresponds to the time Reeve made four straight monthly appearances in *Hearst's* with Craig Kennedy tales that would have been equally at home in *Cosmopolitan*. No doubt, Reeve was moved over temporarily to induce loyal *Cosmopolitan* readers to take a look at the new magazine, another mark of Reeve's popularity.

The Detective Burns bylines continued into 1913. Three more stories appeared in *The Popular*, in 1913 and '14, all longer pieces split into 2-part serials. The second serial, *The Scientific Gunman: An Adventure with Craig Kennedy, Scientific Detective* (January 1 & 15, 1914), made it into hard covers as *Guy Garrick*, Craig Kennedy's name having been changed. Garrick was not a professor, but an educated young man who had studied "the new criminal science" abroad. The narrator of the book was another journalist, the editor of "*The Scientific World.*" The novel, expanded to over 300 pages, was published by Hearst's International Library, Reeve's American publisher for nine books through 1916, and one wonders whether bringing the material back into the Hearst fold necessitated the character's name change. Garrick also appeared, through 1914, in a series of shorts for *The Red Book Magazine*, but these are told sans narrator. The first *Red Book* story, "The Sleep Maker" (May 1914) was incorporated, with character names changed, into the *Guy Garrick* novel.

These confusing circumstances highlight a major issue facing Reeve's bibliographers. Much of Reeve's fiction was reworked, retitled, and otherwise recycled. For example, starting with his third Craig Kennedy collection, *The Dream Doctor* (Hearst's, 1914), the short stories were stitched together into a pseudo-novel format, the gimmick being that Jameson is assigned by the *Star* to follow Kennedy for a month as he solved various cases. Sometimes, the chapter names correspond to the magazine story titles. At other times, the magazine stories start in the middle of book chapters. And sometimes, magazine stories were expanded into multiple chapters, teasing the magazine collector with chapter names like "The Weed of Madness" and "The Perpetual Motion Machine," which end up being simply parts of other magazine stories. Anomalies, where known, are noted in Section IV of this volume. A complete untangling of the roots and branches of his fictional works, we leave as a long-term exercise for the reader.

Reeve remained popular with the public but one senses, for the critics, the bloom abandoning the rose, as in this comment from the *New York Times* review of *The Dream Doctor* (May 24, 1914):

---

* Curt Gentry, *J. Edgar Hoover: The Man and the Secrets* (W.W. Norton & Company, 1991). In 1921, William J. Flynn was fired as head of the Bureau of Investigation (the original name of the FBI). Burns, a boyhood friend of the Attorney General, replaced him; and was replaced in turn by J. Edgar Hoover in 1924.

† Mott, *A History of American Magazines: Volume IV 1885-1905*. *Hearst's* was renamed *Hearst's International* in 1921 and in 1925 merged with *Cosmopolitan* to become *Hearst's International Combined with Cosmopolitan*.

> The detective, especially the scientific detective, with his array of unpronounceable instruments for his emotional clinics, is becoming a little too pervasive nowadays. His methods are hard to follow, and we begin to distrust his omniscience. These things tend to take the edge off the keenness of appetite with which we were wont to devour anything that called itself "a detective story."

It seemed that *Cosmopolitan* wasn't enough for Reeve. He had the energy and ambition, and perhaps the freelancer's fear of putting all his eggs in one basket, to produce more than the story a month that *Cosmopolitan* absorbed. In 1913, in addition to *Cosmopolitan*, *The Popular*, and *McClure's*, he started a series for *Pearson's Magazine* featuring Constance Dunlap, Woman Detective, whose principal novelty seems to have been in not being a man. She is acquainted with the latest that science has to offer the detective, but to a lesser degree than Kennedy/Garrick.

For a while, it must have seemed that Reeve was everywhere. May '14 was a particularly good month. Reeve appeared in *Cosmopolitan*, *Red Book*, *Pearson's*, and both biweekly issues of *The Popular*. In 1914, he also added *Adventure* to his list of conquests, publishing two 58-page Craig Kennedy stories. The Hearst organization may not have minded the ubiquity of one of their star authors since they were publishing everything in book form, including Reeve's first formal novel, *The Gold of the Gods* (1915), whose plot revolves around an accursed Incan dagger.

The Silver Screen

Then the movies happened. We don't know whose idea it was, but the Hearst name provides a nexus between Reeve and the burgeoning film industry. We do know that Reeve had considered the possibility of film adaptations early on. Of his five sales to *The Popular*, he reserved "dramatic rights" for the first three; that expanded to include "motion picture rights" for the final two (sales made February 28 and December 19, 1913).*

In the early days of film, serials preceded features as a medium, since the "chapterplay" more readily adapted itself to theaters accustomed to showing one- and two-reel shorts. It soon developed that "cliffhanger" endings were the most successful in drawing the audience back for the next chapter. Thus were damsels placed in metronomic distress. Early serials bore titles like *The Hazards of Helen* (1914) and *The Mysteries of Myra* (1916). The best-remembered, though not the best-regarded, is *The Perils of Pauline* (1914), the entrée of the Hearst company into film production, in collaboration with French filmmakers, Pathé. The serial succeeded brilliantly and turned star Pearl White into "the queen of the silent serial." Pathé quickly followed up with *The Exploits of Elaine*, a 14-parter released in late 1914. It featured Pearl White, and increased production values, including a better script, officially penned by Charles W. Goddard, scenarist for *Perils*, and Reeve.† *Exploits* also featured

---

* Data obtained from Reeve's pay cards in the Street & Smith Archives, Syracuse University. See A1: Sales to Street & Smith for additional info.

† Basil Dickey (1880-1958) described co-writing *The Perils of Pauline* with his brother-in-law Charles W. Goddard. Dickey claimed to have written *The Exploits of Elaine* next, based on Reeve's *Cosmopolitan* stories. (Vera Williams, "He Wrote 'The Perils of Pauline.' " *Independent Press-Telegram Southland Magazine*, Long Beach, September 9, 1956.) Dickey has a long history of official screen credits from 1916 forward; as well as pulp credits in *Adventure*, *Blue Book*, *Snappy Stories*, etc.

Craig Kennedy as hero, employing science to alleviate Elaine's distress. The villain was nicknamed "The Clutching Hand," a pulpier notion than Reeve's *Cosmopolitan* readers would have recognized, suggesting the broader appeal of the movie. Reeve novelized the story for book publication in 1915; by Hearst, of course. Success spawned two sequels in 1915. *The New Exploits of Elaine* (10 parts) and *The Romance of Elaine* (12 parts) continued the adventures with a new villain, Wu Fang, added to the mix. Both sequels were combined and novelized as *The Romance of Elaine* (minus five chapters from *The New Exploits*) (Hearst's, 1916). In a strange anomaly, both sequels received separate novelizations for UK publication. *The New Exploits* became *The Romance of Elaine*, while *Romance* became *The Triumph of Elaine* (both Hodder & Stoughton, 1916).

Nineteen-fifteen was the year Craig Kennedy finally made it to the stage. The idea had been long in developing. In June of 1911, James K. Hackett, an actor with a personal fortune, announced that he would appear in a dramatization based on the *Cosmopolitan* stories. But it wasn't until 1913 and '14 that the play got underway, garnering notes in stage news columns. The title was announced in March 1915: *The Man in Request*. By this time, Hackett was producing; Brandon Tynan wrote the adaptation and directed. The actor chosen to play Craig Kennedy was Calcutta-born English actor, Norman Trevor, who had appeared on the American stage since 1913. Trevor must have wanted the role badly because, to accept it, he turned down an invitation to cross the Atlantic with celebrated theater manager Charles Frohman, who was making his annual pilgrimage to London to see the new plays. At the end of May, the Craig Kennedy play opened up a New England tour with a new title, *The Bannock Mystery*. It received extremely poor reviews from its first performance in Hartford, Connecticut, Monday evening, May 24, probably its first public performance anywhere. The review in *The Hartford Courant* called it "among the three or four worst plays ever presented." The plot was incomprehensible; the prompter was too much in evidence; and Reeve's scientific crime-catchers didn't translate to the stage. The play was presented in Detroit at the end of June before being shelved. Hackett intended to restart in a few months, but apparently never did, so the play never made it to New York City. It may appear that Trevor made a poor choice, but Fate had a card to play. Frohman sailed on the last voyage of the *Lusitania*, which sank after being torpedoed by a German submarine on May 7. Frohman was killed, affecting Trevor so badly, he didn't act again for many months after playing Craig Kennedy.*

As for Reeve, he had started an association with film that would last his lifetime. At the same time, his publication habits shifted. He appeared to be writing less for magazine publication. Other than the near-monthly Craig Kennedy story for *Cosmopolitan*, and the occasional reprint, Reeve has no known magazine appearances for 1915 through the middle of 1918. After being everywhere, he'd suddenly shrunk to a single magazine market. If the *Elaine* films were that lucrative for him, he may have been taking a breather. The last books for Hearst's International came out in 1916. He returned in 1917 with a novel featuring Craig Kennedy, *The Adventuress*, published by Harper & Brothers, a reprinting of

---

* Basic facts were obtained from syndicated stage-news columns, e.g. *The Stage and Stage People*, *The Oakland Tribune*, July 11, 1915. See the Bibliography for further listings. Additional details on Trevor came from two *NYT* profiles, "Chance and Norman Trevor" (February 18, 1917), and "The Story of Norman Trevor" (November 11, 1917).

a newspaper serial concerning a murder in a family-owned munitions firm and the theft of a new invention, the "telautomaton." Harper, taking over from Hearst's, continued collecting Reeve's *Cosmopolitan* shorts into hard covers. How much of a distraction Reeve's film work may have been in this period is hard to guess.* *The Romance of Elaine* was released June 14, 1915, but Reeve was not associated with another film until a 15-part serial, *The Hidden Hand*, starring Doris Kenyon, and co-written with Charles A. Logue, was released in late 1917. Reeve bylined the newspaper serialization, which never came out as a book. Reeve and Logue also teamed up with *Elaine* star, Pearl White, in a whopping 20-part serial, *The House of Hate*, released in March 1918 which featured a young scientist named Harry Gresham.†

End of One Era

If there had been a calm in Reeve's career, it ended in the second half of 1918. His last story for *Cosmopolitan* appeared in the August issue, thus ending his, and Kennedy's, remarkable run of 86 stories.†† Reeve's departure shortly preceded the arrival of new editor Ray Long who was, over the following thirteen years, to gain fame as the country's highest-paid editor, and one of the best. Long agreed to a contract with W.R. Hearst on Armistice Day (November 11) and took control of *Cosmopolitan* on December 18.††† Notwithstanding the short gap between the two events, it's worth considering whether Long's arrival and Reeve's departure were more than coincidental.

The two men were already acquainted. Long had published six Guy Garrick stories in *Red Book* in 1914, during the middle of his seven-year reign as editor. At the end of the sixth, "The House of a Thousand Murders," ran an announcement that the magazine, with the following issue, would start a new detective series by an English writer, Frank Froest. Considering Reeve's success elsewhere, this was a relatively abbreviated run. But whose idea was it to end the series? In a *Fortune* magazine profile (March 1931), Long's philosophy was paraphrased thusly:

> The publication graveyards are crowded with periodicals which have discovered something that the public has wanted and kept on giving it to them long after the desire for it *has* passed. . . . Thus Mr. Long really functions as a sort of literary barometer, knowing when the rain is coming before the drops have begun to fall. He must be able to predict in advance the point of popular acceptance and the point of popular satiation.

---

* John Harwood, "Arthur B. Reeve and the American Sherlock Holmes," *The Armchair Detective*, October 1977, writes, "Because of Reeve's work in bringing the use of science in the war against crime to the public notice, he was asked to help establish a spy and crime detection laboratory in Washington during World War I." We have been unable to identify the source of Harwood's information. It's plausible that Reeve lent his name to such a cause for publicity purposes, but since he was not in fact a scientist, but merely a well-read layman, it's unclear what practical purpose he could have served. The organization would most likely have been the precursor to the FBI, but Reeve is absent from major histories of the FBI.

† According to user-posts on the Internet Movie Database, imdb.com, a near-complete copy of *The House of Hate* has turned up in the Moscow Film Archive, although we'd hesitate to call Reeve a worldwide phenomenon on that basis.

†† Total includes 82 in *Cosmopolitan*, 4 in *Hearst's*.

††† Ray Long, *20 Best Short Stories in Ray Long's 20 Years as an Editor* (Crown Publishers, 1932). Introduction, vi.

Though Reeve's name never came up, the profile described Long's start at *Cosmopolitan*:

> When Mr. Long took over *Cosmopolitan*, it was full of Robert W. Chambers and Gouverneur Morris, and consisted largely of sex against a background either of high adventure or of high society. Realizing that this type of literary ware was already going into a decline, Mr. Long promptly imported James Oliver Curwood and Peter B. Kyne (from the *Red Book*) and relieved the somewhat stifling atmosphere with the clear, cold Curwood-Kyne breezes from the open spaces.

On the basis of these clues, one could make the case that Long had tired of Reeve at *Red Book* and wasn't about to renew the acquaintance at *Cosmopolitan*. Or that Reeve, on catching wind of Long's impending hire, quit before getting his anticipated walking papers. It's also possible that the timing of Reeve's last story, August's "The Love-Game," was tied to a longer-term contract whose renewal went on hiatus pending the installment of a new editor. Reeve's career, especially through his most successful years, is marked by runs of stories with individual magazines rather than scattershot success.

The situation, when considering a cross-section of his work, looks a little different. At the time of that last *Cosmopolitan* story, he was back in the pulps, appearing in *Detective Story* with a short (August 27, 1918 issue), and two 4-part serials, *Craig Kennedy and the Film Tragedy* (starting July 16), which took the reader backstage into the filmmaking world, and *The Soul Scar* (starting September 17), wherein Kennedy switched his methodology from scientific apparatus to the theories of Freud and Jung. And then Reeve's magazine writing went on hold. The fourth installment of *The Soul Scar* (October 8) marks his last known magazine fiction for five full years. It's entirely plausible that Reeve took Long's impending arrival at *Cosmopolitan* as the catalyst to terminate what had become a tiresome routine in favor of the lure of the movies. But more on that shortly.

One event that must have provided a nice financial windfall at the time his run at *Cosmopolitan* ended, was the publication in 1918 by Harper & Brothers of the twelve-volume *Craig Kennedy Stories*, a reissuing of Reeve's major works-to-date in matched maroon hardbounds with gold spine lettering. The set includes the bulk of the *Cosmopolitan* stories. (The last ten *Cosmopolitan* stories were issued as *The Panama Plot*, a separate book issued in 1918 and not part of the *Craig Kennedy Stories*.) The remainder of the set includes the *Elaine* novelizations, *The Gold of the Gods*, and two books *without* Craig Kennedy, *Guy Garrick* and *Constance Dunlap*. Well, ten out of twelve ain't bad. The set was heavily advertised in leading fiction magazines of the day, *Adventure*, *Blue Book*, *People's*, etc., and, judging from how commonplace and cheap these books still are in the used book market, they must have sold in large numbers. It seems just to deem the set the cornerstone of Reeve's legacy. The separate volumes that were reissued in the set are far scarcer and, had the set never been published, Reeve would have melted into the past a far less accessible figure. The existence of the set insured that he would be easily discovered and rediscovered by readers over the years. Contemporary reprints of Reeve are, for the most part, the texts of the twelve volumes.

All told, Reeve was doing quite well financially. He bought a home in Northport, just across Long Island from Patchogue. He called it his "royalty house," since it was paid for strictly out of book royalties. He expected the income from his next book to finance a garage.* Reeve struck up a friendship with one of his famous readers, Teddy Roosevelt, whose Sagamore Hill estate lay several miles to the west, on Oyster Bay.

While Reeve's magazine writing when on hiatus, his film writing career bloomed. Between March 1919 and September 1920, seven Reeve collaborations were released, five 15-part serials and two features. Industry-wide, the output of serials in 1919 doubled the previous year.† Clearly, Reeve exploited the opportunity.

The first of the seven to hit silver screens was the serial *The Master Mystery*, the film which introduced legendary magician, Harry Houdini, to film audiences. Houdini's knack for dramatic escapes seemed tailor-made for the cliffhanger format of the chapterplay. He and Reeve collaborated on the script, their first of three.†† They must have hit it off, with both men sharing a debunker's view of spiritualism. The film featured "apparently . . . the first movie depiction of a robot," Q, the Automaton,††† although Q is eventually exposed as a man controlling robot armor from within. *The Master Mystery*, as did the rest of Houdini's abbreviated film career, fell short of expectations which, in part, is attributed to the failure of Houdini's illusions to trump the illusion of film itself.

The next release, *The Carter Case*, put the scientific detective front and center. The chapter titles, "The Phosgene Bullet," "The Nervagraph," "The Wireless Detective," etc., sound like they sprang directly from the pages of *Cosmopolitan*. Reeve being Reeve. One ad read, "See the Absorbingly Interesting Uses of Scientific and Chemical Apparatus." *The Carter Case*, released (March 17, 1919) just two weeks after *The Master Mystery*, was co-authored with John W. Grey. The pair had incorporated as "Arthur B. Reeve and John W. Grey, Inc." on December 20, 1918. The address, at 116 West 39th St., Manhattan, was to remain Reeve's office for many years.††††

A month after *The Carter Case*, another Reeve and Logue effort was released. The popular *The Tiger's Trail* starred serial-queen Ruth Roland imperiled between Hindu tiger worshippers and western outlaws. If the subject material sounds off-trail from Reeve's specialties, it's because the original story by Reeve, *The Long Arm*, was an urban melodrama, completely rewritten by Pathé story editor, Frank Leon Smith.†††††

The public then got a four-month reprieve from Reeve before his next Houdini collaboration, the feature-length *The Grim Game*, debuted. Grey was back as Reeve's co-author, the first of four straight films from the pair. In the film, Houdini plays a man wrongfully imprisoned for murder who escapes to find the real killer.

In January 1920, Reeve and Grey returned with the serial *The $1,000,000 Reward*; then in April with the third of the Houdinis, the feature *Terror Island*. It was the last Reeve-Houdini teaming, although Houdini would release three more movies in 1921-23. *The Mystery Mind*, a serial, was released in September. It starred former hypnotist and vaudevillian, Dr. J. Robert Pauline, in a story revolving around hypnotism. Reeve and

---

* Fanny Butcher, *News and Notes of Books and of the Authors*, *Chicago Daily Tribune*, August 10, 1918.

† Kalton C. Lahue, *Continued Next Week* (University of Oklahoma Press, 1964); 71.

†† Lahue, 66.

††† Mike Ashley, "The Houdini Chain," *Postcripts* 6, Spring 2006; 85.

†††† "New Incorporations," *NYT*, December 21, 1918.

††††† Per personal correspondence with silent serial expert, Ed Hulse.

Pauline teamed up again in 1921 for a series of hypnotism comedies for Educational. The first two were to be titled "Spoofing Spooks" and "Fixing Fakers," themes obviously dear to Reeve.*

In February 1920, Reeve signed a contract with Goldwyn Pictures to produce four five-reel Craig Kennedy movies during the year. In April, preproduction was wrapping up at studios in Flushing, Long Island. Decisions were being made on director, cast, and script. Reeve and Grey were there to guarantee fidelity to the Kennedy canon.† Follow-on details for the Goldwyn films, and the Pauline comedies, are not available. Whether they were made, and whether released, is presently unknown.

Reeve's film involvement seemed to take up his time in 1920 and '21. He vanished from the magazines between late 1918 and late '23, save for a pair of non-fiction pieces, in 1919 and '20. His only new books from 1919-21 are film-related: a pair of Grosset & Dunlap novelizations (*The Master Mystery* and *The Mystery Mind*), and a Harper & Brothers reprint of *Craig Kennedy and the Film Tragedy* (retitled *The Film Mystery*, Reeve's original title). In January 1922, a three-dot item mentioned that Reeve had connected himself with a detective agency in New York City in order to study the "new criminal" first hand.†† It may have been his first step in remaking himself from a scientific-detective specialist to a student of Prohibition's crime wave. His views would quickly get a chance to air themselves.

In 1922, he wrote a series of articles for the Hearst papers on the closely-followed William Desmond Taylor murder. Taylor was a Paramount film director who was shot to death on February 1, 1922, a crime which remains unsolved. Bruce Long, editor of the Internet 'zine, *Taylorology*, summarized Reeve's series:

> Shortly after Taylor was murdered, Reeve was hired by Hearst to write a series of widely-syndicated newspaper articles speculating freely about the Taylor murder case. Each of Reeve's articles mentioned drugs, primarily to blame Prohibition for causing increasing drug usage. Reeve wrote from New York and had no personal contact with anyone involved in the Taylor case—he wrote his speculative articles merely in response to the stories and rumors appearing in the press.†††

He wrote a series of articles on the Hall-Mills double-murder later in the year. This case had the advantage of being in his backyard, as it were, Brunswick, New Jersey, a few miles southwest of Manhattan. Reeve always seemed ready to opine on the cases in his locality.

Reeve's absence from the magazines in this period was replaced by his work directly for newspaper syndication. In September-October 1921, a Craig Kennedy novel, *The Black Menace*, debuted as a serial. This was followed in April 1922 by another serial, the 30-part *Mysterious Messages*. The ad copy labeled it "Greatest New Love Serial Story," and a puzzle-solving contest ran in conjunction. In June, Guy Garrick returned in an 18-part story, *On Wings of Wireless*, "the story of super-criminals who seize upon the radio as a tool in their colossal crimes." None of these three works were ever reprinted as books.

---

* "Hypnotic Movies," *The Waterloo Times-Tribune*, June 12, 1921.

† The contract is reported on in "Craig Kennedy Tales To Be Filmed," *The Hartford Courant*, February 29, 1920. Additional details were found in the *Literati on the Coast* column in *The Washington Post*, April 25, 1920.

†† *A Reader's Notes* (column), *The Indianapolis Star*, January 31, 1922.

††† Bruce Long, "Did Drug Gangsters Kill Taylor?" *Taylorology* 94, October 2000.

Starting in late '22, came a series of twenty "Romance-Mystery Novelettes" featuring Craig Kennedy. Some papers ran the novelettes as two-parters, others spread them out from Monday to Saturday. Six of the stories were reprinted in the book, *Craig Kennedy Listens In* (Harper & Brothers, 1923), meaning that Reeve had another two books worth that never again saw the light of day.

A Return to Magazines

In late 1923, Reeve rediscovered his bearings as a magazine writer. His comeback, so to speak, was "Thicker Than Water," a Craig Kennedy story in the *Everybody's* of September 1923. *Everybody's* had been a prestigious magazine in the muckraking era, but its circulation had slipped badly during World War I; it went through a variety of changes in content and format during a protracted period of decline.* In 1923, it was pulp-size on slick paper, and predominantly fiction. As Sam Moskowitz pointed out, Craig Kennedy was not *Everybody's* first scientific detective. Stoddard Goodhue's Dr. Goodrich, "the new scientific detective," appeared in six stories from December 1921 through June 1922, and another two in early '25. Reeve published six Kennedy stories in *Everybody's* from September '23 through February '24, during the period of Goodhue's absence, although we probably shouldn't conclude too much from that. For Reeve's part, the series demonstrated what had become a pattern: that Reeve, with few exceptions, didn't sell stories on the one-at-a-time plan endured by most freelancers. His success at *Cosmopolitan* must have spoiled him, and led him to insist on better deals.

The month after he first hit *Everybody's*, Reeve inaugurated another series at *Boys' Life*. *BL* began publication in 1911 as a magazine catering to a number of youth organizations. It was sold in 1912 to the Boy Scouts of America, and became their official magazine, subscribed to by members of the Boy Scouts. Its circulation rose rapidly. In 1923, spurred by a $100,000 gift to the National Council of the Boy Scouts, the magazine attempted to reach beyond its Boy Scout subscribers. A key use of the gift was to upgrade the quality of fiction by contracting with better authors. The aim was "to drive out pot-boilers, dime novels, and all the mass of Dead-Eye-Dick-and-his-kin cheap thrillers." Reeve appears to have been the prime beneficiary, as he is the featured writer under the new regime.† His three-part serial, *Craig Kennedy, Radio Detective* began in the October issue coincident with announcement of the gift. Kennedy and Jameson were together as usual, but the real star, intended to appeal to the youthful readers of *BL*, was Craig Kennedy's nephew, Craig Kennedy Adams, or Ken Adams, as he was more commonly known, a lad with a none-too-surprising propensity to get into trouble. Ken and "Uncle Craig" featured in eight stories between October '23 and December '24, two serials and six stand-alones, Reeve's only experience writing directly for the youth market.

In November, Reeve hit yet another new market, the flimsy saddle-stitched biweekly, *Mystery Magazine*, a distinctly low-rent magazine that is difficult to find today owing to its extreme fragility. *Mystery Magazine* was edited by the prolific dime-novel author, Luis

---

* Mott, "Everybody's Magazine," *A History of American Magazines: Volume V:* Sketches of 21 Magazines 1905-1930; 85-86.

† "Scouts Mobilize Authors to Fight Dime Novels," *The Davenport Democrat and Leader*, October 21, 1923. (Reprinted in Volume 1 with "The Polar Flight of the ZR-10.") Other popular authors who appeared in *BL* at this time include W.C. Tuttle, J. Allan Dunn, Rafael Sabatini, and Zane Grey.

Senarens, and, though it later became a regular pulp, had the appearance of a dime novel with cheaper cover art. It was an ironic destination for Reeve coming on the heels of the good fight against the scourge of dime novels. It was also an odd destination since Reeve was still riding a wave of prestige, as his preferential treatment at *BL* demonstrates. Odder still was the presence of a co-author, none other than Mrs. Reeve, Margaret W., Arthur B.'s wife of eighteen years. Mrs. Reeve had dabbled in writing on her own, selling the occasional story to women's magazines. The couple collaborated on "I'll Win! I'll Win!" in the November 1, 1923 issue, and then in February/March with a two-part serial. After the magazine converted to pulp format, Reeve returned with "In the Rush Hour" (January 15, 1926), featuring another Reeve heroine, Mary Mannix, a doctor turned detective.

Nineteen-twenty-four turned into another productive year. The series in *Everybody's* wrapped up with "Counterfeit Beauty" in the February issue. Perhaps that opened up the free time needed to write the original Craig Kennedy novel, *Atavar, the Dream Dancer* (Harper & Brothers, 1924), about a man found murdered the morning after dining with a dancer in a jazz club. In July, he hit *Detective Story* with a short, "Craig Kennedy's Greatest Mystery." Then, in August he initiated yet another new series of Kennedy stories in the venerable *The Country Gentleman*, a farm-oriented periodical which dates it first issue January 6, 1853. From 1911 forward, under new management, *CG* rose from modest circulation to a half-million by 1921, and continued to rise, selling well outside its rural constituency. During these years of success, it featured quality popular fiction by the likes of Zane Grey, Courtney Ryley Cooper, Albert Payson Terhune, and Max Brand.* *CG* hired a new editor in 1924, Loring A. Schuler, and this may account in part for Reeve's arrival. Reeve published nine stories in *CG* in a little over a year's time, starting with "Frozen Paper" in the August 30 issue, all with an agricultural theme. This may sound rather offbeat for the highly-educated city-dweller, Craig Kennedy, but Reeve had covered agricultural issues in his journalism days—e.g. "The Potash Industry and the American Farmer"—and had a lifelong interest in the subject. Reeve himself was no longer a city-dweller, having bought a house on the Long Island Sound. "The city is no place to think," he explained. "But, after all, most people don't want to think. They do not dare to be alone for fear that they will think. So they have the radio, the movies, the automobile to help them escape. They have a passion for going places and seeing things, mainly to keep from thinking."† He developed an interest in scientific (of course) farming. As his *New York Times* obituary (August 10, 1936) reported, "Mr. Reeve was an enthusiastic horticulturist and won many prizes at flower shows with his dahlia exhibits." A 1932 story listed him as a ranking member of the Englewood (New Jersey) Dahlia Society. The CG stories were quickly collected as *Craig Kennedy on the Farm* (Harper & Brothers, 1925). The book received a brief mention in the *Times*:

> The Long Island real estaters do not miss many tricks. When Arthur B. Reeve went out there to get atmosphere for his latest book, *Craig Kennedy on the Farm*, they convinced him that the best way to get the full benefit of atmosphere is to buy the land under it, which he did. And now we hear that Mr. Reeve has gone into the real estate business himself and has become a member of the Long Island Board of Real Estate.

---

* Mott, "The Country Gentleman," *A History of American Magazines: Volume II 1850-1865*; 432-436.

† *Trenton Sunday Times Advertiser*, May 22, 1932.

We presume that he sells lots with atmospheric rights reserved.*

Country Gentleman wasn't exactly a slick when Reeve's series began; it was an over-sized nickel weekly printed on quality pulp-paper. But it was a prestigious magazine. When his tenure at *CG* ended, Reeve's career as a fiction writer for quality publications all but ended. From there forward, he was primarily a pulp writer. Which is not to say he wasn't making good money in the '20s, but the slicks paid more, usually a lot more. The days of the magazines making his name had ended. Now the pulps would make their name off of him.

A prime example is *Flynn's*, a new pulp that debuted in late '24. Bob Davis set up the magazine for Munsey's Red Star News Company, but the official editor was William J. Flynn who, among real detectives, rivaled William J. Burns in fame. Flynn had been Chief of the Secret Service for five years; and Director of the Bureau of Investigation for two, before being replaced by Burns, after which Flynn started his own detective agency. The cover of the second issue of *Flynn's* (issue of September 27) featured not only Craig Kennedy, but a photograph of Arthur B. Reeve himself, his writing hand guided by the fictional Kennedy. At Reeve's other elbow is a variety of scientific apparatus. The Reeve story was "Air," the first of four stories comprising "Craig Kennedy and the Elements," the other three being "Fire," "Earth," and "Water." In his introduction to *The Fourteen Points* (Harper & Brothers, 1925), which collected the *Flynn's* stories in hard covers, Davis recounted the casual visit by Reeve that led to the series:

> February, 1924. Enter the creator of *Craig Kennedy*, middle-aged blond, blue eyed, *sans* youthful illusions, but with a trace of dignity and perhaps thirty additional pounds of adipose tissue careful distributed. . . . he lugged a large portfolio under his arm. It was bulging with the paraphernalia of authorship: his own books, other people's books, manuscripts, a volume on chemistry, reports from Scotland Yard, tracts on prison reform, a steel engraving of Bertillon, three pamphlets written by Lombroso in his youth, to say nothing of numerous memoranda and notes for stories in process of acquiring birthright. Whereupon I took his picture in the act of invading my privacy.†
>
> "I have nothing to sell," said he, an observation which placed me instantly at ease and was probably the reason for the more or less flippant dialogue that ensued.
>
> I invited him to sit down and rest his portfolio.
>
> "What's the matter? Is old Craig Kennedy written out? Have you emptied your box of tricks?"
>
> "No one man," responded Mr. Reeve, setting his glasses firmly on the bridge of his nose, "can empty a receptacle into which the entire human race is pouring its best suggestions."
>
> He sat down rather languidly, doffed his Fedora, and passed a plump hand across a high, slightly bald forehead. . . . there lingered in the blue eye that gleam which comes only from men who are born with imagination.††

---

* *Books and Authors*, *NYT*, December 27, 1925.

† The photo accompanies *The Fourteen Points* intro, but is too indistinct for reproduction herein.

†† In one ad for the newspaper serialization of *The Fourteen Points*, the entire Davis intro is reprinted: *The Bee* (Danville, Virginia), June 11, 1925.

Later in the conversation, Davis suggested the series, to which Reeve readily assented. What a turnabout. It was Davis' rejection of "The Silent Bullet" which had led to Reeve landing in the slicks instead of the pulps; now, with Davis recruiting him for *Flynn's*, it was if Reeve had finally sunk back to his natural place in the universe. Still, the featured presentation showed that Reeve was still a star, if only a falling one.

In an afterword to "Air," Flynn remarked:

> In the foregoing story you have had the opportunity of welcoming Craig Kennedy back to magazine fiction. Kennedy has been on a long vacation. Magazine readers who have missed him are going to discover that he has not been idling away his time. Together with Jameson he has been poring over records and notes of hitherto unpublished problems. The pick of the lot he is now presenting in FLYNN'S.
>
> Kennedy is back! And deep in his eyes, lit by the hatred of a strong, clean man for the sneaky and the underhand and the evil, there glows the purifying flame that marks the defender of the right.

No doubt, the "long vacation" referred to Reeve's five-year absence from the magazines, but that was well-past in October of '24. Kennedy's return would only have been a scoop to readers who hadn't noticed him in *Everybody's*, *Boys' Life*, *Detective Story*, or *Country Gentleman*.

Following the "Elements" came four stories comprising "Craig Kennedy and the Compass," to be followed in turn by "Craig Kennedy and the 'Six' Senses." The sixth sense, Reeve's only addition to Davis' original concept, was *common* sense, however, not clairvoyance, or even *uncommon* sense, either of which sounds inherently more dramatic.*

Reeve had had a day when the dazzle of erudition obscured inherent defects in his fiction. That day passed, probably imperceptibly. In a letter published in the October 3, 1925 *Chicago Daily Tribune*, Reeve responded to literary editor Fanny Butcher's query of what book he would rather have written. He replied:

> Now it can be confessed. If it were possible I would call the spirit of Charles Dickens from the vasty deep and make it my very own. In other words I would rather have written *Edwin Drood* than *The Fourteen Points*, *Bleak House* than *Atavar*, created Inspector Bucket than Craig Kennedy. After I had done that I would envy the writers of *The New Knowledge* (Robert Kennedy Duncan) and *Creative Chemistry* (Edwin E. Slosson). Then I would fain acquire the mind and spirit of a philosopher such as Herbert Spencer.
>
> This may all seem incompetent, immaterial and irrelevant. But I envy first the man who creates on paper living types of living men and women; second, the man who understands and can thrill at the great outstanding fact of this modern age, science; third, the man who has the power and ability to delve into the depths of what it is all about.
>
> I think if I were Dickens, Slosson and Spencer I might begin to write.

---

* Woodrow Wilson, Reeve's former professor, listed his famous "Fourteen Points" for resolving World War I in a speech given January 8, 1918. Wilson died on February 3, 1924, the same year Reeve's *Flynn's* series started. The precise choice of title for the book collection may have been a small tribute, and a reason why Reeve contrived a fourteenth story.

Of course, what writer wouldn't prefer Dickens' gifts to his or her own? But when Reeve writes "I envy first the man who creates on paper living types of living men and women," he zeroes in on his inadequacies, suggesting that he'd come to terms with his limitations.

After Reeve's series in the various magazines wound to conclusion in the middle of '25, his magazine writing went on hiatus again. In 1926-27, he published only one original short story, the Mary Mannix adventure from *Mystery Magazine*. Other opportunities emerged to occupy his time.

The most compelling was the continuing success of his first *Boys' Life* story. The series wrapped up in the December 1924 issue. By September of '25, the leadoff story, *Craig Kennedy, Radio Detective* was being produced by Universal as a 10-part serial. It was shot in Universal City, near Hollywood, with some location work done on Long Island. Kalton C. Lahue described the film thusly:

> *The Radio Detective* brought the character Craig Kennedy back to the screen—as a friend of the hero, Eastern Evans (Jack Daugherty), this time. Evans, in addition to holding the secret of a marvelous invention which would revolutionize the field of radio, was a Boy Scout leader. Naturally, an unscrupulous syndicate wanted the invention, known as "Evansite," and tried many scurrilous tricks to obtain possession of it. Jack Mower, as Craig Kennedy, and a group of Boy Scouts banded together to help Evans foil the criminals. The serial appealed mainly to two groups: radio addicts and Boy Scouts.*

The film was released on April 26, 1926 with Reeve's name prominent in the marketing.† Reeve enjoyed boasting of his manifold success with the story, as evidenced by this blurb from the *Books and Authors* column in the August 23, 1925 *New York Times*:

> Arthur B. Reeve seems to be almost as efficient as his favorite hero, Craig Kennedy. He confesses that he recently collected seven times on one story, *The Radio Detective*. He first sold it to *Boys' Life*. Then he sold the motion-picture rights to the Universal Pictures Corporation and was engaged to write the continuity of the story, thus getting two helpings of gravy from the movie people. Then he novelized the screen version of the story and had it syndicated to newspapers. And finally, the story is to appear in Mr. Reeve's new Craig Kennedy book, which is a juvenile entitled *The Boy Scout's Craig Kennedy*, which Harper & Brothers will publish in September. That makes only five payments according to our count, but Mr. Reeve says he got seven and he ought to know. Perhaps he acted in the screen version and it may even be that he directed it. Radio rights and foreign translation rights are still to be heard from, but we may rest assured that Mr. Kennedy will get his.

Reeve lists all seven sales in his *Writer's Digest* article, "How Writers Make Good" (August 1930), the additional two being a lengthening of the original film treatment and newspaper syndication of same. He added, "By the time I had footed up the seventh payment on that story it was netting me around fifteen dollars a word"—a far cry from the original "not much more" than 2¢ *Boys' Life* had originally paid. Reeve ended the article by concluding

---

* Lahue; 127-128.

† See the cover of *The Radio Detective* handout in Section II: Art Gallery, pg126.

that a single work could make an author "rich for life—if the author understands the secret of the capitalization of the written word."

Reeve understood the secret. It's just that Craig Kennedy wasn't fascinating enough to achieve the immortality of other characters who found their way into all available media, Sherlock Holmes and Tarzan being the most obvious examples. Reeve can't be faulted for oversight, though. In July of '26, a Craig Kennedy play was announced for Broadway's crowded schedule. It never got off the ground. Also, from June through December 1926, a syndicated Craig Kennedy comic strip hit the daily papers. Written by Reeve and drawn by future comic book artist, H.J. Flemming, the strip presented two- to four-week story arcs featuring Kennedy and Jameson hot on the heels of mystery, advancing the solution at a one-clue-per-day pace. As one newspaper hyped its coming: "An announcement of greater interest to more readers could hardly be made. The Craig Kennedy detective stories and films have won a large part of the human race as readers of the work of Arthur B. Reeve."* Extravagant praise, but such laudatory comments were not uncommon. Reeve had become an institution. The strip cannot be considered a complete success, however, considering the amazing longevity of many other strips whose duration is measured in decades. And not to forget his traditional arenas, late in the year Reeve published an original Craig Kennedy novel, *Pandora* (Harper & Brothers), about Pandora Paget, a young smart-setter who appears to be working for "The International Catalytic Company of Centrania" in a plot against the government.

Universal must have been happy with the success of *The Radio Detective*, for Reeve was soon back in the film theaters, as co-author (with Fred McConnell) of *The Return of the Riddle Rider*, a sequel to the 1924 western serial *The Riddle Rider*. "The Riddle Rider" was a local newspaper editor who donned a disguise to champion the people. The first chapter of *The Return* bore the intoxicating title, "The Riddle Rider Rides Again." Westerns were obviously not Reeve's forte, so whether he had much to do with the story, or whether Universal simply saw value in attaching his name to the film, is hard to say. As Reeve might have pointed out, if capitalization of the written word is good, so too is capitalization (in economic terms) of the author's name.

Promises Unfulfilled

Nineteen-twenty-seven shows a near-complete absence of Reeve in the public eye. Apart from *The Return of the Riddle Rider*, released on March 8, 1927 but obviously written some months prior, and a reprint of a 1910 *Scrap Book* article in the obscure pulp *Thrills*, there is nothing. In July, Reeve had his New York driver's license revoked for Driving While Intoxicated.† It must have been embarrassing for a man in his position, but the incident never attached itself to his reputation. It may have portended the bad luck to come. . . .

The best clue to his 1927 activities came in a February 1928 lawsuit filed against movie producer, Harry K. Thaw, by Reeve and one John S. Lopez, otherwise unknown in this narrative. It seems that Reeve and Lopez had been collaborating on a novel. Simultaneously, Lopez wrote a scenario (screenplay) for Thaw, of The Lyndhurst Productions Company,

---

* "Craig Kennedy's Detective Stories In Pictures To Be a Feature of Journal," *Hamilton Evening Journal* (Ohio), June 5, 1926.

† "746 Drivers Lose Licenses in State." *NYT*, July 15, 1927. Reeve is listed among 35 drivers in the Manhattan district who lost their licenses. Reeve's office address, at 116 West 39th St., was listed as well.

a new company with a studio at Belle Harbor, Long Island. *The Rajah's Ruby*, for which Lopez received $300, became one of Thaw's first two movies. Both early films "dealt with the spirit world," and the exposure of fake mediums. (Neither were ever sold.) Thaw was so pleased with Lopez's work, he asked for twelve more scenarios for two-reel films, all based on the same subject. Lopez demurred, owing to his commitment with Reeve. On Thaw's suggestion, Reeve was brought into the deal, and the two writers contracted with Thaw to do the scenarios for $500 apiece. The scenarios were delivered, but Thaw only paid for the first two. At the time of the suit, Thaw had abandoned anti-spiritualism movies and was engaged in a new venture "to deal with the more dramatic events of his own life."*

And what might those have been? History records that Harry K. Thaw was the millionaire heir to a Pittsburgh fortune who, in 1906, shot to death famous architect Stanford White in the rooftop theatre of Madison Square Garden. The motive had been a complicated bit of jealousy over a chorus girl, Evelyn Nesbit, who White had deflowered and Thaw had married. It was the most celebrated crime case of its day. Thaw was eventually found not guilty but instead committed to the Matteawan State Hospital for the Criminally Insane. Over the years, he was in and out of asylums, and in and out of one sort of trouble or another, all of which was reported on in great detail in the newspapers. And this was the man Reeve contracted with. It's hard to believe that, as well-informed as Reeve was, particularly in crime cases, he wouldn't have known who Thaw was. We must assume that he did, and took a calculated risk: because Thaw, buoyed by his inheritance, had money; because that goldmine of the movies had gone west and Thaw represented a chance to stay involved in New York. Whatever the reason, it must have been a humiliation to a champion of reason like Reeve to have been taken in, ultimately, by a certified lunatic.

We don't have a clear picture of Reeve's finances, but the Thaw affair may have been a contributing factor when Reeve filed for bankruptcy in September 1928.† He'd had a fallow '27, and the Thaw scenarios may have eaten up the second half of the year while producing no income, and costing him attorney's fees. The bankruptcy petition listed $600 in assets ($300 in household effects, $200 due from his attorneys, and $100 in royalties due from Harper & Brothers), and liabilities of $39,271.82. An astonishing balance. One suspects the contribution of bad investments, unsustainable debts, or long-term living beyond means—but the details are wanting. The filing listed his address as Miller Place, a hamlet some eighteen miles further east on the Sound from his last known residence at Northport.

Nineteen-twenty-eight was not to be another year of invisibility. In fact, Reeve appeared in print a lot. The year resembled his "comeback" season of 1923/24 when he went from absent to seemingly everywhere at once. It strongly suggests that Reeve could "turn it on" when he needed to, and find print markets that would welcome him. His famous name and

* The basic information comes from "Harry K. Thaw Sued By Two Scenarists," *NYT*, February 26, 1928. Additionally, "Thaw Slapped By a Woman," *NYT*, June 16, 1927, indicates that Thaw was producing two-reel comedies. Thaw won the first round, making Reeve one of the few people to lose to Thaw in court ("Thaw Finally Wins a Verdict," *The Clearfield Progress*, February 12, 1930). The ruling was based on the fact that Reeve and Lopez had delivered two scenarios, for which they were paid, and ten plots, which were insufficient to meet the contractual obligation for scenarios. Reeve apparently dropped out of the case at this point, while Lopez soldiered on, getting a higher court to direct a new trial. The disposition of his case was described in "Thaw Movie Suit Up in Winchester," *The Washington Post*, March 27, 1935, by which time the case had migrated to Frederick Circuit Court in Winchester, Virginia. Lopez received a $7000 judgment.

† "Reeve Files As Bankrupt," *NYT*, September 14, 1928.

solid reputation would have made a perfect calling card to editors. It also suggests that Reeve, in his heart, had left the magazines behind and only returned when the film business or other better alternatives could not sustain him.

His first appearance of the year—for which we have a record—was a syndicated newspaper series, *Masterpieces of Mystery*. The feature, which reprinted vintage mystery fiction, listed Reeve as editor and copyright holder. It was a good fit for Reeve. He was well-read in his own field, as he revealed in his essay "What Are the Great Detective Stories *and* Why?" (*Scientific Detective Monthly*, January 1930):

> I may as well confess that my first inspiration came from Poe's "The Murders in the Rue Morgue," followed by impressionable reading of Conan Doyle's "The Sign of the Four" and Anna Katherine Green's *The Leavenworth Case*. (I had devoured "Nick Carter" in earlier years.)
>
> Then, for a short period, I resisted reading detective stories. I felt that, if I did not read them, I certainly could not plagiarize them. But I found that we are all unconscious, subconscious plagiarists; that, as the editor said to the young author, "Some parts of your story are good—and some are original." So I began to collect mystery fiction, hundreds of volumes of it.

Soon thereafter, Reeve hit the newsstands in the May and June 1928 issues of *The Underworld*, a new pulp (first issue: May 1927) that reprinted mystery fiction acquired cheaply, authors from Arthur Machen to Arthur Conan Doyle. Reeve's contributions were a pair of Constance Dunlap stories from *Pearson's*, stories easily available in Volume 12 of the *Craig Kennedy Stories*. They couldn't have been worth much to *The Underworld's* publisher, J. Thomas Wood.

Reeve returned to *Detective Story* in the July 7 issue with the first of six Craig Kennedy shorts that ran intermittently through the October 27 issue. Reeve received a respectable 3¢ a word, a penny more than *Detective Story's* minimum rate of 2¢ a word at that time.

Another set of Kennedy stories started running in the only other weekly detective pulp, *Detective Fiction Weekly* (formerly *Flynn's*), with the September 28 issue. Seven stories appeared in *DFW* over the next year including one 3-part serial, *The Mystery Ray* (Feb-Mar 1929). Craig Kennedy was advertised on several of the covers. *DFW* gave Reeve a shot with a new editor, Howard Bloomfield, who succeeded William J. Flynn earlier in the year, probably due to Flynn's ill health. Flynn died of heart disease in October.

Reeve didn't disappear from the film business in '28, notwithstanding the Thaw fiasco. His author-credit appeared on a 10-part serial released on June 1, *The Mysterious Airman*. The producers were the Weiss Brothers (Louis, Max, and Adolph), who had been making and distributing films since 1919. Their main office was in New York, though production took place in Hollywood. It was the first of several junctures between Reeve and the Weiss family. On October 29, Universal released a 15-chapter serial, *Tarzan the Mighty*. Reeve wrote the newspaper serialization, which bears his byline. His authorship has been questioned, but since he had a preexisting relationship with Universal (from *The Radio Detective* and *The Return of the Riddle Rider*), and had experience writing film novelizations, it may simply have been a convenient hire for Universal.

The *DFW* stories were Reeve's only magazine appearances through most of 1929. In April and May, Craig Kennedy was back in another comic strip. Ads for the strip indicated it was exclusive to the *Syracuse Herald*, where our examples were discovered. The strips ran one-week story arcs and were text heavy, with lengthy descriptive passages underlying each panel. Kennedy and Jameson are central, but the illustrations are practically all-clue and no drama. The strip disappeared after four weeks, making it even less successful than the 1926 attempt.

In late '29, after the *DFW* series had run its course, Reeve began showing up in disparate magazines. The first such was *Radio Digest Illustrated*, October 1929, where Reeve shared the Table of Contents with Amos 'n' Andy and Xavier Cugat. The issue inaugurated a 6-part serial, *The Gigolo Mystery*, which didn't turn out to be as racy as the title implied:

> Who sealed the lips of the adventurous society girl of St. James, whose lifeless body was found on the sinking Gigolo off the North Shore of Long Island? Arthur B. Reeve, author of the famous Craig Kennedy detective mystery stories, brings together a most remarkable group of characters in this amazing tale of intrigue, of love and crime in subtle conflict. You will be thrilled and fascinated as the tale unfolds. It begins here.

The heading to the story emphasized Reeve's connection to the movies. The serial ran through the March 1930 issue.

Starting in November, Reeve landed in Clayton's *Clues* for five straight biweekly issues. *Clues* offered a 2¢ minimum at that time, putting them in a class with *Detective Story*.

In December, a new chain of four monthly titles, the Tower Magazines, was launched. They were distributed nationally, exclusively through Woolworth's stores. The bedsheet-sized magazines carried a mixture of fiction and non-fiction. Some of the author names would have been familiar to pulp readers, and the magazines were considered a bridge between the pulp and slick worlds. One of the new titles, *The Illustrated Detective Magazine*, included Reeve in its first four issues with a Craig Kennedy reprint from *Cosmopolitan*, and an associated feature, "Craig Kennedy's Illustrated Detective News," a spread with true-crime stories and photos. The news page listed Craig Kennedy as editor, which could only have confused readers as to whether the ubiquitous Kennedy were real or not; a longstanding question as revealed by the editor's introduction to "The Black Hand" in the September 1911 *Cosmopolitan*:

> Is Craig Kennedy a *real* detective? Does he actually live and have his being and solve crime-problems as Mr. Reeve says? A surprisingly large number of our readers have asked these questions. One reader—a minister, by the way—said that if Kennedy were a real man he had a "job" for him.

And to those readers who thought Craig Kennedy *and* Sherlock Homes were real people, there were probably no insoluble crimes on Earth, if only those two could have teamed up. Reeve seemed to enjoy having Craig Kennedy as his alter ego. His articles sometimes bore titles like "We're All Detectives Under the Skin, Says Craig Kennedy." In a famous signature book, he wrote, "With Kindest Regards of 'Craig Kennedy' himself."[*]

The Weiss Brothers must have liked Reeve's work on *The Mysterious Airman*, because one of their next pictures, *Unmasked* (released December 15, 1929) starred (the fictional)

---

[*] "Boston Student Has Signatures of Famous Men," *The Daily News* (Huntingdon, Pennsylvania), March 26, 1930.

Craig Kennedy in the lead role. The film was noteworthy on two counts: it was the first feature-length film with Kennedy, and Reeve's first association with a talkie.

A Magazine Made-to-Order

With a date of January 1930, famed science fiction editor/publisher, Hugo Gernsback, launched a new title, *Scientific Detective Monthly*, a bedsheet-sized pulp-paper magazine. It was primarily fiction with a healthy dose of non-fiction features. The concept was made-to-order for Reeve and, indeed, he figured as prominently as Gernsback in the magazine. A banner across the top of the cover heralded Reeve with the title of Editorial Commissioner. In writers' magazine solicitations the Reeve touch was explicitly called for: "Stories of the Arthur B. Reeve 'Craig Kennedy' type can be used as an example of what is wanted." Inside, following Gernsback's opening comments, Reeve provided a 2500-word history of detective fiction, "What Are the Great Detective Stories *and* Why?" The introduction to the article flattered Reeve's contributions to the field and the new magazine:

> Mr. Arthur B. Reeve is without question the greatest living author of scientific detective literature.
> Mr. Reeve first started to write his famous stories for the *Cosmopolitan* and has continued to write these stories ever since.
> Mr. Reeve, as the creator of Craig Kennedy, has perhaps done more for the dissemination of science through the medium of detective stories than any other man alive. Mr. Reeve has always kept within the strict bounds of science; the various instruments and apparatus which he describes in the detection of crime are real scientific instruments, and he has never utilized fictitious methods.
> Only during the past five years have the police departments of our large cities taken to science in the solving of various crimes, and it may be said that Arthur B. Reeve has been responsible for a goodly share of the present adoption of the most important adjuncts to every efficient police department. As Editorial Commissioner of this magazine, it will be Mr. Reeve's duty to scan all the manuscripts before they are printed, in order that only first-class material shall find its way into the pages of *Scientific Detective Monthly*.

Reeve's article hinted at his conflicts over changes to detective fiction since he had entered the field. He referred to "the modern 'smart-aleck' detective so popular with the mystery book clubs," implying a "high art" tradition of detective fiction, of which he considered himself a torchbearer, being eclipsed by disreputable "popular art," the hardboiled school. Reeve's remark betrays a rigidity in the face of change which has doomed his relevance by this time. As the article was being published, *The Maltese Falcon* was running as a serial in *Black Mask*. Reeve's confusion is explicit by the end of the piece:

> Once I thought this was an age of science, and that, consequently, the mechanism of detective stories had undergone a considerable change since the time of Poe and Gaboriau; in fact, that a modern detective story, if it at all aimed at popular favor, should be based on scientific lines. Later on, I departed from that idea. But I wonder which is right?

An original Craig Kennedy short, "The Mystery of the Bulawayo Diamond," followed the article. Reeve had a story in every issue, but the rest were all reprints of early *Cosmopolitan* stories suggesting that Gernsback was unwilling to pay Reeve much more than *Scientific Detective's* paltry ¼-½¢ word-rate for original fiction (the rate for reprints may have been even less).

After five issues, the magazine changed title to *Amazing Detective Tales* for another five issues before folding. Reeve's position remained the same throughout. A pair of authors who shared the pages of the magazine with Reeve for all but the tenth issue were Edwin Balmer and William B. MacHarg with their stories of detective Luther Trant. This is a convenient point to discuss their relationship to Reeve.

Who Invented the "Scientific Detective"?

In his 1913 article, "In Defense of the Detective Story" (*The Independent*), Reeve wrote of the origins of adding science to crime in detective stories:

> It began when several writers tried to apply psychology, as developed by Prof. Hugo Muensterberg of Harvard and Prof. Walter Dill Scott of Northwestern University, to either actual or hypothetical cases of crime. Cleveland Moffet made an early use of it in a story, and some years ago two writers collaborated in the creation of a psychological detective for a popular magazine. But that was only a beginning.
> . . .

The "two writers" were undoubtedly Balmer & MacHarg. They published a dozen Luther Trant stories in *Hampton's* between May 1909 and October 1910. Trant uses a variety of scientific instruments to expose the thoughts and emotions concealed in the brain. Sam Moskowitz first noted the obvious influence of the Trant stories on Reeve. The stories share the same general approach and, beyond that, the first published Craig Kennedy story, "The Case of Helen Bond," borrows the plot and gimmick (the word-association test) from the first Trant story, "The Man in the Room."*

When Reeve later expanded on the subject of detective fiction ("When The Criminal Takes To Science and Its Effect on the Fictionist," *The Forum*, July 1919), he titled one section "The First Scientific Detective Story" and took claim to the crown: "When I wrote my first *Craig Kennedy* story, 'The Silent Bullet,' in 1909 . . . I had endeavored to write the first purely scientific detective story." Here we enter the debate, instigated by Moskowitz, over whether Reeve began to obscure the record in order to cement his reputation as creator of the "scientific detective."

"The Silent Bullet" was in fact the second Craig Kennedy story published in *Cosmopolitan* but the first story in Reeve's initial book collection, *The Silent Bullet*. Moskowitz implies a consciousness of guilt on Reeve's part in swapping the order of the first two stories in *The Silent Bullet*, by removing the obviously derivative "Helen Bond" from the first slot, thus attempting to avoid comparisons between himself and Balmer & MacHarg. The other stories in *The Silent Bullet* all follow the publication order in *Cosmopolitan*.†

---

* Sam Moskowitz, *Strange Horizons* (Charles Scribner's Sons, 1976); 126.

† Moskowitz further suggested that the similarity between "Helen Bond" and the first Trant story may be the reason Bob Davis turned it down. But Reeve's remarks about Davis ("How Writers Make Good," *Writer's Digest*, August 1930), which undoubtedly was Moskowitz's source, don't mention the name of the story. It's

Years after the *Forum* piece, Reeve supplied a 200-word biographical brief to accompany his sole appearance in *Dime Detective* (October 1, 1933). He wrote:

> Princeton, '03, where he created the name "Craig Kennedy" and used character first in *Nassau Literary Magazine*.
> Studied about everything with an 'ology or an 'onomy on the end of it—which accounts for the scientific in Craig Kennedy.
> Went to New York Law School and was fascinated by criminal law. Hence conceived the incongruity of combining science and law with a Nick Carter who should have both the University and Third Avenue Theatre melodrama in his make-up.

However, without providing a direct quote, Moskowitz bolstered his case against Reeve by claiming of the brief:

> Arthur B. Reeve attempted to establish priority over Edwin Balmer and William B. MacHarg for the creation of a scientific detective by citing this early story, difficult to check outside of Princeton University's own library. *It is not the same Craig Kennedy and it is not by the remotest logic a detective story.* [italics in original quote]*

It's clear from the full context of Reeve's remarks that the early "Craig Kennedy" (published in a 1901 story) is simply a character name and that the "Craig Kennedy" of detective story fame developed later. Furthermore, there's no substantive reason to challenge Reeve's word that Craig Kennedy, detective, was born in 1909.

Ultimately, the best defense of Reeve lies in the very pages of *Scientific Detective Monthly* where, according to the magazine, as Editorial Commissioner he approved "all the manuscripts" for publication. He's therefore in print as conferring favor on Balmer & MacHarg, with the "incriminating" "The Man in the Room" in the March issue (although the magazine didn't indicate they were reprints). Reeve also makes a mature point about plagiarism in "What Are the Great Detective Stories *and* Why?" (quoted on page 28), that all writers draw upon their predecessors, consciously or not. It doesn't sound as if Reeve would have avoided the role of Balmer & MacHarg in his own creative evolution—had the question ever been put so directly.

At most, we might conclude that Reeve drew, at least in his mind, a distinction between the Psychological Detective, as Trant was advertised in *Hampton's*, and his own, broader, Scientific Detective; and that, when he wrote in 1919, the creation of the "scientific detective" in *the public mind* was exclusively of his own doing. In fact, at that time, as the ads for the *Craig Kennedy Stories* indicate, Reeve was far more interested in promoting himself as "the American Conan Doyle."

Reeve Battles Crime

Reeve's work appeared in five magazines with December 1929 dates: *Illustrated Detective*, *Radio Digest*, two biweekly issues of *Clues*, and in Street & Smith's *Best Detective* with a

---

the 1919 *Forum* article that makes the linkage between "my first Craig Kennedy story" and "The Silent Bullet." Bob Davis almost certainly rejected "The Silent Bullet." As did many other editors, according to Reeve.

* *Strange Horizons*; 132.

Detective Story reprint from 1918. He had four appearances with a January date: *Illustrated Detective*, *Radio Digest*, the last *Clues* story, and *Scientific Detective*. February and March show three appearances each, with only *Clues* absent from the list. For that brief stretch of time, Reeve was a prolific man of the magazines again. But it was the last time he would have that kind of sustained presence. Henceforth, his publishing record thins out. For example, the remainder of 1930 shows no original fiction. This was due, no doubt, to Reeve's new career in which he penetrated a new medium, making the leap from *Radio Digest* to the actual airwaves.

Around March or April 1930, he hatched up an idea for a new radio show, which was approved by John Elwood, vice president of NBC. It got off the ground fast. Starting in July, the nationally-broadcast show on NBC's WJZ network, bluntly named "*Crime Prevention Program*," debuted with Reeve as host. Intended as serious crime prevention education, the 30-minute show covered issues promulgated by the New York City Commission on Crime Prevention, a citizen's advisory group to the Police Department, and the newly-created Police Department Crime Prevention Bureau, one of a wave of such organizations that had sprung up in the bigger cities. Reeve created the show and co-wrote it with NBC continuity writer, Finis Farr; before beginning the series, the pair took an intensive training course with the police. The show's format consisted of three parts: a drama featuring a detective named Thurlow Wade, followed by a crime prevention talk by a guest speaker (five to six minutes), concluding with a two-minute editorial by Reeve.* The Wade feature would always lead off the show because "more people are to be interested by entertainment than by any other means." If detective fiction had been a vessel for imparting science, Reeve was simply changing the broth.

Crime Prevention Program ran on Monday evenings at 8:30 into October, then switched to 10 p.m. on the WEAF network, another NBC affiliate.

Reeve and Farr worked closely with the NYPD in developing the Wade stories, which were based on actual cases, and meant to impart principles of crime prevention. Police Commissioner Mulrooney was an enthusiastic supporter and assigned an employee to comb the files for useful material. Wade was portrayed by radio veteran, William Shelley, and supported in the stories by Police Lt. MacDonald, played by Tim Daniel Frawley. Wade was certainly one of radio's earliest series detectives. A syndicated newspaper article described the character: "Thurlow Wade . . . appears as a leisurely person, wealthy and independent, devoting his studies to a perusal of crime and the ways of criminals. Wade has developed a remarkable faculty for remembering faces and his keen gaze can penetrate almost any disguise."†

The show's guest speakers included Mulrooney and other top executives of the Police Department, state attorneys, judges, and other prominent civic leaders. Reeve, in his December 26 commentary, branded organized crime the greatest crisis facing the U.S. since the World War, and claimed it cost the country billions of dollars a year. "What we need most of all is a 10-year program to save civilization." He urged creation of a national

---

* See Section III – E: Radio for a list of guest speakers.

† "N.B.C. Lifts Crime Plots From Police," *The Syracuse Herald*, August 3, 1930. Additionally, Farr was author of a radio program called *Mystery House*; he later wrote for NBC's crime drama *Mr. District Attorney*. Shelley later played villain Killer Kane on *Buck Rogers in the 25th Century*. Frawley was later the voice of sponsor Blue Coal on *The Shadow*.

foundation to unite the local crime prevention bureaus.* His language grew increasingly apocalyptic, as in this passage from a syndicated interview, "Who Will Break Gangster's Grip?," published in February:

> We are witnessing the creation of a new feudal system, an extragovernmental government. It would not surprise me at all if 100 years from now our descendants looked back upon the creation of a new dynasty—new families, new social sets, a new "Four Hundred," in short, a new "aristocracy"—an outgrowth of the racketeers.†

When no one volunteered to start the foundation, Reeve must have concluded that he was just the man to spearhead such a sweeping effort. Thus on the last airing of *Crime Prevention Program* (March 20), he announced the creation of the Crime Crusade Foundation. (This was just after the debut of Reeve's last association with Universal Pictures, the 10-part serial, *Finger Prints*, for which he supplied the story.) Reeve's ambition seemed unbounded. "The primary object is to organize a vast body of members with a power against which even entrenched and financed crime cannot stand. Our aim is a Million Members the First Year." He described the structure of the organization:

> Among the Sections of this Crime Crusade Foundation, which is being headed by an executive committee of twenty-one nationally prominent men and women, including many of our guest speakers are the following fifteen, each section with its own chairman and committee—Sections on Banking, Insurance, Better Business, Chambers of Commerce and Boards of Trade, Labor, Civic Associations, Professional Men and Women, Prison and Corrective Organizations, Crime Prevention Bureaus, Boys' Clubs, Big Brothers and Big Sisters, Boy Scouts and Girl Scouts, Women's Clubs, Educational Organizations, and Religious Organizations.

The Foundation would publish a weekly magazine, *The Crime Crusader*. The magazine would sponsor a new radio program to supplant *Crime Prevention Program*, to be called the *Crime Crusade Radio Hour*. The Crime Crusader Newspaper Syndicate would feed stories to the press. There would be a series of ten "short reel talking pictures," "sponsored by one of the big advertisers," which Reeve would write and also appear in. "The biggest job of the next decade is to wipe out this Black Menace of Crime—this Ten Year Plan of the Crime Crusade Foundation."††

There would also be a book on the history of racketeering. Reeve had never published a nonfiction book before, though he'd never retired as a journalist. In a March 25 letter to Critchell Rimington, Associate Editor of the publisher John Day Company, Reeve wrote,

---

* "Crime's Gauntlet Flung Down To U.S. Criminologist Says," *The San Antonio Express*, December 27, 1930. Reeve was already famous; the radio show made him more so. A column item (*Bo-Broadway, The Chester Times*, February 5, 1931) reported on his "daily mail weighted with epistles from cranks and crooks." One letter from Illinois was 125 pages, a single word to a page; another from two farm hands in Pennsylvania volunteered to be his day and night bodyguards; another letter came special delivery, urging Reeve to warn New York about the greater threat from the Soviets.

† Carol Bird, as told to, *The Oakland Tribune*, February 1, 1931.

†† Details about the plans come from two Crime Crusade Foundation brochures, undated but which reprint addresses from the final March 20, 1931 airing of *Crime Prevention Program* and a March 22 newspaper article by Reeve. The address of the Foundation was 150 Broadway, NYC. Reeve was listed on the letterhead as Founder. (Archives of the John Day Company, Princeton University Library.)

"This book will be in the nature of a semi-official volume for the Crime Crusade which will help to put it over big. If you don't do it, someone else must; only I prefer that you should, inasmuch as you spoke first." Whether "speaking first" means that Rimington instigated the idea, or was simply the first to reply to Reeve's overtures, is open to conjecture. Probably the latter. At any rate, Reeve treated the book as an important project. In the letter, he wrote that he had "a mass of material I have been gathering for years for just this purpose." He suggested the title "The Royal Road to Rackets," same as he used for "the leading article in a new magazine which I have just been commissioned to prepare." What this new magazine was is a mystery—Reeve noted that it was not *The Crime Crusader*. They settled on "What Price Crime?," the title of Reeve's March 22 article in *The New York Herald-Tribune Sunday Magazine*. It fit Reeve's thesis better. The newspapers played up violence and colorful characters, but for Reeve it was mostly about the money, the invisible tax on ordinary citizens. Rimington may have had divergent ideas, describing *What Price Crime?* (in a May 19 letter) as a "blood and thunder" book.*

Reeve insisted on, and got, a $500 advance, the same amount, he claimed, as he was getting from Harper & Brothers, though they hadn't issued one of his books since 1926. The contract, dated April 1, called for the complete manuscript to be delivered by June 1, certainly a rush job for a 60,000-word research project, but Rimington may have wanted to strike while the iron was hot. The John Day Company had been preparing a 25¢ pamphlet about Al Capone, but had to drop the project in February when Capone was unexpectedly arrested and imprisoned. By May 19, Reeve's due date had slipped to July 1.

In a June 23 letter to Rimington, Reeve upped the ante. He revealed that he really had in mind a series of three nonfiction books of a "social-philosophical" nature. *What Price Crime?* was merely the first. The second would be "a study of the vast, hidden forces that America is swayed by and has always been swayed by"; "a true history of the United States," which no one had ever written. "Every standard history of our country is not only false but grossly false. We live in fool's ignorance of our own prejudices." And the subject of this "rather sensational study": the influence of religion in politics. The title he fancied was "Render Unto Caesar." Reeve's third "pet subject" was sex: "I have some rather sensational and scientific facts about women—and men." He envisioned a "three-year program" to complete the work. But at the same time he didn't want to abandon mystery fiction. He foresaw three Craig Kennedy novels coming out in the same period. Six books in three years: "it would make a mark." The plan lacked only the opportunity, i.e. commitment from a publisher.

Reeve had long betrayed a messianic view of his own intellectual potential. There was a hint of it in his high school valedictory remarks, in his call to embrace destiny's duty for the 20th Century. And in the comprehensive essay on the human brain he tried to sell Bob Davis in 1907. His 10-year anti-crime program aimed at nothing less than "saving civilization." Now he was ready to write the first true history of the United States.

Alas, the big plans for the Crime Crusade Foundation—the magazine, the movies, the radio show, the book, the organization itself—seemed to have quickly boiled down to just Reeve's writing. There's no evidence the other plans really got off the ground. Reeve's big ambitions, perhaps frustrated in the civic arena, transmuted into another form—or back to his natural form, as a writer—the "three-year program." We don't know why *Crime*

---

* Correspondence between Reeve and editor Critchell Rimington, also come from the Archives of John Day Company.

Prevention Program went off the air. When NBC moved it to a later time-slot in October, that may have been a sign its novelty had worn off. In fact, the notion of a wider crime prevention effort, which arose in December, may have been Reeve's rebellion against the notion that *Crime Prevention Program* had run its course.

Rimington's reaction to Reeve's big ideas is absent from the record. Caution was the likely response. A July 20 letter from Reeve accompanied several chapters, giving Rimington half the book at that point. The complete manuscript had been delivered by early August. It fell to John Day president, Richard J. Walsh, in an August 5 letter, to deliver Reeve bad news. "I am greatly disturbed by [the manuscript]. It seems to me that to put this in a book in anything like its present form would be very bad for us and very bad for you." Walsh guessed that Reeve had gotten "so close to a great mass of material that you have lost your critical faculty." Specific problems were enumerated: confusion in the use of the term "rackets"; summarizing newspaper accounts the public is familiar with, and failing to go beyond them; recklessness in charges against, for instance, President Hoover; superficial handling of large problems, like juvenile delinquency; hastily-written, bad English with a lack of clarity. After the assault, Walsh sounded a note of conciliation: "Now this is very severe criticism for me to hand out to so old a hand as you, and I would not dare to do it unless you were an old hand, and accustomed to the difficulties of the written word." He suggested either setting the manuscript aside for three months before rewriting it for the company's spring list, transferring the contract to another publisher, or repackaging the material as magazine or syndicate articles. In a follow-up letter, Rimington expressed regrets, alluding to Reeve's "personal complications" as a probable major factor in the book's shortcomings. "Personal complications" may have been Reeve's attempt to mask his embarrassment. Other commitments undoubtedly played a large role.

While *What Price Crime?* was in development, Reeve started to publish a series of sixteen 3000-word stories for newspaper syndication under the rubric *Craig Kennedy and the Gangsters*. The first one appeared July 4, and weekly thereafter. Prohibition had already inspired a new genre in the pulps, gang fiction which invited the reader inside the underworld—*Gangster Stories* (first issue: November 1929), *Racketeer Stories* (December 1929), *Gang World* (October 1930), etc.—and Reeve added his own spin. The stories were an explicit outgrowth of *Crime Prevention Program*. The first, "The Murder Contract," opens with an assassination attempt on Kennedy in a radio station studio. Jameson immediately gets to the point: "I knew it! I told Craig his Radio Anti-Racket Program was getting over with the gangsters—as well as the public!" The Craig Kennedy stories once represented the dramatized experiences of medical examiner, Otto Schultze; now Craig Kennedy heightened Reeve's reality. The series provided a guided tour through the rackets, e.g. "The Fixer," "The Gun Broker." The stories stand alone but have continuing characters, in particular Reeve's mob boss Tony Magnifico—the "Big Fellow"—and Roslyn Miller, a gangster's girl. Themes and characters from *Craig Kennedy and the Gangsters* would turn up in Reeve's later pulp stories.

In an August 15 letter from John Day, the subject is Rimington's return of some Craig Kennedy stories, which Rimington hoped to discuss when next they met—which may have put the official kibosh on Reeve's six-book plan. In the end, the contract for *What Price Crime?* was transferred to a new publisher, The Mohawk Press, subjecting them to the terms, depending on what negotiations had yielded. The arrangement can't have been all rosy, judging from Rimington's regrets in a letter of November 24:

I haven't heard any of the recent developments of the reorganization of The Mohawk Press, but I wanted you to know how disturbed I was over the trouble, and I trust you realize that we had no idea that there was anything in any way out of order in their organization. At the time of our negotiations with them we had nothing but the finest reports.

In fact, The Mohawk Press would be defunct by the end of '32. But Reeve's book had been salvaged. Mohawk brought it out in late '31 under a new title, *The Golden Age of Crime*. It was a history of Prohibition's unintended consequences, racketeering, echoing the theme of his reporting on the William Desmond Taylor murder (1922), wherein he blamed Prohibition for increased drug use. As he described it in an interview, two notorious crime cases bracketed his three months of work on the book: "Strangely enough the [Benjamin Collings murder] occurred the night I finished my book, *The Golden Age of Crime* [September 9, 1931]. I had started to write it when Starr Faithfull was killed [June 8, 1931], and I had to stop the job to cover that case."* The work on Starr Faithfull (and *Craig Kennedy and the Gangsters*) accounts for Reeve's initial delays; the September 9 date suggests he did a month-long rewrite for Mohawk. The book was not widely reviewed, surprising considering Reeve's name and the weightiness of the subject. That only suggests that Reeve never resolved the problems that doomed it at the John Day Company. It all sounds so predictable. The deadline was short, Reeve overscheduled himself with other irresistible opportunities, the finished product was thus deficient. The Crime Crusade Foundation may have been another victim of Reeve's workload.

Passages from *The Golden Age of Crime* fill in Reeve's perspective and experience with the issue. For starters, he got as close to the problem as he knew how:

> Go, as I have done, day after day, to the lineup each morning at Police Headquarters in New York, or in any other city; ask Warden Lawes of Sing Sing to show you about the famous old state prison, or ask the same of any prison warden in any other state, and you will be astounded and alarmed as I have been time and time again when you learn the ages of the offenders. Mere boys and girls! Fifty, sixty, sometimes seventy per cent and higher, under the ages of twenty-one or twenty-two! [pg20]

Reeve, the friend to presidents, returned to rarefied circles:

> We were discussing the [public tolerance for racketeering] one day in the office of Chief Inspector John O'Brien—the Chief, his old bosom friend, [New York Police] Commissioner Mulrooney and myself.
> "No man or no business that is thoroughly honest," said Mulrooney positively, "can be racketeered successfully for long—unless it wants to be." [pg129-130]

Reeve became well-known among the criminal class, too. He quoted from a long profile of *Crime Prevention Program* that appeared in *The Evening World* (September 6, 1930):

> Arthur B. Reeve came into the WJZ studios one day this week, his face wreathed in smiles. He had just been paid one of the most startling compliments ever given to the writer of a radio program.

---

* *Trenton Sunday Times Advertiser*, May 22, 1932.

He had received three distinct, unmistakable overtures from gentry "outside the law," asking him if he wouldn't like to "chisel in" on their rackets at an alluring figure. The offers were stimulated by the radio crime-prevention series and the racketeers had sent their emissaries to the author of the sketches with an open suggestion that he would be an invaluable ally in covering up their activities because of his ostensible connection with the forces of law and order.

Reeve expressed his appreciation of the left-handed compliment, but his answer was uncompromising: "I will not be intimidated, threatened, cajoled, or persuaded to depart one hair's breadth from the purpose for which I established these programs."

Reeve added:

> . . . there was a great deal more to the story than the reporter told. It was an opportunity to become a cog in the wheel of the Beer Racket. . . . It was an offer of more money per week in the shape of an interest in a night-club not too far from the Fifth Avenue headquarters of the National Broadcasting Company at a minimum figure that was more per week than I have ever made in any month or some years of my life. [pg50]

In a 1932 interview, Reeve used his newfound authority as a platform for his political views.* Officially, he'd been a Progressive, but switched to the Republican Party ca. 1915.† He donated money to Republican events. His fiction, as well as *Crime Prevention Program*, identified him as a true blue law-and-order man; which may be another reason why changes in detective fiction passed him by. The hardboiled dick inhabited a gray area between law and lawlessness, mingling easily with the underworld. That wouldn't have been Reeve's inclination. In the interview, he expressed his pessimism. The courts and public were too lenient. Congress was passing too many laws. Things were only going to get worse. . . .

> "That is until we get back to the faith of our fathers."
>
> "The faith of our fathers? You mean a revival of religion?" he was asked.
>
> "Well, not just like that," he remonstrated. "It sounds too much like a revival meeting. I do not mean any emotional movement that will die away as quickly as it came. I contend that men must get back to the fundamentals of religion, to the rock of faith, to the belief in God. What can you do with men who have no character and no belief in God?
>
> "To my way of thinking, the real cause of crime has been a decay of religion and the cause of increased juvenile crime the break-up of the home. Family life has almost vanished nowadays, and home is just the place to stay, when you have no other place to go."

Reeve had started out a Presbyterian. He and his family converted to Catholicism in 1926. Reeve continued:

> "It would be practically impossible today to get together a group of men who

---

* ibid.

† He's listed as a Progressive in *Who's Who 1914-15*; a Republican in *Who's Who 1916-17*.

would write the Declaration of Independence and the Constitution of the United States. We haven't the character nor the principle our forefathers had. We are just incapable of writing those two documents of human freedom.

"Money has been the main factor in our moral let-down. We've had too much money. It has been our greatest curse, and probably the depression will do us a lot of good.

"In fact, that's the very reason why Great Britain has saved her soul. She came out of the war broke and saved herself. We came out rich and lost our ideals, principles, everything.

"How much we talk nowadays about social justice and how little we practice it! And how much we have experimented both with social justice and with economics. Experimented with no brains, I should say. You just cannot throw out the accumulated experience and knowledge of the race and get anywhere. What we need to do is to go back to the economics of Thomas Aquinas, the greatest human economist who ever lived. It would not hurt to have a little more of the spirit of St. Francis, either. St. Francis with his birds, his fish and animals."

Kidnappings, Real and Fictional

Reeve published a new novel in 1932, *The Kidnap Club*, his first original since *Pandora* (1926). His new publisher, The Macaulay Company, announced the work in March. *The New York Times*, in the *Book Notes* column of March 17, crassly characterized it as "The first of what is considered likely to develop into a swarm of mystery and adventure stories based on kidnapping." The timing certainly merited a raised eyebrow. On the night of March 1, Charles Lindbergh's baby had been snatched. The *Times'* observation conjures an image of Reeve typing around the clock since the sensational news broke to be the first to cash in on the tragedy. But it was just a coincidence. What the *Times* writer had been unaware of was that the novel received near-simultaneous publication in the April '32 issue of the pulp *Complete Detective Novel Magazine*. Pulps, like most magazines, were sold a month or more ahead of the issue date, putting Reeve's novel on the newsstands near the time of the Lindbergh kidnapping. Macaulay released the book at the end of March. But the subject matter of *The Kidnap Club* doesn't resemble the Lindbergh kidnapping, anyway. The victim is the daughter of the chairman of the "Crime Prevention Campaign." Reeve's novel is a usefully paranoid fantasy that arose out of his own recent experiences and the fact that he had a teenage daughter by 1932.

Reeve's address, noted in April 1930 and September 1931, had been East Setauket, about four miles west of Miller Place, his given address at the time of the '28 bankruptcy.* In another strange coincidence—although the timing is unclear—Reeve and family relocated from Long Island to New Jersey in 1932, moving into Lindbergh's first home near Hopewell in the Trenton/Princeton area. Hopewell was the site of the Lindbergh kidnapping. Soon

---

* "Reeve Fire Called Arson," *NYT*, April 25, 1930, lists East Setauket; in the 1932 interview, Reeve said, "The Benjamin Collings murder [September 9, 1931] took place right in front of my home at Setauket, L.I. Our house was directly on the Sound, and in the Summer one hears all kinds of noise from the water, coming from merry-makers amusing themselves." All indications are that Reeve lived in the same Long Island Sound area from 1918 until his move to Trenton—with one exception. When he served as foreman of a Federal Grand Jury in Brooklyn (January 1921), he lived in Brooklyn, which registered surprise in *The New York Herald*, Brooklyn being deemed too suburban and undramatic for a writer of detective stories—as opposed to Greenwich Village or Chelsea.

thereafter, the Hopewell residence was designated a summer home, and the family moved to their winter retreat at 615 Greenwood Avenue, in a historic district of Trenton, Mrs. Reeve's hometown.

Reeve had foreshadowed the nostalgic pull of the old college haunts in "Water" (*Flynn's*, November 8, 1924), wherein Kennedy and Jameson travel to Princeton on a case. It's one of the few stories to provide any of Kennedy's background, revealing that he and Jameson attended college there. Dialogue from Jameson opens the story:

> "What a delightful relief, Craig, to get out of the sordid city, back again in a community where it's not all what you have, but what you are!"

Later, Jameson narrates:

> I always had a weakness for the old town, more especially since it was more than a college town. It had what neither the city nor even a little village has. Cities too often are centers of aliens with a fringe of Americans. Princeton was a center of learning with a fringe of culture.

After making the move, Reeve admitted: "The main reason why I have come to Trenton is to be near Princeton, which has drawn back to her more of her graduates than any other college in the world."*

At any rate, *The Kidnap Club* began a lengthy association with *Complete Detective Novel Magazine*. Each issue of the pulp published a lead novel and several shorts. With the exception of a radio-themed short in the December 3 *Argosy*, all of Reeve's 1932 magazine stories appeared in *Complete Detective Novel*, including five shorts and another lead novel, *Murder in Green*, in the September issue. *Murder in Green* was never reprinted as a book.

Perhaps of most significance with the *Complete Detective Novel* stories, the erudition of the "scientific detective" school is a distant memory. Reeve's storytelling would now be resigned to the action-oriented style favored by the pulps. In truth the transition was many years in the making, but it must have been galling to Reeve, to surrender the thing that made him special. Perhaps the failure of *Scientific/Amazing Detective* hammered the final nail in the coffin. Reeve's specialty had been put front and center, and the center didn't hold.

In November 1932, Reeve incorporated himself again, as "Arthur B. Reeve, Inc." The nature of the business was listed as "motion pictures, plays, radio productions," which sounds far more ambitious than his remaining career was destined to achieve. At about the same time, Reeve made a series of Saturday evening guest appearances on newspaperman Heywood Broun's fifteen-minute radio show, although the content of Reeve's contribution isn't known.

The Return of "The Clutching Hand"

Our record for the first seven months of 1933 show no publications—book, magazine, or newspaper—and no film work. Reeve resurfaced in the August/September issue of *Complete Detective Novel* with a Craig Kennedy lead novel, *The Electric War*. He likely

---

* *Trenton Sunday Times Advertiser*, May 22, 1932.

completed the story three to four months before the magazine date but, considering Reeve's top writing speed, that doesn't account for much of his elapsed time. Between the publication of *Murder in Green* and *The Electric War*, he published only two shorts. We don't know whether this is due to his slowing down, or whether other works done in this time perhaps went unsold.

The Electric War pitted Kennedy and Jameson against an old nemesis, The Clutching Hand, first encountered in *The Exploits of Elaine* two decades earlier. The novel was reissued between hard covers in April 1934 and renamed *The Clutching Hand* (The Reilly & Lee Company). Wrapping up 1933 were a pair of appearances in new markets. Reeve, unexpectedly, made the cover of the October 1 *Dime Detective Magazine* with a novelette, "The Golden Grave," the only sale he ever made to Popular Publications, the three-year-old company that had added new dash and excitement to the pulps as the Depression came about. The story was, per the new Reeve, action-oriented. Robert Sampson summed up new versus old in his study of scientific detectives:

> "The Golden Grave" is far distant from the former adventures of our Professor Kennedy, calm and steely-eyed, working grave miracles in his Coolidge collar. Dusted thinly through the narrative glitter shiny bits of science fact, like memories almost lost. A sprinkling of fact does not make a scientific detective story, however. And, really, who cares about the Latin name for rattlesnake, as the nude corpses pile high and Kennedy rushes up the street and down the street.
>
> In the true scientific detective story, the science must be real. It must achieve something, resolve something. Its function is to shed light, not merely to be decorative, in the manner of a fan-dancer's tassels. There is little science detection in "The Golden Grave"—only the pretend of it.*

Gang Pulp

The other new market for Reeve in late '33 was *Gang World*. The pulp had been one of Popular's original four titles, but folded after the November '32 issue. Spencer Publications re-introduced it with the December 1933 issue, presumably after purchasing the title. Spencer was part of the new Martin Goodman chain that issued pulps under a variety of publisher names. Reeve is buried in the back of the issue with a short, "Gawd Hates a Rat!," which reads like a real gang-pulp story. The story takes place in the world of mob boss, Tony Magnifico, but lacks the muckraking aspect of *Craig Kennedy and the Gangsters*. Reeve's resistance to the "smart-alecks" of the fiction world was breaking down.

January 1934 was Reeve's last "lucky month," as measured by newsstand appearances. He had three. In *Black Book Detective Magazine* (another Goodman pulp), Reeve made the cover with a 46-page story, "The Inca Dagger," an action-oriented rewrite of his first true novel, *The Gold of the Gods* (1915). He was back in *Complete Detective Novel* with a short, "Murder in the Rumpus Room," which featured a new character, "Scarley Scott: Soul Detective." Scarley's nickname was "The Idler," owing to his status as career student. Scott had a confidante from college days, a newsman, to remain at his side and narrate the story. Where have we heard this before? All in all, it was a bit of the old Reeve, although

---

* Robert Sampson, *Yesterday's Faces, Volume 2: Strange Days* (Bowling Green University Popular Press, 1984); 44.

the concept of "soul detective" is never explained. The story has other touch points to Reeve's past. Scott's uncle is John Hawtry; the murder victim of *Atavar* is Guy Hawtry. "Murder in the Rumpus Room" has a character, Paul Fentress, a member of the "Pittsburgh steel and iron Fentresses," reminiscent of Harry Thaw. The story also has a veiled sarcasm, if one chooses to read it that way. Scott orders his "man" to dispose of a pile of newspapers: "Wickham! You may carry out that pile of wood pulp and put it in the rubbish!"

The third appearance of the month came in a new detective pulp, *World Man Hunters*, from another new publisher, Fiction Guild, Inc. The magazine ran from January to March, and Reeve featured in every issue. The January issue advertised his story, "Murder Around the Corner," as "The Return of Craig Kennedy"—not that he'd gone anywhere. The story was an explicit continuation of the *Craig Kennedy and the Gangsters* series, although at twice the length. The editor's introduction promised " 'the inside' on the new rackets of a great city and the methods Kennedy employs to combat them." Tony Magnifico, and his Campo Club, which comes up the *Gangsters* series, figures in. *World Man Hunters* also advertised Kennedy as the "scientific detective" but, although Kennedy signs on as scientist, he quickly downgrades its importance:

> . . . "You see, I'm a scientist. I do things on the basis on which all science is built."
>
> Dimples looked a bit nonplussed. "How's that?" she asked, not quite taking it in.
>
> "On the basis of reason." Kennedy smiled again. "Of course, this didn't need so much science as it did straight thinking and keen observation."

The story is close in spirit to the gang pulps—a near-dead genre in 1934—peppered with rackets, punks, bloodstained sidewalks—the usual accouterments of the gang story. Jameson is absent—gone on a world cruise, according to Kennedy. Dimples appeared again in the March issue, described as Kennedy's "thrill girl."

It wasn't much help to Reeve to hit every issue of a magazine, if the magazine was to fold after three issues. And *World Man Hunters* was no *Cosmopolitan*. In the June 1934 *Writer's Digest*, Harriet A. Bradfield reported on *World Man Hunters* and its companion title, *The World Adventurer*: "I understand that much of the material used in these magazines has not been paid for; and in as much as no forwarding address is known . . . it looks as if authors were rather out of luck." Was Reeve paid? We don't know.

After the three appearances in *World Man Hunters*, Reeve disappeared again from the newsstands. He resurfaced in August 1934 in the cheap gang pulp, *Complete Underworld Novelettes*, with a Guy Garrick story that appeared side-by-side with stories like "Tong Vengeance" and "Gangland's Judas." In the story, Garrick finds himself on a Brooklyn gang's "sucker list." He queries a police detective about the others on the list:

> "How many of these names have been checked off—many?"
>
> "A good many, Garrick! The last was that Wallabout slugger who squealed to the D.A. Bumped off, if you recall, yesterday. Oh, there's been plenty of others, business men who have squealed, kick-back men who have welshed—"

Tough stuff. The following month, Reeve had a short in *The Underworld Detective*, by the same publisher (Carwood) as *Complete Underworld*. *Underworld Detective* was a continuation of *The Underworld*, which Reeve hit twice in 1928, but it was no longer a reprint magazine. In both *Complete Underworld* and *Underworld Detective*, Reeve was labeled "Creator of Craig Kennedy." That honorific was as important as his name, and may have done more to sell the stories than the stories themselves.

Like "Gawd Hates a Rat!," these gang stories are a long way from the staid and formal style of Reeve's *Cosmopolitan* stories, fueling the speculation that Reeve's uncharacteristic later fiction was ghostwritten. The obvious objection is that *Craig Kennedy and the Gangsters* provides a transition. Another argument is that Reeve was hitting the lower-paying markets with these stories. *Gang World*, *World Man Hunters*, the *Underworld* titles, were bottom-tier pulps, offering a half-cent to most of their contributors. Seemingly not an amount worth splitting with a ghostwriter, especially the $25 sale of a 5000-word short.

Further ambiguous evidence appears in the form of small inside jokes buried in the stories. For example, "Guy Garrick, P.D.," the *Complete Underworld Novelettes* story, has a character named Will Foster. In real life, artist Will Foster illustrated Reeve's *Cosmopolitan* stories. In "Gawd Hates a Rat!" an employee of the Campo Club takes protagonist Kirk Van Kirk's walking stick:

> "I say, sir, but that stick of yours is some heavy! What's it made of, sir?"
> "Paper," replied Van Kirk, rather pleased Harry had noticed it. "Made under hydraulic pressure in the shop by a convict in the Charlestown State Prison, out of gang stories my ghost wrote which he admired. Has a rod of iron down the middle."

Reeve learned of the technique of making walking sticks from paper in a letter from a convict who later sent him a stick made of Reeve stories. Reeve cited the incident in a 1922 letter to Arthur Bartlett Maurice, at the time literary editor of *The New York Herald*.* Later, Van Kirk talks about a budding playwright gathering material about the New York underworld:

> "He wanted to ghost-write the gang stuff for me or I was to do it for him, I never could make out which, for five grand and a cut-in on the royalties."

In another scene, a lawyer says to Van Kirk:

> "I'll tell you, Mr. Ghost Writer. . . . You see, I know a thing or two, Mr. Van Kirk. I know you—er—assist in the production of plays and pictures and stories of the underworld."

These confusing quotes are incidental to the central action of the story, which makes them even more tantalizing. Van Kirk is either a ghostwriter, or has a ghostwriter, but in any event produces stories of the underworld. Why would a writer drop hints about ghostwriting unless he was a ghostwriter? "Gawd Hates a Rat!" is in its entirety hard to follow, which is not an accusation leveled at Reeve very often. His journalistic credentials were impeccable, and his writing usually clear-cut. If a case could be made on the basis of *feeling* that Reeve employed ghosts, this would be it. The inside jokes are Reeve's fingerprints on the work, but they could have been part of a synopsis passed to a ghost, or added in a rewrite.

---

* Reprinted in this volume. Maurice solicited the recollections of numerous authors on the subject of correspondence received from readers.

Perhaps we should conclude that Reeve's research into the gangsters and rackets of Prohibition gave him the knowledge and patois to write in a new-sounding way; or that his true-crime credentials made his name attractive enough to the gang pulps to put a ghostwriter behind him. Which is no conclusion at all.

Ghosts in the House

Reeve had another story in an August '34 pulp, *Thrilling Detective*, his first such in another big, new chain of the '30s, Standard Magazines. Standard started a companion title, *Popular Detective*, with the issue of November '34, and Reeve hit seven of the first eight issues, his last sustained run in a single magazine. All were Craig Kennedy stories. With *Popular Detective*, we finally have documentary evidence that Reeve became involved with another writer. In correspondence from Leo Margulies, former chief editor of the Thrilling chain, to researcher, J. Randolph Cox, the story came out:

> Arthur B. Reeve and I became rather good friends towards the end of his days. I learned to love the guy. And Craig Kennedy was, to me, one of the great names of all time. I even contemplated doing a magazine to be called: CRAIG KENNEDY MYSTERY MAGAZINE, but couldn't convince my boss.* But I tried to carry-on the name and got some old unsold Kennedy short stories turned over to me. Reeve was very happy to permit me to have them rewritten into short novelets. And after I'd run six of them, around 10,000 words each, they'd make a book. And he wanted another book. . . .
>
> But of this I can assure you, for my Craig Kennedy stories, I only had one author work on them—Ashley T. Locke. He was a competent pulp writer around that period and I had used him often, and he got on well with Reeve. They split the proceeds—all I purchased were magazine serial rights only.†

Margulies elaborated on the possibility of Reeve collaborating at other times:

> . . . as far as I know, Reeve never sold the character or by-line. Reeve was a proud man, and after I had convinced him it was okay, he was happy to work with Locke. And if Reeve tried it again, it certainly was without my knowledge. Most assuredly I would have known. Then again --------?

Of course, most of the questionable stories under discussion were published prior to Reeve's involvement with Thrilling. And, if Reeve had worked with ghostwriters, it might not have been a fact he divulged freely.

Reeve ended the year with a syndicated newspaper article on the new Department of Justice building in Washington, D.C.†† On the first day of his visit, he spent "hours" talking

---

* His boss was Standard Magazines publisher, Ned L. Pines. Pines and Margulies must have known that the Craig Kennedy magazine idea had essentially been tried—and failed: *Scientific Detective Monthly*. Of note, from about 1945-48, a little-known 48-page digest, *Scientific Detective*, was published out of New York under several publisher names. A half-cent market, it included a fair amount of reprinted stories; however, in the nine issues currently listed in the FictionMags Index, Reeve is not to be found.

† Leo Margulies, letter to J. Randolph Cox, January 28, 1975. The *Thrilling Detective* story was about 5000 words and probably not one of the group rewritten by Ashley T. Locke.

†† "Reeve Sees Crime Foes," *The Los Angeles Times*, December 16, 1934.

with J. Edgar Hoover, director of the Bureau of Investigation. (It became the *Federal Bureau of Investigation* in 1935.) The hook to the article was the frequent interruption of the interview by important phone calls, as in this passage:

> A buzz on the telephone. He reached for the instrument. Staccato questions, quick answers. I caught the name of "Baby Face" Nelson. Only a few weeks before "Pretty Boy" Floyd had been shot down in a field of Ohio. The mantle of public enemy No. 1 had fallen on "Baby Face." I was all ears.
> "Just a lead that he's in South Dakota," vouchsafed Hoover. "This morning a report from Iowa. Both fake leads, I think." He returned to talking of the work.

Old acquaintance Critchell Rimington, of the John Day Company, wrote Reeve on December 12. He'd been following Reeve's series, "The New Deal Against Crime," appearing in the *New York Evening Post*. He wondered whether Reeve had reconsidered rewriting it as a book, making it "less journalistic in approach." Accordingly, Reeve forwarded his clippings. However, Rimington replied on December 20 that he was leaving the company, wasn't sure whether he would remain in publishing, and was withdrawing his interest until his plans became settled. He also dangled the possibility of Reeve rewriting a "record of prison experiences from J.A. Johnston, Warden of Alcatraz." But neither book came to fruition with Reeve's byline. (Johnston's book was published with no listed co-author in 1949.)

As 1935 began, Reeve hit *Complete Detective Novel* one last time, with "The Royal Racket," a short featuring an old name with some familiar initials, Clare Kendall. Clare had actually been Reeve's first female detective, appearing in newspaper syndication in early 1913; predating Constance Dunlap, who first appeared in the September 1913 *Pearson's*. Clare then surfaced as a supporting character in "The Abduction Club" (*Adventure*, February 1914). Reeve must have wanted to do more with her, for when Constance Dunlap ended her run in the August 1914 *Pearson's*, the next issue had a Reeve story featuring Clare Kendall, advertised by the magazine as a new series. But there was no continuation. "The Royal Racket," borrows its title from the third *Craig Kennedy and the Gangsters* story, and also has a gang theme.

That January/February issue of *Complete Detective Novel* turned out to be its last. Reeve had been accustomed to inaugurating new magazines—*Flynn's*, *Scientific Detective*, *World Man Hunters*, *Popular Detective*—now he was closing them out. But it wouldn't have mattered much financially. The pulp had been reduced to a half-cent market by then. Reeve's name turned up in a three-dot column in the January 1935 *Writer's Review*: ". . . ARTHUR B. REEVE who, tired of waiting in an editorial office for an appointment with an editor, decides to demand the installation of bunks . . ." An oh-so-brief comment, yet suggesting so much: the fall from glory, the sense of humor unimpaired, dignity intact.

Top of the World

The Kidnap Club, back in March '32, provided a near-miss between Reeve and the Lindbergh baby snatch, but the trial of Bruno Hauptmann, the accused kidnapper, resulted in a direct hit. The trial was held at the Hunterdon County Courthouse in little Flemington,

New Jersey, northwest up the highway from Reeve's home in downtown Trenton. The trial got underway as the new year of 1935 began. A *New York Times* story reported on the extensive communications infrastructure being installed to handle the mob of press descending on the town. Reeve received mention as one of the celebrity journalists in attendance, sharing company with Kathleen Norris, Alexander Woollcott, Fannie Hurst, and others.* Reeve covered the trial for a Philadelphia newspaper. The trial concluded with Hauptmann's conviction and death sentence at 10:45 p.m., February 18. In a February 27 letter, Reeve wrote Margulies from his sickbed. He described the ill health that had plagued him throughout the trial:

> The last Sunday night before the trial ended I was caught in the middle of the night with an acute attack of cardiac asthma. Couldn't get my breath. Like steel bands around my chest. Face blue. Covered cold sweat. Gasping for air <u>to live</u>. They called a doctor and a priest about two in the morning. . . .
>
> I came back. Doctor said bed for a week. Monday morning he came about ten. I felt the iron man again. The moment he shut the door I was up, shaving, and drove 25 miles to Flemington . . .

Reeve's symptoms had first appeared in the fall of '34. He was a cigarette smoker and that may have been a factor.

Reeve's excitement in covering the trial could barely be contained in words:

> . . . My last story, a valedictory. Stuck around half the night, waiting verdict. Meanwhile Red Gallagher and Frank Toughill and myself snipped a telephone wire than [sic] ran down outside my window in court. Drew in the live ends. Our wire upstairs, anyway. Clipped in. We had a direct wire from inside the court room to the city desk in Philadelphia! Bunched up under eagle eyes of state troopers and deputy sheriffs, after court doors locked when jury came in, Red and I whispered running story of verdict to Toughill under table. Slammed AP fake report extras Life Imprisonment, scooped all the other papers AP, News with indoor wireless, everybody, one of big unprincipled scoops of modern news.

He summed up the whole experience: "Leo, that was living!" But there was more at stake than just the trial. Reeve sounded desperate: ". . . now with all these doctor's bills, nurses, damned creditors and so on I have got to make money." He believed that his reinvigorated fame had brought Craig Kennedy back to life. He reminded Margulies of the Craig Kennedy magazine idea. "I may go in the gutter but Craig isn't going in the gutter." The trial had been a highpoint for Reeve during a protracted period of financial and physical decline, but he still had a few more cards to play. . . .

Final Affairs

Reeve hit his last new market with the novelette "The Death Cry," which made the cover of the May '35 *Weird Tales*. Moskowitz reports that Reeve's agent, Otis Adelbert Kline, sold *WT* editor, Farnsworth Wright, on the idea of a Craig Kennedy story with weird trappings. Reeve was paid $150. For *WT*, it offered the promise of luring detective-story readers to

---

* "Huge Wire Service Set Up For Trial," *NYT*, January 2, 1935.

the fantasy magazine. In the story, Kennedy finds himself hotel-mate to a vampire killer in the Catskills, which turns out to be—merely—a blood-drinking Sino-cat with a "terror-inspiring leap." Many readers were not amused. Wright addressed their complaints at length in *The Eyrie* (July), the *WT* letter column. The July and August issues sampled reader reaction. Julius Hopkins summed it up best: "I like the vampire stories to have genuine vampires—not the ones with scientific explanations, for they take away the true weirdness of it all." Other readers were less diplomatic. "I am completely disgusted."— J.A. Williams. "Good old *Weird* is going to the doggies with silly detective stories."—Veith Dall. The cruelest blow came from prolific letter-writer Jack Darrow: "I've read stories in detective magazines that were weirder." The story's rational explanation may not have been true to the *Weird Tales* tradition, but it was true to Reeve. Unlike his British exemplar, "the American Conan Doyle" was no spiritualist.*

The string of Craig Kennedy collaborations in *Popular Detective* played out through the June '35 issue. That story, "The Navy Murder Case," was his last magazine appearance. Reeve did indeed get another book out of the deal. The first four novelettes were issued by Macaulay as *Enter Craig Kennedy* in late '35.

And so ended Reeve's magazine career. The rest of 1935 is a near-blank. According to *Who's Who in America 1936-37*, Reeve worked as supervisor for the Federal Writers' Project in Trenton. The FWP (a division of the Work Projects Administration) was established July 27, 1935 to support writers during the Depression. Their main product was the *American Guide Series* which published state histories. Reeve may have spearheaded the Trenton section, but when *New Jersey: A Guide to Its Present and Past* was published in 1939, Reeve's name was absent. At any rate, it's hard to imagine him taking on a job with a New Deal agency unless his writing career was stalled. It hadn't completely. He published another novel, *The Stars Scream Murder* (March 1936), one of D. Appleton-Century's "Tired Business Man's Library." The story had Craig Kennedy using astrology to solve a murder, which doesn't sound like an idea Reeve wished upon himself. Reeve had another film credit, too, the 15-part serial, *The Clutching Hand* (released April 18, 1936), based on the book of the same name. It was his third film with the Weiss Brothers. The co-authors were Leon D'Usseau and Dallas M. Fitzgerald. The 305-minute serial was later released as a 74-minute feature, suggestive of the amount of needless activity in the former.

Reeve died at home in Trenton on August 9, 1936, age 55, of cardiac asthma. The February '35 letter to Margulies makes a convincing case that he'd been flirting with the end of life for some time. Reeve's funeral was held in Port Jefferson, Long Island, near his former home; he was buried at nearby Laurel Cemetery, Northport. He left behind a wife, a mother, a son, a daughter; and one last novel, which remains unpublished.

His obituary appeared in newspapers across the land, fitting since so many papers had carried his fiction and crime reporting, while often couching his name in easy assurance, in the vein of "written by Arthur B. Reeve, who scarcely needs an introduction."

A Short-Lived Revival

But when Reeve died, so did his career; a foolish observation except when we consider writers whose works and characters outlive them, sometimes even growing in popularity.

---

* Sampson was suspicious about authorship: "it does not read as if Reeve contributed anything to the manuscript but his name." (*Yesterday's Faces, Volume 2*; 45.) But there's no hard evidence of "collusion."

This was not to be Reeve's—or Kennedy's—fate. Reeve all but took Kennedy to the grave with him. Most of the books were already out of print; the remainder soon joined the silence. Reeve went from American institution to forgotten man of antiquity virtually overnight.

The *Craig Kennedy Stories* haunted the used bookstores—they still do. Reeve's short stories receive occasional reprint in anthologies, especially "The Silent Bullet" and "The Black Hand." But Reeve had trouble making money for himself at the end of his career; he didn't make much for anyone after his death. He did receive one posthumous tribute. In 1944, the Weiss brothers bought the rights to the Craig Kennedy stories. Louis Weiss' son, Adrian, took over the company in 1948 with the aim of developing properties for television. In 1952, the low-budget *Craig Kennedy, Criminologist* went before the cameras. Twenty-six episodes were produced for syndication. Veteran actor Donald Woods played Kennedy; the role of Jameson went to Lewis G. Wilson.

The first thing to notice about the show is Kennedy's change in title from "scientific detective" to criminologist. "Criminology" is a term of 19th Century origin, well-established by Reeve's time as a writer. Recall that Kennedy sought to become the first professor of criminal science, in essence, a criminologist, one who studies crime and its prevention; but *Cosmopolitan* tagged him with "scientific detective," a distinction better serving the stories. Lest we think, however, that the television producers were setting the record straight by reverting to Reeve's original intentions, TV's Craig Kennedy was barely even a scientific detective, much less a criminologist. "Criminologist" was probably chosen because it sounded more modern; "scientific detective" must have sounded alarmingly quaint by 1952. *Craig Kennedy, Private Eye* would have been a more accurate title for the show.

In the show, Kennedy works out of a high-rise office, taking cases for hire. His door reads:

CRAIG KENNEDY
L.L.B., M.S., M.D.
CRIMINOLOGIST

. . . As if the string of degrees were essential to solving the none-too-profound murder and crime puzzles the show presented. The script is enlivened with wisecracking banter between Kennedy and Jameson, and Woods and Lewis do a nice job of breathing life into the characters. The shows pump up the action: occasional gunplay, swinging fists from Kennedy, Jameson knocked senseless with the butt-end of a scythe, etc. The main nod to science—other than the beaker which emits chemical vapor under the main titles—is Kennedy's surveillance system. He has a television monitor set up in the office to let him see who's at the door.

Legacy

What do we conclude about Reeve's career? He was an experienced journalist when the Craig Kennedy stories were launched in *Cosmopolitan*. Reeve did a good job of drawing contemporary science into his fiction—and his timing was right. The readers were quick to embrace Craig Kennedy. Perhaps the scientific element flattered their pretensions to worldliness, even if they didn't always understand it. Reeve's great error was in failing to develop the literary sensibilities that would have allowed Craig Kennedy, the character, to outlive the scientific vogues that informed the plots. "The British Sherlock Holmes," that is, the real one, casts a long shadow. Holmes is a fascinating and endearing character—even if you never fully accept his ability to identify any tobacco product from its ash. You *want* to believe—because you like him. Craig Kennedy is easy to admire, but difficult to like. The human connection is absent. He's a savant who comes down from academia's mountaintop to impart inscrutable wisdom. You want to like him; you want him to become human again after he's exercised that super-efficient intelligence for the good of the law. After reading enough stories of his adventures, you realize you will never know him. And perhaps that's why he passed from the limelight.

For a while, it looked as if Reeve's career might skyrocket in every direction. He helped make Pearl White into the queen of the cliffhangers. Then feature films became ascendant, and the serials faded to matinee attractions. The film business moved west. Reeve missed another opportunity to raise his game. He never did find a regular-paying gig as good as the near eight years with *Cosmopolitan*. Those eight years generated books, movie opportunities, secondary sales, and on and on. It made Reeve's name and the name of Craig Kennedy. After it had ended, Reeve's career looks more like the nomadic existence of the freelancer, moving from one opportunity to another. Reeve was a pro, though. He kept his name in the game. However, one can't avoid the suspicion that the two decades, post-*Cosmopolitan*, were a series of futile attempts to recapture past glory. Many sales, many deals, must have been based more on Reeve's name than his ability to deliver the goods. He made it to the top again—briefly—with his national radio show. From it, he attempted to launch the ambitious Crime Crusade Foundation. Had he pulled it off, had Reeve possessed the energy of ten men instead of three, he might have gone down as one of the legendary figures of the '30s, "the detective-story writer who took America back from the racketeers," or some such. Instead, he slipped down into the literary netherworld of the pulps, faking the leaner, harder storytelling styles of younger, more creative writers. His waning years look increasingly dissipated. The Depression was tough on Reeve, as it was on most writers.

What was really going on in Reeve's career? We're left with numerous unanswered questions. Why did he leave *Cosmopolitan*? What was his relationship with Ray Long, Houdini, Harry Thaw, Hugo Gernsback, and the other interesting figures he crossed paths with? Why did he go bankrupt? Did he collaborate with writers more than is presently known? The record begs for explanation, but Reeve is near-silent on his own life.

He leaves a legacy, albeit mixed. Critics have not found favor with his fiction. Bob Sampson, for example, in reviewing Reeve's output, steered clear of harshness for the most part, but wrote of the *Country Gentleman* stories: "There is no great pleasure in savaging stories as poor as these. . . . The stories almost flash to life. . . . But they don't. They lie there, flaccid, distorted."* Van Dover wrote: "In preparation for this study I read through 15 of Reeve's books, and the work of reading consistently defeated my intention of championing him as an undeservedly neglected author."† No, Reeve's legacy is not with literature, it is with history. Craig Kennedy captured the public's fancy. He was fresh, modern—if only for one of history's fleeting moments. He will live forever in the annals of fictional crime fighters, if not in our hearts.

---

* *Yesterday's Faces, Volume 2*; 35.

† *You Know My Method*; 232, Note 2.

I

NONFICTION

McClure's Magazine, October 1912

Detective Burns' Great Cases
The Mystery of the Double Eagles

Note: Names, dates, and places are, for obvious reasons, either changed, concealed, or omitted in this amazing revelation of how William J. Burns thwarted one of the cleverest crooks who ever tried to beat the government at its own game of guarding the millions of dollars in one of the large branch mints.

"THIRTY THOUSAND DOLLAR SHORTAGE DISCOVERED AT THE MINT. Require ablest and best talent in the government service." Never had the Secretary of the Treasury received a more alarming message than was flashed to him some ten years ago from the Director of the Mint himself.

Consider for a moment what this simple telegram meant, coming from the Director at a time when he happened to be visiting one of the leading branch mints of the country.

From the massive granite and sandstone exterior of the great United States treasure-house to the minutest electrical device, the mint bespoke national security and national strength. It was supposed to represent the utmost progress in protective systems and mechanisms of the time—safety raised to the nth power.

The very external aspect of the mint seemed to say to the world that such a thing as theft was impossible. Huge doors proclaimed by their very ponderosity that it was their sole duty to guard the nation's treasure. Guards were stationed at every remotely vulnerable point. Apparently, nothing that human ingenuity could devise was lacking.

From the moment the bullion entered on the various processes until it returned again to the outside world as gold coin, all sorts of delicate tests, checks, and balances had been devised to protect the government. No bank is so exact, no record is kept so clean, as in the United States money mills. Every ounce of metal, every penny of coin, must be accounted for invariably before the cashier of the mint can call his day's work done.

Consider this, also. Far from the street lay the great vaults where the mass of money was guarded with vigilance surpassing that bestowed on almost any other house of treasure. In this secret realm no visitor could enter. Millions were stacked ceiling-high where public curiosity could not see them, though it might dream futilely of the fabulous wealth behind the impregnable walls. Sentinels, mechanical as well as human, defended it at every avenue of approach. Not even the officials, except those immediately identified with that particular department of the mint, might be permitted to enter the proscribed zone.

Guarding the vaults were doors of armor-plate, swung on the latest kind of concealed hinges, locked by massive combination locks with time-clock attachments, proof against fire, against earthquake, against burglars. Against burglars? Six heavy bags of five thousand dollars each in double eagles were missing! There was the telegram, which the Secretary hurriedly turned over to the chief of the Secret Service:

"Thirty thousand dollar shortage discovered at the mint. Require ablest and best talent in the government service."

If that could happen once, what would prevent its happening again? If it could happen with thirty thousand, why not with three hundred thousand—with three million? The message was enough to send shivers up the spine of the Treasury Department, despite the torrid temperature of Washington at the close of the fiscal year on June 30. The chief of the Secret Service did not pause to read the message twice. There was just one man in the service at the time to whom all such difficult and knotty cases were turned over. He handed the telegram to Burns.

As he was whirled across the country the great detective spent the hours gazing at scenery that he did not see and turning the matter over in his mind. This much he knew. Some one trusted and high in the government employ itself had gone wrong. Fifteen hundred double eagles had been taken by some one on the inside. A black stain on the amazingly clean record of the mint in handling billions upon billions of dollars must be erased. Even before he arrived on the scene, Burns knew that this must prove a historic case.

II

Burns began first what he calls his "secret investigation." When he arrived on the scene, he did not let a soul know who he was or why he was there until he had looked the ground over. He began by placing everybody who was in a position to know anything about the crime under suspicion, and then, by what is known as the "process of elimination," arriving at the possible suspects. He looked over the mint itself where the loss had occurred, investigated the methods of conducting business throughout the day, absorbed everything that might or might not prove evidential. After going over the mint thoroughly, he watched carefully for days how business was transacted, the number of clerks around, all sorts of things, until he might almost have been learning to run the mint himself.

Let us say, for the purposes of this story, that the superintendent of the mint was Mr. Atchison—"Mr. A." Atchison enjoyed the distinction, at the time, of being the ablest man who had ever held the position anywhere in the country. He was a large, fine-looking man, middle-aged, with a clear eye, a hearty voice, and a grip of the hand that left you with no doubt as to the power of the man behind it. He was known as a man of the greatest integrity and honor, extremely careful in the conduct of the affairs of the mint, a man who had shown great interest and intelligence in keeping up the good record of efficiency which had been set for the institution under him.

The chief clerk, "Mr. B."—or let us call him Mr. Braden—was also a man of high character and standing in the community. He had come to the mint on the recommendation of some of the most influential men in that section of the country, had risen from the position of cashier until now he was assistant superintendent. He was a tall, rather spare, engaging chap, who by the sheer force of an attractive personality had won for himself membership in some exclusive clubs of the city, though he lived with his family in the suburbs. There was something about Braden of that solidity which one sees in the successful commuter— grave, but not aloof, capable, methodical, a man who had raised himself in the world and felt a pardonable pride in his position.

Mr. Colton—or "Mr. C."—the cashier, also bore a reputation for the highest integrity. Colton was one of those men whom, if he had come to the ordinary man and had asked a little favor, the ordinary man would have been proud to accommodate. He would have felt a little flattered merely by having been asked. Colton was still young, ambitious, and eager to get ahead, and his position as a church member and a leading citizen in the section of the city where he lived stamped him as a "comer." He was respected highly by those who knew him, and his appointment as cashier a year before had been only what they expected.

In fact, all three, Atchison, Braden, and Colton, as well as the other employees, seemed impeccable. Many of the two hundred-odd employees had records of long and faithful service in this mint, some of them as high as forty or forty-five years. Men who had worked there from ten to thirty years were common among them.

And yet, when the Director of the Mint from Washington had been present for the government in its usual settlement with the various mints in the country, he had found that this particular branch mint showed a shortage of thirty thousand dollars.

More than that, investigation had disclosed the fact that the shortage was in the vault of the cashier. The Director had made absolutely sure that the cashier was actually short before he had wired the facts to the Secretary of the Treasury; there was no question about it. In this mint there were several large vaults, belonging to the assayer, the receiver, the coiner, the melter and refiner, and the cashier. It was Colton's vault alone that had been found to be short.

There was a time-lock on the vault, too, and no person had the combination except Colton. The only copy of it was in a sealed envelop, and that was in the custody of Atchison, to be used only in case of accident or the sudden death of the cashier. There was no evidence, as yet, to show whether or not the copy of the combination sealed in the envelop had ever been tampered with. Therefore the discovery of the shortage was all the more sensational.

Burns went over the life and habits of Colton, the cashier, with a microscope. Apparently he was a man of the best record and connections, just the sort one would pick out instinctively as the man through whose hands all the money that was to be paid in or out should go. All this time Colton betrayed not the slightest outward symptom of uneasiness, although he knew that the shortage had been found, and must have suspected that he was being watched. What a surprise it would have been to the community to know that everything in Colton's vault down at the mint was not correct!

There was another peculiar coincidence in the situation, too. For instance, on the day the shortage was discovered, it had happened, as it so often happens in such cases, that Colton had been ill, very suddenly taken with a bad case of tonsillitis. Thus it had been that the cashier was not present when the shortage was discovered. But the superintendent and the chief clerk had been there.

Many things about the mint interested Burns. For example, the system of accounts was somewhat intricate, in order to secure absolute accuracy in handling such large sums of money. Just to illustrate with what minuteness business was done, there were reports in weight in standard ounces of metal, its cost value and the nominal value of the coin made from it, the number of ounces being multiplied by the value of one ounce of metal at the time, worked out to the millionth of a cent. That was in order to arrive at the "seigniorage," the profit the government makes in coining metals.

All accounts of various departments ultimately went through one office, where they were compiled and sent to Washington daily, weekly, monthly, quarterly, and annually, according to the nature of the reports. Finally, at the close of the fiscal year two officers were detailed by the Bureau of the Mint to examine the accounts, weigh the bullion, count the coin in hand, and report the results of this examination to the Bureau in Washington. Everything was done with scrupulous exactness and precision.

There was nothing of this mass of detail that escaped Burns in his hunt for the criminal who set these checks and balances in defiance. He noted everything, such as the "delivery" every morning, as it is called, when the coiner delivers to the superintendent the coin that has been made the day before in his department, which is then placed in the vault in the cashier's office. Representatives of the assay department, of the superintendent and of the coiner, had to be present at the "delivery." The coin had to be receipted for to the coiner, and brought in sacks on trucks to the cashier's room, where each sack was counted and weighed in the presence of the three men, tied with a stout string, and sealed with a lead seal stamped with the superintendent's name, secured so that if the sack was tampered with it could be seen.

A glance at the conduct of a mint is a romantic revelation of a fairy world where gold and silver are the stock in trade, as in other more sordid businesses it is mere iron pig or bolts of cloth. For instance, a citizen with gold to sell, a miner perhaps, would go to the receiving-room. There he would find a long counter on which was a scoop into which he would dump his dust, nuggets, or old gold. Back of this counter he could see desks and tables, interspersed perhaps with trucks actually loaded with real gold bars, a fortune casually wheeled about like a sack of oats.

It is not a part of this particular story, though it is a romance in itself, how the gold is carefully weighed in the weighing-room next to the receiving-room, the various processes through the laboratory of the assay department in the basement, the assay furnaces, the delicate scales and weights of the adjusters, the melting and refining department, the settling and silver reduction tanks, the ingot melting-room, the rolling-room with its long, gleaming strips of rolled gold, the annealing-furnaces, the coiner's department with its coin-presses, the milling, and reeding-machines, the weigh-room with its ingenious counting-boards—a long process, ending with the cashier's vault hiding its mystery of the missing double eagles. Mystery it was, too; for so carefully were all these processes carried out that, with a wastage allowed by law of one thousandth to the melter and only half that to the coiner, the infinitesimally small amount of only six or seven per cent of even this legal wastage occurred.

But it was in none of these departments that Burns knew he must look for the thief. Altogether, there were as many as seventeen watchmen, of whom twelve worked at night, eight on the inside and four on the outside. No clue to the mystery was coming from them—at least at the start—and Burns still was going alone and single-handed in his quiet study of the situation. Each watchman, he observed, had a certain station on the different floors and a specific round to make each half hour, ringing a bell to notify the man at the door that he had attended to his duty. Failure to ring the bell caused investigation. In certain rooms, such as the refinery, no watchman ever might go alone. They had to go in pairs. There was also a system of electric alarms throughout the building, so that every one might be notified in case anything went wrong at any point.

A word about the mint itself. It was a huge square building of granite and sandstone, with a long and impressive flight of steps leading up to the main door under its massive Grecian columns. On two sides of the building ran street-car lines.

It was the general layout of the interior of the building that, the more Burns pondered over it, proved to play a large part in the solution of the crime. Entering the front door, the visitor looked down a wide corridor before him, crossed at right angles at the end by a transverse corridor running the width of the building from right to left, after the manner of many large public buildings. Directly before him, at the far end of the main corridor, was the door of the cashier's office, the office being at the back of the building and extending from the center to the right wing, along the far side of the transverse corridor. It was in this right wing, at the back, that the cashier's vault which had been rifled was located.

To the right of the main corridor as one entered, in the front of the building, and consequently lying opposite the cashier's office along the transverse corridor, was the numismatist's room, where coins and medals were kept in a museum. To the left, as one entered this main corridor, was the office of the chief clerk, Braden, with a door leading into the main corridor, as well as another leading into the transverse corridor. This office extended from the front of the building to the transverse corridor. Next to and communicating with it was the office of the superintendent of the mint in the very left-hand front corner of the building, opening into the long transverse corridor.

Opposite these two offices, which occupied the entire front of this wing of the mint, and ranged along the other side of the transverse corridor, was the receiving-room at the extreme end, opposite the superintendent's office; the weighing-room, opposite the chief clerk's office; and then the cashier's department, extending through the other half of the back of the building. All three of these departments, the cashier's, the weighing, and the receiving, communicated with one another.

III

Burns' first and most natural query had been: Was it possible to manipulate the books? That proved to be easy to settle, in spite of the intricate system. And it was settled quickly in the negative. No, the books were perfect. According to Colton's own accounts, there was a thirty-thousand-dollar shortage!

Even the cashier himself could not conceal, or had not concealed, the fact that there ought to be thirty thousand dollars more in gold pieces in the vault than there actually was. Blazoned in damning figures on the books themselves was the mystery of the missing double eagles.

Here Burns began his clear and clever reasoning. With an instinct that led him unerringly to the heart of the matter, he quickly came to the conclusion that it was absolutely impossible for any one to have taken the money in business hours, during the day. The next question was: If the money had not been taken during the day, how was it possible to manipulate the time-lock after the cashier's vault had once been closed?

Burns then tackled the time-lock on the cashier's vault, and he soon discovered that he was on the right trail. Some one had filed the dog-locking device so that it could be operated by one who knew the combination, hidden in Colton's mind and sealed in the superintendent's envelop. It made no difference whether the time-lock was set or not. It was out of business. When it was apparently set it really did not lock the combination. No one ever discovered it, for no one ever tried to open it out of hours, except the thief.

The time-lock was taken to a jeweler, and later a government expert—one of the best in the country—was summoned from Washington. Burns and the expert found that the thief had bent a little arm in the time-lock in such a way that it did not strike the proper part to lock the tumblers. The arm had been bent first with the idea of rendering the time-lock inoperative, so that the thief might return at night, work the combination, and so get into the vault. Later, apparently, he had bent the arm farther down in order to be able to work the combination after two days, say on Sunday or a holiday. But he had cracked the nickel, as Burns and the expert discovered, had found that filing the dog-locking device was sufficient, and had bent the arm back again.

Next Burns devoted his attention to the vault itself. He found that at this time and for several months it had been congested with money. All the stationary pigeonholes or receptacles for the sealed bags, each compartment holding a bag of gold with five thousand dollars in it—in one section in fives, in another eagles, and in another double eagles—were full. Therefore, in order to put more money into the vault, two trucks had been pushed up against the east side of it, entirely out of the way. Of course there was no likelihood of wanting to use the money on the trucks or in the pigeonholes back of them. There were plenty of other bags that could be readily got at for any usual demand. These trucks remained stationary until the final accounting, and, in all, some three million dollars accumulated on them.

In counting over the bags, keeping the amount on the trucks separate from the bags in the pigeonholes, the men who did the work found that the three million was intact. Some of the men who helped to carry out the gold remembered, however, six vacant holes near the floor, behind the place where the trucks generally stood. Burns was now getting closer and closer to the truth.

He had already learned from the superintendent how the shortage had been discovered when he and Braden had been counting the money in the vault the day Colton was sick.

Braden had just written down some figures when Atchison leaned over. "There is a shortage of thirty thousand here," said the superintendent keenly.

"No, I think not," replied Braden, continuing to figure; "or perhaps it is due to the cash drawer; or there may have been a mistake in the count."

"Not a bit of it, Braden," replied Atchison promptly. "That count is right."

Count and recount as they might, there was no straightening of it out. There was the mystery at the start, and that was as far as anybody had got when Burns arrived at this point. The money was gone—that was all there was to it. No one believed that it had been spirited away, but then, no one knew what to believe.

"I satisfied myself thoroughly," says Burns, "that it was not even possible to bring the money out into the cashier's office in the daytime, then hide it until night. Every afternoon, before the doors were closed, the cashier and the chief clerk counted every dollar, and, in the presence of the cashier, every day the O.K. of the chief clerk was placed on the cash."

Burns went out and took a turn or two up and down the street; then stood in the shadow of the high Doric columns, thoughtfully revolving the matter over and over in his mind. For it is his theory, in every important case, to put himself in the place of the thief. Point-blank he asked himself, "If I had access to this mint at night from the time of the chief clerk's O.K., and after the mint is closed, to midnight, what possible chance would I have to steal thirty thousand dollars?"

The more he thought of it, the clearer it became, until finally he put the case hypothetically this way: "In order to do that, it is necessary to have entrée to this mint at night under proper pretext, to have entrée to the cashier's office at night under proper pretext, to be able to carry a valise or suit-case in and out of the mint at night under proper pretext. If I had this entrée I could then go ahead. It would then be necessary to manipulate the time-lock in such a way as to render it inoperative. I should also have to know the combination of the vault.

"If that were all true, then I could come into the cashier's office at 4:30 p.m., when the clerks had all gone. At that minute the watchman on that floor, who is as regular as clockwork, has lighted the lights in the cashier's office and has left on his rounds, not to return for twenty-eight minutes. That would give me a chance to open the vault."

Burns then sauntered in and traced out the hypothetical course. Some one, he continued to reason, came in at half past four, opened the vault, took out one or two sacks—never more, for they weighed nearly thirty pounds—and carried them out. Then he hid them in a box-counter in the cashier's office under some empty coin-sacks.

Instead of going out to the main corridor by the natural way, he must have gone on through the weighing-room to the receiving-room. In this way he would be out of sight of the watchman who was always at the main door in the main corridor, looking right down to the cashier's office. In the receiving-room he would then have to climb a counter, and could leave by a door opening into the transverse corridor. Directly across from this door, only ten feet away, was the office of the superintendent. This office had a door opening into the office of the chief clerk. If the gold were hidden, it might be done up in some sort of package and carried out that night or the following day. Probably the thief returned at, say, eleven o'clock at night, when there was a shift of watchmen. He must come in, go to his office on a plausible pretext, get the two sacks hidden in the cashier's office, and in that fashion make his get-away.

This was clear and clever reasoning, and it told Burns much. But it did not catch any criminals—because, as you see, the route taken by the thief involved the offices of Atchison, Braden, and Colton, all three. Burns had his suspicions, and the reader probably has his. At any rate, Burns' were right. It was a question of building up the evidence.

IV

Burns was now ready to come out of cover and begin his "open investigation." Up to this time he had been lying low, but he had now reached a point where certain phases of the case could be inquired into only by his coming out. For instance, he had not yet even been introduced to Braden, though he had been watching everybody and everything in and about the mint.

"I have never met you, Mr. Burns," said Braden one day soon afterward, "but I think I ought to introduce myself. I'm glad to know that you've been detailed on this case, for I've heard and read a great deal about you."

Burns shook hands, and as he did so he noted Braden's clear, steady gaze into his own eyes. And that is something for any man to do; for, if there is one thing above the many that impress you about Burns, it is those boring steel points of eyes of his which cut into your very soul like a bit and seem to strike home at what is lying hidden there.

"I'm satisfied," Braden added, "that you'll find the thief, and if there's anything I can do to aid you, command me."

"Thank you, Braden," returned Burns; "I'll be glad to call on you later."

It is always easier to pick criminals and pile up evidence in predigested detective stories than it is in real life. Burns had made up his mind long before he came out into the open, but there were still some small matters that he did not quite fully see. So it wasn't long before he decided to take advantage of the chief clerk's considerate offer.

"You're the best posted man in this mint on the conduct of the business and things in general," wheedled Burns, to start with. "Now, Braden, as man to man, give me the benefit for a moment of your intimate knowledge. Tell me, how do you yourself think it in reason possible for any person to steal that money? Of course, there must be some person whom you suspect. Who is it?"

For the first time Braden was reluctant to speak. It was quite obvious to Burns that he had his suspicions, and also his reluctance was quite as obvious.

"Yes," he parried; "but you know yourself, Mr. Burns, that it is a serious thing for one in my position to condemn a man on suspicion, and, and—well, I should hate to do it."

"But you must do it," urged Burns, with a becoming show of warmth; "it is your duty."

Braden still hesitated, but it was evident that a name was all but bursting from his lips. Burns pressed him. Finally, with reluctance, he whispered the name of the cashier.

"Yes—Colton," mused Burns. "There was nobody in a position to do it except the cashier. But then, Braden, can't you see the utter futility of any one like Colton expecting to be able to get away with it? What puzzles me is how he could manage it."

"Well, I've figured out several ways. For instance, there are a number of large depositors who do a good deal of business with the mint. One concern alone does from $50,000 to $200,000 a year. There might be some mix-up there."

After going over the drafts and the action that had to be taken on them by the chief clerk himself, as well as each step in the delivery of the money, Burns readily convinced Braden how impossible it was for Colton to do anything in that way.

"Well, then, how about this?" suggested Braden, his reluctance all gone now. "The cashier, when he is filling a truck in the vault with his assistant—you know, he is never alone—could surreptitiously miscount the sacks when the other fellow was off guard, and place a couple of extra bags on the truck. Then, as it was going through the office, he might secretly shove off the sacks, hide them, and later get off with them."

"But there are too many clerks around," objected Burns. "No; you'll have to do better than that."

"Well, how about this?" pursued Braden, thoroughly warmed up to the detective job. "Why couldn't he have the other man stand in with him—put on, say, two extra sacks—and then later the two of them divide up?"

Burns picked that to pieces, too, until even Braden had to admit the folly of Colton's dreaming of such a thing. Then he began a little quizzing on his own account, "Braden," he asked casually, "while you were counting the cash with Colton every day, why did you fail to look behind the trucks in the vaults? It was your duty not to take for granted that everything was there. It was your duty to count all, all—not part, no matter what Colton said. It was your business to see whether the pigeonholes behind the trucks were filled or not. Now why didn't you discover the shortage before?"

The chief clerk shrugged his shoulders. "I took it for granted that they were all there," he answered weakly.

Right here Burns stuck a pin. The failure to look back of the trucks each day showed conclusively one of two things: either some one was outrageously derelict, or he purposely avoided finding the abstraction of the bags.

"Why," continued Burns, "what was the use of counting at all, if you overlooked half a million dollars or so hidden by the two trucks?"

"I didn't think it was necessary to look behind there," reiterated Braden more strongly. "I trusted Colton, and—oh, say, here's another possibility that has occurred to me. Why couldn't he have taken out two sacks, put the money on the cash-table in the vault, and then carried in something—anything, potatoes maybe—to fill up the empty sack before he put it back?"

"Impossible," ejaculated Burns skeptically. "How could he seal it?"

"Well," exclaimed Braden, somewhat nettled, "if you explode all my theories, I must confess I have no others to offer. I can't see how else he could have done it. What's your own theory?"

Burns briefly outlined the case he had worked out.

"Impossible," interrupted Braden. "Why, the time-lock was on, Mr. Burns. He couldn't come back and open it. No; there are no other theories if you reject those I—"

"Think it over," cut in Burns, turning on his heel.

Burns stuck to his theory, too. He went to the men who, covering the period from the previous settlement to the discovery of the shortage, had been on watch. He asked them if they had ever seen any one there after the mint was closed. Some said they never had; others said they had on a few occasions. But all said that whomever they saw never carried a package, a valise, or a suit-case in or out after the mint was closed.

If that were true, then the whole theory that Burns was working up fell to the ground. The men went further and assured him that every package had to be shown to the man at the door. That also exploded the theory. But Burns did not believe it was true. He took the men one at a time, and finally found that there was really only one whom he knew must have been the man on duty when the package or grip, whatever it was, was carried in and out. He took this man aside and told him directly, bringing his cutting eyes into play again, that he suspected him of being part of the conspiracy to loot the mint. That was startling news to the doorman, and he did some quick thinking as well as vigorous asserting of his innocence. Burns told him that he had stated positively that no one had ever gone in or out with a grip, whereas Burns knew better—that some one had.

The watchman looked at him blankly; then a new light seemed to come over his face. There was no fake about it. He had forgotten, but now he actually remembered that an officer of the mint several months before had brought a suit-case one night after seven o'clock, and, with his office door open, had disrobed almost in the presence of the watchman, put on a dress suit, and had gone out to attend a reception. About eleven o'clock he had returned, taken off the suit, put it back in the suit-case, and taken it away with him. This happened on several occasions. But he had taken nothing out except the suit. The man was sure of that. So was Burns, up to a point.

This, then, was an important clue. The man had taken nothing at all until, say, the last few times. It was all cleverly done to "educate" the watchman to see him going in and out with a suit-case at night.

V

The trail was now hot. One day Burns went to the cashier himself. "Colton," he demanded, without any warning, "who changed that lock on the vault?"

"Why," replied Colton thoughtfully, "when I became cashier about a year ago the combination had to be changed. It must have been done by a locksmith."

At once Burns began to trace this assertion down through the labyrinth of fact. It didn't take him long to find that the accounts showed no charge whatever for the services of a locksmith.

Burns confronted the cashier with this fact from his own records. Then Colton said he had made a mistake. He now recalled that when he had assumed his duties, he had asked the chief clerk, whom he succeeded as cashier, what to do about the combination.

"Oh," said Braden, "there isn't any need of getting a locksmith; I'll help you change it."

Together the cashier and the chief clerk had set the combination. Burns made the cashier show him exactly how he claimed it was done.

It seemed that there were four numbers in the combination, the first and last being fixtures, so that only two had to be set by Colton himself. According to Colton, Braden had stood in a certain position while he had tried to fix the second number after the first fixture. As often as he tried, he failed. Something was wrong with the tumblers. At last Braden had said he thought he saw what was wrong.

"Upset it, Colton," he had ordered, "and begin all over again. I'll tell you when the tumblers catch. First the fixture. There. Now try again. Four turns to the right, remember, and set it wherever it happens to be. There—slowly—no—whoa!—a little more, there. The tumblers catch all right. Set that number down, whatever it is. Now twice the other way—and set it at just whatever it is when the tumblers catch—there."

Burns continued to ponder the matter. Suddenly the truth flashed on him. There were only two numbers to be set, since the first and last were fixtures. In some way, Braden had made scratches on the back of the lock which would indicate to one who had made them where the combination was being set by some one else on the other side. One scratch was at twelve, the other at ten. Twelve and ten were the second and third numbers in Colton's combination. From the position which Colton said Braden had assumed, Burns saw that Braden could manipulate the tumblers so that whatever number Colton set the combination at would prove a failure. Then, after Colton had tried again and again and failed, Braden had worked the scheme of telling him that the tumblers caught at the twelve and then at the ten. They caught because Braden did not manipulate them at those points. Braden had forced a card on Colton!

"Now," reasoned Burns, "that filing of the dog-locking device could all have been done a year ago, when Braden himself was cashier. Therefore Colton's story is quite plausible, and he might not have noticed it, since he would have no occasion, if he were honest, to discover that the time-lock was inoperative after he thought he set it."

More than that, it was found that Braden had often been found, when he was cashier, working over the lock, which he always said was out of order.

Piecing his case together bit by bit like a mosaic, Burns next investigated to determine who had arranged that the watchman should be so occupied that his place was vacant for twenty-eight minutes in the afternoon when he started on his rounds to light the gas. The superintendent told him that Braden had said that by a rearrangement they could do with one less watchman. The scheme seemed so well worked out that Atchison had said it was all right.

The mystery was gradually clearing itself up. Braden had first filed the dog-locking device, then he had worked Colton for the combination. The next step was to "educate" the watchman to see him go in and out at night with a suit-case. There was still no chance to get away with anything unless the vault was congested. Braden had accomplished this as cleverly as he had the shifting of the watchman. "Mr. Atchison," he had said, "of what use is it to unseal and seal the other vaults every time we have a little gold to put in or take out? Now, if we take two trucks and put the extra money on them we shall no longer have to break the seal of another vault, but we can put the trucks right into the cashier's vault."

Thus the complete case finally unraveled itself. Step by step, Braden had been working toward a robbery since he himself had been cashier; step by step he had been weaving a web about Colton which should involve him. It was a diabolically clever scheme. It squared with the facts so far. Would it square with new facts?

Patiently Burns set about ferreting out new facts. He questioned every man who might by any possibility have seen anything. From start to finish, he found that he had erected an iron-bound, rock-foundationed case. Colton was innocent.

One night, several months before, four watchmen just going on duty happened to be sitting in the main corridor, with the regular man at his accustomed position at the door. One of them recalled that another was reading from the newspaper an account of the St. Patrick's Day celebration.

"What's that noise I hear in the cashier's room?" he asked.

"It's the chief clerk," replied one of the others.

A moment or two later he thought he heard a noise in the weighing-room.

"What's that?" he asked quickly again.

"Don't know," replied a third. "Keep still. I want to hear about the parade. Go on."

The man who was reading resumed. Just then, from his place near the corner of the main corridor and the transverse corridor, where he was sitting with his chair tilted back against the wall, the first watchman who had heard the noises caught a fleeting, diagonal glimpse down the transverse corridor, as of some one crossing it.

A few minutes later Braden came out of his office with a suit-case. He was white as a ghost. He had had a big scare thrown into him by the presence of five watchmen. The man on the tilted chair thought the man at the door would stop him. But he didn't; instead he merely nodded. He had been "educated."

Another link in the chain Burns was laboriously forging. Out on the big stone steps, that night, Braden had chanced upon one of the outside watchmen. The man had hurried up to help him with his suit-case. "No, no, no," insisted Braden. The man was equally insistent. But Braden won, and jumped on a street-car going to the ferry.

More than that, on the street-car he had had a dispute with the conductor, who wanted to shift the suit-case out of the aisle. The conductor, having once before had words with him, took out a note-book secretly and jotted down in it the date and time with the words, "That crank from the mint," in case the "crank" should lodge a complaint with the company.

At the ferry another watchman, going home, noticed him carrying a suit-case wrapped about with a newspaper as if to hide something bulging. Even the conductor on the other side of the ferry remembered Braden's taking a car home.

Even more than that, it was found that, a couple of weeks before the annual counting of the money, Braden had taken his family several hundred miles on a visit, while he had gone by another route, quite evidently for the purpose of hiding the money.

Here was a chain of evidence whose every link clanked ominously as Burns had forged it since that offer of assistance. You recall that offer of Braden's? "It is my theory," says Burns, "that every criminal leaves a track. This fellow left deep furrows. Any man who is a student of criminology and human nature could have at once detected that Braden had overshot the mark. He looked too straight. He was too persevering in it. It was so marked. I was satisfied beyond question that he had come to me for a purpose. But he had put his foot in it. Then, again, when I asked him of his suspicions, he acted as if he told the name of the cashier reluctantly. Any person sufficiently versed in the investigation and detection of crime could have seen that he had no compunction of conscience whatever. He promptly named the cashier as soon as it was decent to do so, and I apparently acquiesced."

The case was complete. Burns was ready to act.

One day, when he knew Braden was at his club, he called.

"Tell him I can't come out now," Braden sent out.

"Go back and tell Mr. Braden it is very important," Burns ordered the boy.

"He says he is sorry," reported the boy, "but he is in conference."

Burns entered. There was Braden sitting, smoking and joking, with a number of prominent men of the city. He jumped up apologetically. "Beg pardon, Mr. Burns," he said, "but I didn't understand it was you."

"Well, Braden," whispered Burns, drawing him aside, "I've got the thief."

"You have? Good! Let me congratulate you, old man. Never doubted you'd do it. When did you get him?"

"Just now."

"Indeed? Who is he?"

"You."

VI

This is the point where a short-story detective quits with the capture of the real criminal and the vindication of the innocent suspected man. But Burns was just beginning.

"Say, you're joking," protested Braden coolly.

"Not much," reiterated Burns sharply.

"You saw those men in there?" hissed Braden, changing his tactics. "They are some of the most powerful fellows in the city. They can make and unmake people. I can make you lose your job, Burns."

"All right; go ahead, Braden," persisted Burns doggedly. "But you're going with me first."

"You're making a big mistake."

"I'll take a chance on that, but I'll take you, too."

Then, for two days and two nights, there was a battle of wits in Burns' room in the hotel, where he took Braden a virtual prisoner.

It was a dramatic situation, these two men facing each other, with the heart of a great city pulsing about them, and yet alone, each straining at the last ounce of mental power in him. They were "sitting in" a game in which the stakes were Braden's freedom and reputation against justice. Burns knew that, even with a plain open-and-shut case, there were so many slips in a jury trial that only overwhelming evidence would do.

Each eyed the other's every move keenly. Cool and calm and conscious of his power, Burns played his cards. Braden, desperate, deliberate, stood pat. Nor was it an ordinary player who faced Burns. Braden kept his head. He smoked sparingly, drank lightly, and slept almost with one eye literally open, weighing every word of his opponent, watching every action of the detective, and asking himself over and over and over again, "I wonder just how much he *does* know?"

For Burns had been busy flashing a dark lantern on the shady spots in the man's life.

Now, in that hydraulic fashion of his, which has squeezed many a confession out of the most recalcitrant of criminals by the sheer weight of the evidence, he was adding pound after pound of pressure.

He went over the whole case, from the discovery of the shortage, through the various steps down to the now cleared up mystery of the missing double eagles. Braden denied it without the flicker of an eyelash.

Burns drew two cards. He told Braden how he had unearthed the fact that twice before he had been using money that belonged to the government, how he had worked the schemes, how he had covered them up, and how, twice, he had had to get up out of a sick-bed to make good on these "loans" and prevent discovery.

Still Braden did not throw down his cards. Burns finessed. He told him how he had even worked out a scheme to defraud the government, involving checks on the New York sub-treasury. He told him how he had imitated the signature of Atchison so perfectly that even Atchison could not have picked a flaw in it. He told him how the scheme had fallen through because Braden could find no one whom he could trust in New York to work the scheme from that end.

Hour after hour, Burns increased the hydraulic pressure of the facts he had dug out. Would Braden be able to resist?

Burns went back into the man's life before he had come to the mint. He told Braden that he had also been a defaulter in one position, that he had hypothecated warehouse receipts in another. He told him how no one had dared prosecute him on the latter two charges.

All this and more he rammed into Braden. But at the end of the forty-eight hours of mental dueling in the hotel room Braden was still standing pat.

Yet there is nothing of the bloodhound about Burns after he has run his man to cover. "I see what's the matter with you," he finally remarked to Braden, never raising his voice. "You're afraid to talk frankly because you think I'll trick you into an admission. Now, I'll agree on my word as a gentleman that anything said between us will not be used against you. We can discuss your case freely."

There could be no doubt that Braden was cornered at last. He was beaten, baffled, betrayed by the facts at every point, weak, nervous, yet still game.

At the end of the second night he asked desperately: "If I give back the thirty thousand, will you let me go free?"

Burns had begun to feel for the man in his power. But there are "some things no fellow can do." "No," he answered; "you'll have to go to court and plead guilty. But I'll get the Department of Justice not to press the two minor cases where you misused government funds, since you afterwards made restitution."

Braden was visibly weakening.

Just then a Secret Service man came in with an evening paper. In spreading headlines it told of the confession of a man who had stolen $228,000 in gold bars from a smelting company. The paper seemed to be roasting the man, not for the theft, but for confessing.

Braden read it attentively.

"That's what they'd say about me," he remarked thoughtfully, as he laid the paper down. "No; do your worst—I won't say another word."

With that, Braden closed up like a clam.

So began a long battle for justice against this clever crook. First he was convicted and sentenced for two years each, on the two minor charges of misusing government funds.

But for the theft of the thirty thousand dollars he was tried, and after a bitter fight the jury disagreed. Again he was tried, and again the jury disagreed. Braden's "most powerful fellows in the city" were powerful enough for that.

It was after the second failure to secure a conviction that Burns returned to Washington. James M. Beck, who as federal District Attorney in Philadelphia had prosecuted the hundred-dollar Monroe-head counterfeit case, was Assistant Attorney-General then, and on that day was acting Attorney-General.

"It's too bad we didn't get a conviction," remarked Mr. Beck.

"Well," explained Burns ruefully, "you see, the government is too penurious in conducting its cases to watch the jury. If we had had money enough to keep off the jury-fixers we would have won."

Mr. Beck simply reached for his pen.

"I'll make out an order for the money," he said. "You go back there; we'll hire new lawyers as special district attorneys and keep the jury safe this time."

Then began a final battle royal with the jury-fixers and the corrupt attorneys who were fighting for Braden and the gang with which he was friendly. By the way, his own attorney was afterward sentenced for fourteen years in another matter, and several of the "big fellows who could make and unmake people" have also been unmade themselves.

Braden got nine years altogether. The débâcle of this clever crook was complete. The mint breathed easier. Burns had cleared up and fought to a finish the alarming mystery of the missing double eagles.

Harper's Weekly, July 4, 1913

The Infallible Finger-Print

"Suppose the telephone rang, and Brooklyn asked, 'Have you anything on 25 over 27, 10 over 1, 18?' What would you do?" The speaker is a square-shouldered man with a kindly keen twinkle in his eye. He stands in a room where a double line of a couple of dozen or so fixed desks and chairs face him, like a school-room. On the walls are a black-board, charts, and enlarged photographs, while at one side is a battery of stereopticons, indexes, and files.

The uninitiated visitor rubs his eyes at the sight of the "pupils" in this school-room. They are grown men, fine-looking, intelligent fellows. And the charts and photographs—they are not like anything he ever saw in a school-room anywhere else before. There are fragments of noses, ears, eyes, foreheads, mouths. There are curious collections of drawings, and enlargements of gently curving lines that resemble the scroll-like patterns on the old maps denoting the borders of bays, gulfs, and oceans. What are all these hieroglyphics—a physiology lesson?

The "scholar" jots down the cryptogram message; and there is no uncertainty in his manner or face as he does so.

"I should look in the twenty-fifth pigeonhole of the twenty-seventh horizontal row of the cabinet," he begins. "Under nine ridges on the right index finger, over on the middle, under on the left index."

So he rattles on.

Training Men to Hunt Men

By this time the reader has no doubt got his bearings. This is not a class in physiology. This is the new school for detectives at the headquarters of the New York Police Department in the imposing new granite and marble building on Center Street. Captain Joseph A. Faurot, head of the Bureau of Identification, the expert on finger-prints, the portrait parlé, and all manner of latest ideas in identification and apprehension of criminals, is "quizzing" a class of detectives, who are studying in this unique school all the mysteries of the new idea in tracking criminals. This New York school, in which the course lasts some five or six weeks, is a replica and extension of one that has existed for many years for the training of detectives in Paris under the famous Bertillon.

Volumes might be written on the various "lessons" that are crowded into this short course in which practically the entire detective force of New York is being instructed. Most of it is so new that it has not yet found its way into text-books. This article, however, deals only with part of it—with the marvelous new detective chiromancy, with those, ten indelible marks of identification, the infallible finger-prints.

In the history of modern scientific criminology there have been few advances that have had to fight their way more bitterly against prejudice and opposition, and yet have won more surely, than the system of finger-printing. And, more than that, the victory has not been confined to criminology. In all sorts of official and civil life the vogue of the finger-print is to-day gaining rapidly, in the army and the navy, in civil service, in banks, in business.

Photography has failed. Our rogues' galleries, important adjuncts as they still are, have proved to be nothing but nets with big holes of escape through which the clever crook may easily wriggle. The Bertillon system of measurement is all right, if the measurements are correct. But, as we shall see, the "if" looms large. It remained for the finger-print to accomplish what no other system had accomplished. Here, at last, is the system whose introduction marks the end of alibi and alias.

Mark Twain Popularizes the Finger-Print Theory

One of the clearest and most graceful expositions of the finger-print theory is that of Mark Twain's "Pudd'nhead Wilson" in his speech in defense of the twins:

> "Every human being carries with him from his cradle to his grave certain physical marks which do not change their character and by which he can always be identified— and that without shadow of doubt or question. These marks are his signature, his physiological autograph, so to speak; and this autograph can not be counterfeited, nor can he disguise it or hide it away, nor can it become illegible by the wear and the mutations of time. . . . This signature is each man's very own—there is no duplicate of it among the swarming millions of the globe!
>
> "Upon the haft of this dagger stands the assassin's natal autograph, written in the blood of that helpless and unoffending old man who loved you and whom you all loved. There is but one man in the whole earth whose hand can duplicate that crimson sign!"

Twenty years ago these facts were not so well known as they are to-day. Now almost any schoolboy knows, at least vaguely, that the surfaces of the hands and feet of men and monkeys are covered with minute ridges which form regular systems, though the ridges themselves are not always perfectly regular. These ridges are studded with microscopic pores, the raised entrances to deep-seated sweat-glands which it may be their purpose to elevate, as well as to aid the nerves in the sense of touch. As the late Sir Francis Galton, who may properly be called the father of the finger-print theory, put it, "Let no one despise the ridges on account of their smallness, for they are, in some respects, the most important of all anthropological data."

These ridges, it is interesting to note, are prominent on the hands and feet of the man-like apes, as well as on the under surface of the prehensile tail of many primates. They are, perhaps, a relic in us of our arboreal days, for they certainly enable us to get a better grip. If they are worn off the grip is bad, and they are most prominent on the hands of manual laborers. Moreover, in certain mild emotions it is the hands and feet that perspire, while the rest of the body is comparatively unaffected. The ridges probably act as little suckers, but not so as to render sluggish an attempt to release the grip. Air is let in along the depressions between the ridges, making possible quick movements.

For instance, it has been found that the fear of falling, as in our "falling dreams," automatically increases the exuding of perspiration. A slightly moist hand gives a better grip than a dry hand. Practically nothing, say the physiologists, has been added to the machinery of the emotions since our forefathers lived and fought and fled in the tree-tops. A damp hand then denoted fear. It does so to-day. And one of the very interesting appliances from the psychological laboratory which it has been proposed to use in the detection of crime, in a scientific "third degree," has to do with this fact of the damp hand.

How to Take an Impression

To return to finger-prints. All that is necessary to take them is a piece of glass, or a piece of polished copper, a bottle of printer's ink, and a roller to spread the ink very, very thinly over the glass or metal. Carefully smoked glass may be used, as well as an ordinary inking-pad designed for rubber stamps; while several prepared papers have been placed on the market, with varying success.

In taking prints, the fingers must first be cleansed so as to remove everything from the hollows between the ridges. There are two kinds of impressions that are then taken, the rolled and the flat. If you place the right thumb with the nail at right angles to the flat surface on which you rest it, and roll it over, pressing only slightly on the bulb of the thumb as you turn it over through a half circle, you will have a rolled impression, giving the full detail of the marking as if a half cylinder has been impressed on the paper.

In taking finger-prints in the standard manner, the right hand is taken first, the thumb, index, middle, ring, and little fingers in order. This is repeated on the other hand in the same order, rolling from right to left on the right hand, from left to right on the left. Finally, at the bottom of a standard finger-print blank, the four fingers of the left hand are taken, and then of the right, holding them all close together and laying them simultaneously first on the ink-slab and then on the paper. These latter impressions are known as "flat" and are taken as a check against getting any of the separate rolled impressions out of order.

All Finger-Prints Run in One of Three Patterns

There are three general types of patterns in finger-prints, the arch, the loop, and the whorl, to which may be added a fourth known as the composite. In the arch the ridges run from one side to the other in parallel curving lines, making no backward turn, and devoid of twists. In some arches the center is raised like a tent, and they are known as "tented arches."

The loop has a pitchfork or hair-pin, making a complete turn, as the name "loop" indicates. Loops are never exactly parallel to the median line of the finger, but turn one way or the other. If the angle is toward the inner side, the thumb, it is known as radial; if toward the outer or little finger direction, ulnar, named after the bones of the forearm, the radius and ulna bones. Sometimes there are two loops, one in each direction, on one finger, known as "twinned loops."

In the whorl the ridges have a vortex arrangement around a central nucleus, the ridges making a turn through at least one complete circuit. In some cases there is a little "pocket" in the pattern of the print, either a central or a lateral pocket. Often two or more of the three general types are combined in one finger, known as a composite. There are also what are called "accidentals."

An Indestructible Signature

The fine work comes in when the markings of a particular print are compared with those of another on file, to prove the identity of the two. For the most minute marks persist, the same, from the cradle to the grave. Fingers grow, but the convolutions of the ridges in childhood are the same in old age, except in size. Faces change, but not fingerprints. Galton once compared prints taken at all ages, and among more than seven hundred pairs found only one small ridge cleft in a child which in later years was apparently united, a change so small as to be negligible. The ridges are like threads in lace. Distort the lace as you will, the threads are still there in the same mutual relations. Fingers grow fat or lean; the patterns remain the same. Indeed, they do more than that. The general pattern is found in the fingers of the unborn babe, and has been studied accurately in mummies from Egypt, thousands of years old.

Identifying Jezebel

Galton calculated that the chance that one fingerprint would be the same as another was one in sixty-four thousand millions; that is, if the population of the world were forty times what it is, there would then be the probability of one person having finger-prints the same as another. Dr. Balthazard, the French medico-legal expert, recently presented to the Academy of Sciences some extraordinary figures to demonstrate the impossibility of error. If the population of the earth is taken as 1,500,000,000, and a generation considered as a third of a century, there would then be some 5,000,000,000 people each century, each with ten fingers, making 50,000,000,000 prints. By dividing each finger-print into one hundred squares, and calculating the possible combinations of variations in the ridges, he arrives at the conclusion that, theoretically, two identical finger-prints would be found only once during a period of years whose ciphers would take up a couple of lines of type—a period longer than that which astronomers estimate is needed for the sun to grow cold.

Thus, as Galton remarked, when Jezebel was devoured by the dogs and nothing of her was left but her skull, the palms of her hands, and the soles of her feet, so that no man might say, "This is Jezebel," in reality that was just how a modern scientist could have been sure that it was Jezebel!

London newspapers awhile ago contained a circumstantial story of how, at last, finger-prints had broken down. Finger-prints of a man accused of a crime were shown to a magistrate to prove that the man had been previously convicted. But it was also proved that this man was serving in the army at the time. A week later, however, finger-prints were vindicated. It was found that the man had stolen the proofs of service of another, and that he had never been in the army.

This was something like a recent case in America, where, for certain reasons, a man gave himself up as a deserter from our army and was sent to a Western United States penitentiary. His finger-prints were taken and referred to the War Department. There it was found that he had never been a United States soldier. Finger-prints convicted this man of innocence, and his scheme fell through. In fact, the system has time and again proved itself so infallible that a writer of detective fiction, in a recent story, could find no way in which to beat the system except to have the clever criminal cut off his fingers and grow new ones by the ultra-modern methods of the new surgery!

· · ·

A Historic Finger-Print Case in India

Among the historic finger-print cases in India was that of the manager of a tea-garden in the Jalpaiguri district. He was found lying in bed, his throat cut, his despatch-box and safe rifled, and several hundred rupees had been carried away. The Indian police at once rounded up a number of suspects. The man had been a hard task-master, and it was thought that perhaps some of the coolies in the garden had murdered him. But, in looking over the ground, the police found suspicious blood-spots on the clothing of the cook.

Not to let any possibility escape, the relatives of a woman with whom the murdered man had had a liaison were placed under surveillance, as well as a servant whom he had once had imprisoned for theft, Kangali Charan. Besides these, a wandering band of natives excited suspicion. Further investigation, however, soon eliminated the band of natives, the woman's relatives, and the coolies. Inquiry showed that the servant had been released within a week, but had not been seen in the neighborhood. The cook asserted vehemently that the stains were of pigeon's blood from a bird that he had killed.

It so happened that among the papers in the despatch-box was a calendar in book form printed in Bengali. It had a light-blue cover, and on this cover two faint brown smudges appeared. Under the glass they were seen to be impressions of fingers, and the chemical examiner of the government demonstrated that they were marks of mammalian blood. The murderer or an associate had placed his bloody thumb on the book while hunting for the key to the safe. In the murdered man's own blood the murderer had signed the warrant for his own arrest. But who was the murderer, the cook or the ex-servant?

The central office of the Bengali police was appealed to, and they hunted through their classified finger-print records. The bloody fingers corresponded exactly with a set on file. Meanwhile the report of the chemical analyst said that the spots on the cook's clothes were really of pigeon's blood. Kangali was finally located a hundred miles away, and taken to Calcutta. There his finger-prints were again taken. The prints on the book, in the police records, and those taken after the arrest, all agreed. The proof was overwhelming—calculated by Sir Edward Henry at over one million to one against him. The judges convicted Kangali of having stolen the property, but held it unsafe to convict him of murder, as no one had seen the deed committed. To-day there would be no such hesitation.

The Convict in the Billiard-Room

The first case in Great Britain in which the evidence of finger-prints was solely relied on to convict a man occurred in 1902. A billiard-room in a house in Denmark Hill had been broken into and robbed, and the thief had used part of a dust-cover in which to carry off the stolen property. There was no clue, apparently, to the murderer. But the police, in going carefully over the billiard-room, found that the woodwork of the window-frames had been quite recently painted and was not yet dry. On this newly painted woodwork they found the fresh imprint of a thumb. Sergeant Collins, one of the officers in charge of the records of finger-prints kept at Scotland Yard, who had had special training in the system, was at once notified, and he immediately photographed the single print—a slender thread, it would seem. Here were, not ten fingers, but only one. Still, there was no difficulty in deciding it to be a thumb, and the left one.

Four nights later a burglary was perpetrated in Herne Hill, and there the dust-cover that had been taken from Denmark Hill was left behind. It was clearly the same criminal in each case. Plate and valuables amounting to six hundred dollars were taken.

It would have taken a long time to go through all the records on file, laboriously comparing this left thumb-print with those filed. Fortunately, it proved to be unnecessary. The police knew the kind of man who would be most likely to undertake such a job, and among those whom they suggested was a man named Harry Jackson. His prints were already on file. The moment Collins saw them he knew he had the right man. But Jackson could not be found in any of his regular haunts.

Six weeks later, in the early morning, a noise was heard on the roof of a public house in Brixton. The constables were called, and a man was seen on the roof. They gave chase, and the man dropped a bag of tools that showed him to be a house-breaker. Over roofs, and finally into a garden, he was followed and captured. It was Harry Jackson.

So far the case had been ordinary enough. But it was novel in this respect—the single finger-print on the window-sill. That connected the man with two previous robberies. The sergeant at once compared it with the finger-print of the prisoner himself and the record on file. The three agreed absolutely.

But would the court accept such evidence? Would it go even as far as in the Kangali case? Here was evidence to establish identity of a kind never before used before a jury in an English criminal court. The prisoner stoutly swore his innocence. Nevertheless, the authorities went ahead and presented their evidence, photographs, and explanation to the jury. The court did accept the evidence, and about a month later, in spite of the man's plea for leniency, he was sentenced to seven years' penal servitude in the Old Bailey. The precedent had been set. The first man had been convicted in England by means of finger-prints alone.

Since then innumerable cases have occurred where finger-prints have identified and convicted criminals—impressions on plated ware, drinking-glasses, bottles, cash-boxes, candles. An empty champagne bottle on the dining-room table of a house that had been burglarized in Birmingham was found to bear a fingerprint. It was sent to London. Within a few minutes a duplicate impression was found in the files, and the burglar was arrested the same day.

In another case two finger-prints on a wine-glass convicted a notorious criminal of a robbery of a West End house where he had paused long enough to help himself to a drink. A cash-box bearing a blurred finger-print was found in the room of a man and his wife murdered in Deptford. Two brothers suspected of the crime were arrested, and the finger-print of one of them corresponded precisely with that on the box. A curious case was that of a thief who climbed a ten-foot gate, but in attempting to reach the ground his foot slipped from the center cross-bar. He had been holding the spikes on the top with his right hand. The ring on his little finger caught on one of the spikes, and his weight, as he fell, tore the finger from his hand. The ring and finger were found by the police, an impression and a search revealed a duplicate record on file, and the man was arrested.

The "Candle Burglar"

Clearing up the mystery of the "candle burglar" added to the fame of the new system. The man was so called because he always had with him a tallow dip. This case involved the robbery of a house in Washington Square, New York, and its solution hinged upon the sweaty imprint of a thumb left by the thief on a soup-ladle. Captain Faurot, who has a memory for finger-prints better than most people have for faces, noticed that the print had the peculiarity of three "deltas." There was no print in the file which corresponded. But some weeks later a man was brought in for loitering about a pawnshop suspiciously. He was finger-printed. At once the peculiarity of one print flashed over Faurot. This was the candle burglar—there were the three deltas. Rather than stand trial, the man pleaded guilty and was sentenced. The soup-ladle he didn't take because it was plated landed him in Sing Sing.

While John G. Milburn, Jr., son of the noted corporation attorney, and his family were in Europe one summer, burglars entered their New York house and stole a number of valuables amounting to several thousand dollars. They even looted a small safe. There was no clue to them except a print of some fingers on a Tiffany glass clock. This became known speedily as the "clock case." From the prints in the dust on the glass, "Black" Cohen was promptly identified by comparison with similar prints on record. He was arrested by the mere lines on his fingers, and confessed. The other members of the gang were gathered in and much of the booty recovered. In another case, the "bath-room burglar," who made a practice of climbing to the roof of extensions and thus getting in by an unlocked bath-room window, was captured.

One of the many cases with a queer little human-interest touch is that which centers about a cut-glass rose-bowl. Three years ago a house in Flatbush, New York City, was entered, and most of the contents of the dining-room were taken. A canary bird, freed from its cage, was flying about the room. But among the things left behind was the bowl, on which the detectives found a blurred finger-print. It was photographed; but, as nothing like it was found in the files, the detectives had to wait. Three months later, in another part of Flatbush, a woman was killed by one of two burglars who had broken into her home. Her son wounded one of them severely, and later both men were captured. The wounded burglar protested that he was not a professional, and declared that this was his first crime. But Captain Faurot quickly discovered the similarity of his finger-prints with those on the glass bowl. He proved to be a convict of long standing.

"Why did you release the canary in that other robbery?" shot out Faurot, when he confronted the wounded man with the evidence against him.

"Well," he replied slowly, realizing that the game was up, "I'd just done time up the river myself, and I hated to see any creature shut up."

So far, finger-prints had secured indictments and convictions after the criminal had confessed or corroboratory evidence had been introduced. But the first case in which finger-prints alone secured a conviction in New York, when offered in open court before a jury, was that of the Italian criminal, Carlo Crispi. One night a loft building on Wooster Street was entered. A glass panel was removed from the door in order to avoid setting off the burglar alarm. The burglar had taken out the putty and leaned the glass against the wall, so as not to break it and attract attention. Then he had opened the door and taken some hundreds of dollars' worth of goods. On the glass were found the imprints of three fingers. The criminal had left something behind that was as good as his card or even his photograph. Crispi was recognized through prints already on file, and was arrested. But, with forethought, he had prepared a very careful alibi, and protested his innocence vigorously. Several persons swore that on the night of the robbery he was at the theater with a party including his wife, that they had returned, and Crispi had gone to bed. The accused man feigned amusement when the glass and marks were produced in court. But Captain Faurot's testimony was a sensational feature. Still the jury appeared skeptical. The expert offered to leave the room, to let any one touch the glass, and then to pick him out from finger-prints. He did so, and one of those in the court-room touched the glass. From a dozen or two finger-prints of those in the room Faurot quickly decided who had touched the glass. He went on to show how many points of identity there were in Crispi's prints and those on the glass—sixteen in one finger alone. Crispi's amusement changed to wonder and wonder to despair. He visibly lost courage before the precise demonstration of the peculiarities of his fingers as duplicated in the prints shown on the glass, broke down, confessed, entered a plea of guilty, and was sentenced. His story of the alibi, perhaps to save his friends, was that he did go to the theater, return and go to bed, but that after his wife was asleep he got up and went out to do the job. Whether that was true or not, finger-prints proved one thing—Crispi was the thief. This case gave the authorities much greater confidence in finger-print evidence.

Finger-Prints on Objects Soon Fade

As a rule finger-prints on objects are valueless, however, after a few days, often hours. For instance, in one case the New York police found finger-prints on a safe that had been broken into. They found that the fingers belonged to a certain man who had a police record. At the trial his lawyer admitted the finger-prints for the sake of argument, but contended that his client might have been at the place some time before the robbery on legitimate business. The police replied that it could not have been so, that finger-prints thus made would have faded away. A test was made. Fingers of various persons were placed on a safe, and then five days later the safe was examined. The lawyer was in high glee when Faurot dusted some powder on the safe and faint smudges appeared. But when the smudges were examined and photographed it was sufficiently evident that the prints had faded so that they were valueless. The lawyer asserted he could identify them, but when he tried he failed utterly. The man was convicted and the fact was established that at least on some substances the oil and moisture left by the fingers are not permanent. In this way the plausible excuse is destroyed that the accused may have visited a place long before the crime on legitimate business.

In one case an express package containing six thousand dollars was opened and part of the money abstracted. The thief had resealed it, but the imprint of one of his fingers was left in the wax. The company ordered impressions taken of the fingers of all its employees. One man refused and ran away; he was overtaken and prints were secured. They proved to be the same as those on the seal; he confessed and returned the money.

The Wide Use of Finger-Prints

New York is probably the first city to use fingerprints in the case of minor charges. In that city they are now used in the night court for women. Two years ago finger-printing was authorized for prostitutes brought into this court, and the magistrate now knows the previous record in every case before him. The record for sixteen months shows that 2,937 persons have been brought before the court on this charge, some as many as ten times.

Prints were taken 5,257 times with 2,320 identifications.

The immigration authorities have tried finger-prints in order to catch foreign criminals, but discarded the system after a short trial, not because it broke down, but merely because the government force was inadequate. Other uses that have been proposed for fingerprints are on passports, in civil service work, and lately for insurance companies. In the latter case it is urged that the dead can be identified and substitution or fraud made impossible, since a dead man's fingerprints are as good as those of the living.

Savings-banks have pretty generally taken up the finger-print lately, in addition to signatures and other identification records to prevent forgeries and frauds. There are now scores of banks in New York and other sections of the country where finger-prints are taken when an account is opened or money withdrawn. In this case the system is a little different from that already described. An ink-pad is used and three fingers of the right hand only are impressed on a card, which is filed with the paying-teller. It has been found that bank employes learn the system readily, that depositors do not object, not even the women. It is a fine system for banks having many illiterate depositors and prevents many swindles. The American Bankers' Association has indorsed the idea, though when it was first proposed conservative bankers believed that there would be considerable opposition due to prejudice since finger-prints were used in police work. Prejudice has been easily overcome and depositors often, realizing the protection, have actually asked for this protection. It is real forgery insurance. There is no record of any one ever having forged a finger-print. It might also be valuable on letters of credit, and one lawyer uses it for the testator and witnesses in signing wills.

Finger-prints are now used in one way or another all over the world, and the recent Men and Religion Movement went on record as favoring finger-printing for everybody. Captain Faurot suggests a central bureau in which the finger-prints of every one might be filed. With the growth in the civil and commercial use of the system, the "stigma" is rapidly passing away. If finger-prints were in general use there would be no more election frauds, no more unidentified dead, no more cases of "lost identity." New uses for finger-prints are constantly being discovered, and students of the system confidently believe that some day it will indeed be universal.

The Independent, July 10, 1913

In Defense of the Detective Story

WHAT IS THE PSYCHOLOGY of the hosts of readers of detective stories? Is it that, as Paul Armstrong says, "we are all as full of crime as Sing Sing and we long to see those who have dared to do the things we all have had glimpses of, even a smothered impulse to do them ourselves—but we're 'too well civilized,' let us say?"

Now and then the newspapers report cases, or alleged cases, in which crooks "confess" to deriving inspiration from this or that literary source. Such was an example not long ago when the driver of a delivery wagon in Brooklyn was arrested as the culprit in a series of house robberies. What differentiated his from other arrests on similar charges was the reported fact that this young man had evidently studied for his criminal profession, as one newspaper put it, "in the most approved modern text-books," or perhaps what might be called the up-to-date correspondence school of crime.

The fact of the matter is that there are two kinds of fiction which every generation reads with avidity—the love story and the mystery story. If all the world loves a lover, so does all the world look with interest and curiosity on the criminal and the detective who traps him. To the normal mind the crook and his captor are always alluring.

I recall once asking Mr. Edison whether he ever read detective stories. With that magic smile that flits over his race when a question interests him, the great inventor replied, "That is about all the fiction I do read." Then he went on, a moment later, glancing about at the appalling mass of scientific books and periodicals in his library, "I don't think I ever felt so badly over the death of anyone not connected with me as I did when Gaboriau died."

Perhaps a little excursion into the history or rather the evolution of the detective story might clear the air a bit. An odd point, as someone once remarked in the *New York Times*, about the entrance of the detective into American literature is the fact that an American took him to France and the French writers sent him back to the land of his birth.

Poe's immortal mystery tales made but slight impression at first on his own countrymen, but they were received with applause in France and under the influence of "The Purloined Letter" Gaboriau wrote his *Le 13me Hussards*. This first of the French detective stories did not reach America, but it was the book of Gaboriau's follower, Du Boisgobey, which was the literary parent of the *Old Sleuth* tales. This was *The Crime of the Opera House*, which set all Paris agog, even after the Gaboriau thrillers, and started the cheap detective story in America.

Before leaving Poe, one cannot resist paying tribute to the real founder of the modern mystery story. Change the setting of "The Purloined Letter" and we have Gaboriau's inspiration. Change the setting of "The Murders in the Rue Morgue" and we have the inspiration for Conan Doyle's "The Sign of the Four." Poe's Dupin is the father of Sherlock Holmes; his "analytical reasoning" is the forerunner of "deduction." If we reimported Poe in the vastly inferior form of the dime novel from France, we reimported him in a vastly better form as Sherlock Holmes from England.

"Old Sleuth" was the nom de plume of Harlan P. Halsey, who was the first to introduce the detective story as the main element of the dime novel, and kept at it himself for twenty years, until a younger generation of writers of these penny dreadfuls took up the work.

It is said that some of this new generation have composed sixty thousand words a week, providing a new plot every seven days.

The dime novel began about 1860 under the guidance of H.H. Beadle, a story of lurid western adventure, on the covers of which appeared a woodcut of a dime, hence the name. Halsey, who helped to throw discredit on the detective story by injecting it into this class of literature, is said to have received his literary training as a butcher in Washington Market. He overcame his fundamental failings in the matter of grammar and spelling after he "broke into" literature by dictating his stories. His first genuine hit was *The Fastest Boy in New York*, which caused him to branch out into more ambitious detective stories as a result of reading the book of Du Boisgobey, the literary parent of "Old Sleuth."

Halsey's success was instantaneous. Immediately another publisher copyrighted the signature "Nick Carter" and that was soon followed by "Old Cap Collier" and "King Brady." Under these names some hundred writers have at various times contributed to the world's supply of blood and thunder.

It did not take long for this "literary" output to slop over into Europe. In England, France, and Germany, translations and elaborations of dime novels have had a wide vogue. Indeed, a society was recently organized in Germany to discourage the publication and sale of the "Nick Carter" and other stories for the express reason that they were said to increase crime by suggestion if not by direct incitement. A large number of publishers have agreed not to have anything to do with such literature and booksellers have combined to discourage its sale.

In Russia nearly nine million copies of such books are sold annually, and are known as "Pinkerton stories." They are flimsy affairs, sold at about three cents a copy, with paper covers embellished with cheap colored pictures of crimes. The titles themselves are hair-raising: *A Nest of Criminals, The Bloody Altar, Kidnappers of Girls, A Sect of Murderers, The Revenge of the Escaped Convict.*

One may agree heartily with the unsparing critics of the dime novels and still disagree even more heartily with those who would condemn also the modern detective story as it appears from the presses of the hosts of reputable publishers. It is said that Nick Carter inspired one of the brightest and wittiest women who write detective stories. She saw the need and desire of readers for literature of that class and determined that it might be wholesomely supplied—and with marked success.

It is often the other elements (besides the high literary quality) that various writers add to detective stories which should be the saving grace even in the eyes of the sharpest critics. Law, justice, and the right triumph in ninety-nine stories out of a hundred of this class, which is a higher average than can be set by any detective bureau in actual life. Whatever the psychology of the reader of crime stories, it is the crime *plus* other elements that fascinate him. Mr. Arthur Train in a recent interview put it:

> No story of crime or of criminal procedure is interesting because of this fact, but in spite of it. Crime and everything connected with it are at their best sordid and repellent. What makes a story based on them at all interesting is that which makes stories of any and all types interesting—interesting personality or conditions.
>
> The criminal is interesting, despite the fact that he is a criminal, because of his personality. Conditions and incidents are interesting despite the fact that they are criminal conditions or incidents, and they must be uncommonly interesting to

overcome the barrier.

Few stories of crime would be interesting that were accurate, true to life records. The story writing impulse must go hand in hand with the imagination. The setting, the background, and the foundation of the characters may be drawn from experience, but all that is only a beginning. The story writing impulse has to be there first and imagination always.

An example of the "other elements" which stories of crime and detection must possess may be cited in the scientific detective story which just now seems to be popular. It began when several writers tried to apply psychology, as developed by Prof. Hugo Muensterberg of Harvard and Prof. Walter Dill Scott of Northwestern University, to either actual or hypothetical cases of crime. Cleveland Moffet made an early use of it in a story, and some years ago two writers collaborated in the creation of a psychological detective for a popular magazine. But that was only a beginning. The fact is that the whole field of science lies open to be drawn on by the clever detective—from finger prints, the portrait parlé, the dictagraph and detectaphone to chemistry and physics in general. Not long ago an astronomer freed an innocent man by calculating the exact date on which a photograph was taken, using the shadows to guide him.

This latest development, far from being harmful, is a decided advance for both the detective story and the detective. More and more the discoveries of the scientists, romantic and thrilling in themselves, are being applied by the forces of law and order in the running down of the criminal. Fiction of this sort is a positive source of good. In the end it will make detectives more and more efficient; will tend to discourage criminals by the sheer weight of inescapable fact. In Europe there has actually grown up a class of scientific professors, a dozen of whom could be named, whose exploits read like fiction. The spread of such knowledge cannot do harm—unless indeed the spread of knowledge itself be harmful.

I recall that the very first scientific detective story which I wrote was returned to me by one editor of a popular magazine with what I considered the most complimentary letter he ever wrote me, that he "couldn't publish a story like that—some darn fool would go out and try to do it." Of course, he had put the cart before the horse. It was not the criminal who might profit.

In one case which "Kennedy" unravelled, he found that the criminal had broken into a safe by using thermite to burn thru the steel. Immediately several people wrote for the formula for thermite. It may be found in several scientific journals. There is not and never was anything to prevent a crook from using it, yet it is not regularly found in the cracksman's kit as a result of a story about it and the detection of the user.

In another story the method of preparation of "soup" or the nitroglycerine used by yeggmen, was mentioned. From the president of a large powder company came this letter:

> I wonder if you have ever considered the possible effect of your stories upon the coming generation of up-to-date yeggs. No doubt some of them combine with an honest desire to get something for nothing, enough intelligence to read high class detective stories. They may pick up a good many valuable little tips from your practical yarns. However, the preparation of "soup" (nitroglycerine) as you give it, while satisfactory, may have a discouraging effect on some inquiring souls. Rubbing dynamite in the bare hands long enough to effect a complete alcoholic solution will

surely give the investigator a severe case of "powder headache" or nitroglycerine poisoning. While these attacks, as you know, are seldom fatal, they are always so excruciatingly painful that the chances are that the investigator will thereafter reform, or at least limit his attentions to those safes which may be opened with the teeth of a hairpin.

Every mention of the dictagraph, the detectaphone, and similar scientific eavesdroppers has brought eager inquiries. In one case a letter from a South Carolina man said: "I have a case in which I can use such a device in procuring the real truth. It will be the means of restoring the character of a young man who is now a victim of a foul conspiracy." In another case a man who was under indictment in Iowa wanted the author to come to his rescue with such of the scientific paraphernalia as Kennedy uses. "I think," he appealed, "that if you will bring the instruments named, I can get enough evidence to clear myself."

Whatever may be said of the cheap crime story, whatever may be said of the crime story of the past—and even that must be read with a sack of salt handy—it remains to be shown that the detective story as it ordinarily appears today is a force for evil. Much more often it serves a decided moral purpose.

Mr. William J. Burns is fond of reiterating the statement that every criminal leaves a track. If it has never been found, it is simply because no one has ever looked for it in the right way. He says that it is a good thing to tell people how hard it is nowadays in the face of modern organization and modern science to "get away with the goods." It is at least an even chance that a good detective story will help the detective as much as it will the criminal.

Today the scientist as well as the detective is on the trail of the criminal. If the fiction writer, by telling the facts in the only way that you can reach a large audience, is writing a "text-book for crooks," let the crooks make the most of it. The detectives have been doing so for some time.

The Forum, July 1919

When the Criminal Takes to Science
And its Effect on the Fictionist

WHETHER IT IS POSSIBLE THESE DAYS for a man to commit a crime of which there is no possible means of detection, and not be found out, is simply the ancient problem of the immovable body and the irresistible force. The criminal, to-day, is bound to be caught, and the more a man studies a crime, the more art he spends on it, the surer he is of detection. That may sound paradoxical, but William J. Burns himself affirmed that proposition to me long ago.

The hardest man to catch is the one who uses the simplest, crudest method. The thug blackjacks his victim and too often goes his way. Take, on the other hand, the bomb outrages that are worrying the police, just now. Those bombs were so very well made that the police are bound to catch the maker. Take again the recent sensational case of Dr. Arthur Warren Waite, the New York dentist who killed his father-in-law and his mother-in-law by arsenical poisoning, and had planned to kill his wife also. An examination of his private apartments brought abundant evidence to light that he had studied crime from a scientific standpoint and had endeavored to penetrate the secrets of the laboratory for the purpose of becoming a highly developed scientific criminal.

He calculated to inoculate his victims causing them to die a commonplace "natural" death. I found in his desk a large number of microscopic slides which he had made—three or four hundred of them—showing germs of tetanus, anthrax, typhus and bubonic plague. He even went to Bellevue and tried to buy a tubercular mastoid bone, for the purpose of inoculating his victims. And yet this man, who might have become a master of scientific crime, used the most primitive poison in the pharmacopoeia when he came to despatch his victims. He needed money. It was the one passion of his life. Money—money, to gratify his extravagant and ever-increasing tastes. And so in his hurry he employed plain arsenic. Had it not been for the sheer intuition of a woman—and that you know is woman's prime gift, mere man is not supposed to have it, and yet there have cropped up here and there instances, such as Lloyd George who is said to have rare intuition—he never would have been caught. Merely suspecting that something was wrong she sent a telegram suggesting an autopsy. And this disclosed the facts.

Scientific Criminals Who Bungled

I never was more disappointed—speaking from a purely scientific standpoint—in a case in my life. Here was a man who might with patience have developed into the arch-criminal of the ages—a very limb of Satan—who would have revealed to the authorities a new realm of detective research, and begun a new era in criminology. And yet because he was a spendthrift and must have money he despatches the victims, over whom he had spent laborious days and nights, by the commonest poison known—arsenic. Arthur Warren Waite lacked two of the great moral virtues—patience and the commonest sort of sense. Perhaps when the perfect type of scientific criminal is evolved he will be found to possess them all—must have them, as the very basis of his equipment.

Sounds paradoxical, doesn't it? But crime is about the most paradoxical thing so far created. The perfect type of scientific criminal may evolve in the course of time, but thus far, at least, the more scientific he is the more sure he is to bungle, to leave some loose end by which he can be caught.

Take the celebrated case of Carlyle Harris who killed a girl by the use of morphine. He simply bungled. He gave her too much. It was noticed that her pupils after death were contracted to pin-points—and that led to discovery. That was the only sign in an unsuspected case.

The reader will remember how that case led to another. Dr. Buchanan, a dentist, when he heard of the Harris case, remarked: "Why didn't he give her a little atropine, and dilate the pupils?" That remark was remembered some time after when Dr. Buchanan himself stood suspected of murder. The body of his victim, as it proved, was exhumed and it was found that both atropine and morphine had been administered, so as to leave no trace even in the eyes. The Doctor was convicted.

What Scientific Crime Has Proved

Scientific crime "such as it is," as the boarder remarked when he passed the butter, if it has proved anything thus far has proved that there is such a thing as being too clever a murderer. Of course the old-fashioned, and still to some extent persistent order of "square-toed" detective will not catch him. But bless you: "the force" is improving all the time. And I am not even thinking of flattering either myself or the small army of detective-story writers when I say that we have simply got to take some credit for this ourselves. I have always found—since I began to write—that I was "great friends" with any real detective. I think I know one or two men at headquarters now, who, in the parlance of the street, would give me almost anything. A young man who had been reading my stories came in to see me from Chicago a year ago and announced that he was establishing a scientific crime-laboratory. He wanted to know what he needed. I introduced him to Osborne, the hand-writing expert—a first step.

To speak boldly I consider Dr. Otto H. Schultze, medical adviser at the District Attorney's office of New York City, the nearest thing to a scientific detective there is in America. Perhaps there will always have to be a doctor in the case. You remember how *Sherlock Holmes* relied on *Dr. Watson*?

I do not investigate crimes myself, only as a looker-on, a gatherer of evidence. I only write about them. And yet often I study the actual crime and figure it out by one of two methods: analysis or deduction. The former method was Poe's; the latter Conan Doyle's.

The Art of Writing Crime Fiction

I chase the criminal up on paper and put him into print, in fictional guise. And it is the most exciting, interesting and complex chase in the world. Say I am working for material on an unsolved mystery. I sit down and figure out a perfect theory that seems to fit the facts exactly and then a new little fact will pop in that upsets everything, and knocks my theory sky-high. And intuition, which is the divine gift of the great detective, must not be allowed to stray. It must be sure and compelling—straight as the arrow to the mark. Yet intuition, or rather what seems to be intuition, too often turns into an infinite capacity for making

Illustration by John Held, Jr.

The hardest man to catch is the one who uses the simplest, crudest
method.

mistakes due to hasty judgment. Then it is so easy by the law of opposites in theorizing to figure out that exactly what might have happened might *not* have. I have sat down and been able to figure out that a certain man could, not by any possibility have done a certain deed—and it has been proven ultimately that he did. And here comes in the advantage the Police Department will always have over a deductive sleuth working by himself—the advantage of organization. Add science to organization and you've got the game beaten.

The First Scientific Detective Story

When I wrote my first *Craig Kennedy* story, "The Silent Bullet," in 1909, it was turned down by every magazine I sent it to, and that was all of them. That story was a commuter. It had the highest mileage of any story ever written. I had endeavored to write the first purely scientific detective story. I had started something—and editors were afraid of it. The detective stories of Conan Doyle are not scientific, but deductive. The "science" in Conan Doyle is of the most elemental sort. Here is a grass blade—somebody has stepped on it. Here are some tobacco ashes, let's work them up. In my Preface to "The Silent Bullet," I introduce the scientific theory for the first time in an argument between *Kennedy* and *Jameson*, his *Dr. Watson*. *Kennedy* says, "I am going to apply science to the detection of crime; the same sort of methods by which you trace out the presence of a chemical, or run an unknown germ to earth."

The only reason why I started writing detective stories at all was simply that I had had a long education in Poe and Conan Doyle—and got to love them. It is so in every avocation. Poets, whom we have always been told are born not made, simply become poets because they love poetry and try to imitate what they love. Thomas Bailey Aldrich, perhaps our rarest lyric poet, confesses this frankly in his early letters. Allied closely to my own field is that of the greatest authority on the supernatural in literature in America who gives the same reason as I do: she came to write about ghosts in literature—as she states in the preface to her authoritative work *The Supernatural in English Literature*—because she came to love the ghosts!

Poe Founds the Detective-Story School

What really happened as we know was that Poe founded the detective story. "The Murders in the Rue Morgue" still stands unrivalled. We in America then did not dream what he had done when he gave us *Auguste Dupin*. On that single story was built up the whole school of French detective-story writers. One sheer laurel to Mr. Poe, at least! Conan Doyle in turn derived his inspiration from the Frenchman, and from both the French and English writers the American writers got theirs. It is thus a peculiar evolution or rather involution which returns to the point from which it started. Undoubtedly the unique example in literature.

It is rare enough indeed to find the detective story that is not lacking in one great quality—scientific imagination. *Dupin*, Poe's man, had it. Dickens was fast tending toward the mystery-story when he died. The last thing he wrote was *The Mystery of Edwin Drood*. There may be a hundred solutions but nobody has ever found one. Perhaps some day when I'm not too busy I'll have *Craig Kennedy* dig up *Jasper* in Chinatown (New York City), fill him up with hop: and make him tell the real truth. I don't believe *Jasper* murdered his nephew. I think the jewelry was planted in quick-lime to throw suspicion on him. If Dickens could have lived ten years longer he would have been perhaps the greatest master of the detective-story that ever lived except Poe—could *he* have compassed another decade. Both of these men were in my opinion far greater geniuses that any who have followed them in this field. And what a supreme, perhaps sublime, master Dickens would have been in the film-world! Because Dickens *thought* in motion pictures. He darkened the shadows and heightened the lights and kept his characters moving. What wonderful "pictures" (I mean "movies") some of his books have made. *Great Expectations*, *Oliver Twist*, too, have made very wonderful pictures—best of them all was the *A Christmas Carol*.

The Old-Fashioned Dime Novel

But to return to our own, American, mutton. Let us consider the old-fashioned dime-novel—beloved as ever by the younger generation to this hour. The very inception of our own school of mystery-writers was here. There are many living who can remember how the dime-novel started with stories of hairbreadth adventure, chiefly of the Wild West. Of course there were pirate stories, and stories of other climes, but our own Wild West was the favorite stamping-ground of writer and reader alike. In the early seventies a change began to creep over the face of ten-cent fiction—by all odds the widest form in which literature circulated in those days. The Wild West was becoming tamed; the mystery of foreign lands had been largely dissolved by exploration. Exit the story of adventure, enter the detective-story. It is not generally known, and I being of the craft will certainly not be guilty of telling tales out of school, but a good many fiction-writers who have since become widely famous were early contributors to this form of literature. There is an old legend to the effect that these industrious persons—and it was probably the most industrious period of their lives—always took Sunday as a day off and made up for it by doing 10,000 words a day for the rest of the week. Upton Sinclair has confessed that he did—and I know of one or two others. So were born the immortal *Old Sleuth* and his enterprising young successor *Nick Carter* and their progeny—"old" and "young" *King Brady*. Out of these finally evolved the "dime novel in cloth-covers," a little less hasty in manner, but hardly less thrilling, at a dollar and a half, as we have it to-day.

And all this body of work can be claimed as a distinctive contribution to American literature.

The mystery-story is our meat.

Scientific Stories Now the Favorites

The boys of to-day are not reading the same things the last generation read. When I was a boy I worshiped Henty as all boys did. The previous generation had the same feeling for Oliver Optic. Boys don't read that kind of thing now. Their stories are built differently. The great sweep of science, beginning with the early Victorian thinkers, has had its profound influence even on the commonest literature. Our boys read scientific stories now. To-day there are whole sets of juvenile books relating adventures in a submarine. Stories about the wireless—the aeroplane—are the things boys devour now—and the detective-story. I know that I have quite a large number of readers among boys.

On the other hand what appeals to women more than the mystery-story? It may seem strange but a large percentage of my readers are women. One would think that the science in the tale would repel these gentle readers, but it seems only to attract them. You ought to look through a bunch of my letters. Seventy-five per cent of them are from women. I suppose the easiest way to account for it is that insatiable curiosity which is perhaps the strongest trait of the sex.

At a dinner of engineers not long ago a discussion about the *Craig Kennedy* stories arose. It was discovered that several of those present had tried experiments suggested by them, and some interesting experiences were related. One man had filled a chimpanzee full of radio-active water and had actually got a photographic impression of the animal!

Did you ever think of the vital American way we live? We are always going after mental gymnastics. Now the mystery-story is mental gymnastics. By the time one has followed a chain of facts through he has exercised his mind—he can't help it. There has never been a time when the mystery-story, in motion-pictures, in plays, in periodicals, in books, was in such demand. The adventure story, the travel story, the story of world-discovery, exploration, are back numbers. To-day it is the mystery-story. To-morrow it will be the mental adventure into those psychic realms we have only just begun to investigate. We have conquered everything; we have discovered everything, but the unseen world. We must find another dimension. And I think the means of expression will be revealed—on the screen!

Letter From Arthur B. Reeve to Arthur Bartlett Maurice

July 17, 1922

My dear Mr. Maurice:

Regarding letters, one of my chief hobbies, I am glad to comply as follows.

Sincerely

[signature]

Arthur B. Reeve.

Where do readers get all the time to write letters to authors?

It has long since come to this, that I feel that a story didn't "get over" if I don't receive a bale of letters about it during the fortnight or month after it is published.

One of the first letters and the most flattering I have ever received was from a rather large manufacturer in Pittsburgh. A poisonous chemical had suddenly appeared in the raw material used in his plant. He asked if Craig Kennedy was a real man, because if he was he had a case for him. His feeling was that "an enemy hath done this." Would I send Craig out to Pittsburgh immediately?

Another of my early letters which I have never forgotten was from Tombstone, Arizona, from a man who was evidently a misogynist. "Don't," he implored, "ever let Kennedy get mixed up with a woman."

I have had irate letters from people whose names I had unwittingly taken in vain for characters in stories. Some time ago I adopted a policy of picking names made up of two last names when I could do so. There are not so many letters but when they come they are more virulent, for the possessors of the names are more than ever convinced that I must have meant them "since the name is quite unusual." An essay could be written on names alone.

My first dictagraph story, in fact <u>the</u> first dictagraph story brought a request from a convict in Iowa for a machine. If only he had one he could clear himself.

Another convict in Dannemora read a story in which appeared thermit, burning holes in chrome steel. He wrote secretly to know the formula so he could burn his way through the steel bars.

A convict in Charlestown liked the stories so well that he wrote he was making a cane out of them under hydraulic pressure in the shop. Later the cane came along. The same man wrote to Booth Tarkington and sent him a cane made of Penrod stories to which Tark wrote back thanking him and promising to use only that when he gave Penrod a caning.

But of all kinds of stories the psychoanalysis stories bring the most and the worst letters. I have come to the conclusion that in the matter of their dreams there is no secret too intimate for some women to take strangers into their confidence--at least epistolary confidence. This alone, also, would make a story.

One most amusing letter was from a fellow in Florida, enclosing a sample of a green window shade material. He wanted to know how to make it transparent. It seemed that a business man in a building next door to his employed as stenographer a girl on whom my correspondent had a crush as he confessed frankly. He wanted to know what took place on the other side of frequently drawn shades. And Craig Kennedy was elected to furnish the peeping Romeo with a scientific X-ray eye.

Now and then come letters correcting scientific slips. I am proud to say that they are not many because once I saw on a newspaper office wall the three rules: Accuracy, Terseness, Accuracy. But for instance. In one case I had Kennedy stain a germ, then call Jameson to see its peculiar, tell-tale spiral motions under the microscope. An eminent bacteriologist in a Wisconsin university wrote by special delivery: ". . . and, you darn fool, don't you know when you use that stain, it kills 'em and they can't wiggle?" I corrected the slip when the story was republished in book form. But it taught me to be accurate about the little things as well as the important things.

I have scores of letters from insane people, in and out of asylums and, I hope, about to get into asylums. There are letters asking advice, letters from people who seek lost friends or relatives, letters from Java, Sumatra, the Celebes and the ends of the earth.

Then there is the autograph hunter. Thousands of boys and girls have taken up autographs in a serious way. They send you cards and specially sized sheets of paper. I sign them all-- but carefully, mindful of the author who did so and later had one turn up at his bank edited above his name--"One month after date, I promise to pay."

In fact, I answer practically all my letters--in time. If for the investment of a two-cent stamp, some stationery and a little time I can make a "Craig Kennedy" fan for life, I feel that it is not a misplaced courtesy.

Letter From Arthur B. Reeve to Arthur Bartlett Maurice

May 13, 1924

Dear Mr. Maurice:

I have your very kind letter asking me for a list of the twenty best, in my estimation, mystery stories in all literature. They are found on the back of the paper jacket of my twentieth and latest, just published, "Atavar".

However, in Lardner's Ringlish Grammar, "all jokeing 2 one side", I suppose what you really want can be said by me best if I give you those mystery stories which have given me the greatest pleasure and profit. I shall, however, practically have to confine them to English. These are the mystery stories to which I have a predilection:

The Murders in the Rue Morgue	Edgar Allen Poe
The Mystery of Marie Roget	"
The Moonstone	Wilkie Collins
Edwin Drood	Dickens
File 113	Gaboriau
The Sign of the Four	A. Conan Doyle
A Study in Scarlet	"
Dr. Jekyll and Mr. Hyde	Robert Louis Stevenson
The New Arabian Nights	"
Dracula	Bram Stoker
Pudd'nhead Wilson	Mark Twain
The Teeth of the Tiger	Maurice Leblanc
The Lone Wolf	Louis Joseph Vance
The Mystery of the Yellow Room	Gaston Leroux
Fu Manchu	Sax Rohmer
The Leavenworth Case	Anna Katherine Green
The Circular Staircase	Mary Roberts Rinehart
Raffles	E.W. Hornung
The Boule Cabinet	Burton Egbert Stevenson
Cleek	Thos. W. Henshew
and The Mysterious Card	Cleveland Moffett

I shall be much interested in your projected discussion of the mystery story in the "Sun" and expect to learn something, for I was brought up to believe that "if you see it in the Sun, it's so."

Sincerely,

[signature]

Arthur B. Reeve.

Scientific Detective Monthly, January 1930

What Are the Great Detective Stories and Why?

WHEN FIRST THE TROGLODYTE told how he carried off his wife and won her—romance began. Then their son, who recaptured their stolen stone-ax by tracking the robber's footprints to his cave, bragged about it in the Neolithic dusk. *He* began telling detective stories.

After creation, the first story is of Adam and Eve—and the apocryphal Lilith. But hard on its heels come Cain and Abel. "Am I my brother's keeper?" was the original lame evasion when the First Officer of the Law confronted the suspect.

The first mystery story is, therefore, theological. Later, the stone-age detective began by following footprints of beasts and men. From ecclesiastical narratives, man developed tales of soldiers. Slowly emerged the mathematicians and philosophers and lawyers. Last to obtain recognition were the scientists.

Galileo was an astronomical detective. Columbus fathered a new race of geographical detectives. Following these, come the great biological and historical detectives. Champollion wrote an archeological detective story around the Rosetta stone and penetrated the mysteries of Egyptian inscriptions. All science, in fact, is a detective story.

You never read detective stories? As well say you never read modern science, never read stories of the human head and heart.

Crime is the most tremendous upheaval of human nature. Excise crime and you destroy drama.

I may as well confess that my first inspiration came from Poe's "The Murders in the Rue Morgue," followed by impressionable reading of Conan Doyle's *The Sign of the Four* and Anna Katherine Green's *The Leavenworth Case*. (I had devoured "Nick Carter" in earlier years.)

Then, for a short period, I resisted reading detective stories. I felt that, if I did not read them, I certainly could not plagiarize them. But I found that we are all unconscious, subconscious plagiarists; that, as the editor said to the young author, "Some parts of your story are good—and some are original." So I began to collect mystery fiction, hundreds of volumes of it.

Whatever we may say of the evolution of the detective story, Poe should be credited with inventing it. We exported him, like raw material, and reimported him in the manufactured goods of Gaboriau and Doyle. Meanwhile we created Nick Carter, Old Sleuth and the whole tribe of dime-novel heroes who are counterparts of the "shilling shockers" and "penny dreadfuls" abroad.

Gaboriau and Doyle rescued the idea from the dime-novel paper cover and put it into cloth at $1.08—now $2. The Bowery and the University met together; science and melodrama kissed.

"The Murders in the Rue Morgue" must remain the patriarch of the clan, for it gave us "Auguste Dupin" and his analytical reasoning. But I also admire "The Mystery of Marie Roget"; because in Poe's handling of the murder of Mary Cecelia Rogers in 1842 he showed how we might handle the Hall-Mills case and the Rothstein case for purposes of literature. I complete my trilogy of Poe with "The Purloined Letter," the triumph of the obvious. It may be that Dupin was more clever than convincing; but he certainly started something.

Poe's genius was at once recognized by the French, and widely imitated. Gaboriau created "Père Tabaret" (a little theatrical, it is true) and his pupil, Lecoq. Among the many volumes of Gaboriau I believe *The Lerouge Affair* of Tabaret and *File No. 113* of Lecoq stand out above others.

In reasoning and deduction Lecoq follows Dupin as a blood bother. But he is peculiarly Parisian. If he did not invent, he at least stuck always to the old rule, "*Cherchez la femme.*" Illicit love is quite invariably the motivation. He is as wrong—and as right—as Dr. Freud with his Viennese philosophy of life. Sex is not the great motivation; it is a largely-promoted motivation. My mild quarrel with Gaboriau is with his prolixity and an overworking of coincidence.

Mr. Edison once told me that practically the only fiction he read was detective stories. "When Gaboriau died," he said with that marvellous smile of his, "I felt as though I had lost one of my own family!"

If I may depart on a slight tangent, I must call attention to the last, and unfinished, work of Dickens, *The Mystery of Edwin Drood*. If Dickens had only lived he would have outshone all others with his marvellous ability to heighten the lights, and darken the shadows.

But to return. Along comes Conan Doyle, the master. I once believed "The Sign of the Four" to be a masterpiece and I believe it yet. The inspiration of "The Sign of the Four" and "The Murders in the Rue Morgue," is to me striking—the intellectual achievement of what Sherlock Holmes calls "deduction" and Dupin calls "analysis." Holmes takes Lecoq to task rather severely in one of his adventures, but their inspiration and methods are essentially from the same source. "A Study in Scarlet" I love; also "A Scandal in Bohemia," because of the woman in it and its comparison with "The Purloined Letter." I feel that *The Hound of the Baskervilles* rises to a very great height and certainly one of the finest episodes in detective fiction is that of Moriarty in "The Valley of Fear" and "The Final Problem."

What's the use? All of them stand out. As for Sherlock Holmes, it is difficult to restrain oneself from being fulsome. Keen and incisive, yet letting us into his mental processes afterwards, and we share the wonder of the faithful Dr. Watson. Sherlock Holmes rings true. I remember one critic betraying himself into calling him "the greatest *living* character in detective fiction"; perhaps because Gillette made him live in the dignity and restraint of the stage. To the modern "smart-aleck" detective so popular with the mystery book clubs, Sherlock Holmes is like Betelgeuse compared with a rush-light on the other side of the earth. The answer is, take any hundred people on Broadway or the *Ile de France*—how many are ignorant of Sherlock Holmes?

Yet it is not that other detective fiction characters are so greatly inferior to him, or that they lack sufficient interest. It is due to the fact that Sherlock Holmes represents a real standard of judgment, an ideal of what a detective should be. Others are judged by him. It is a unique position that he enjoys, and reflects great credit on his famous creator. Sherlock Holmes has universality.

Stevenson created no great detective character; yet, the plot and counter-plot in *The New Arabian Nights* must put the book high in the detective class. I greatly enjoyed "The Adventure of the Hansom Cab." I suppose among the older writers, Wilkie Collins should be counted; but beyond *The Moonstone* I am not so familiar with him.

However, in America, contemporary with Sherlock Holmes came Anna Katherine Green. Among her outstanding creations is the girl detective, "Violet Strange," one of the unique and original detectives of fiction. I like "The Grotto Spectre" and "Missing: Page

Thirteen." But after all I return to my first love, *The Leavenworth Case*. There may be a tendency of modern mystery-mongers to look upon it as mediocre. But I am faithful; it had its part in training me in the way I should go and when I am old I will not depart from it, in an age when most of us are standing on our heads and gesturing with our feet as we cry out, "See how cleverly I talk!"

Foremost, to me, among the French descendants of Gaboriau, grandchildren of Poe, stands "Arsène Lupin," of Maurice LeBlanc. Like Lecoq, Lupin is an old offender. He is a polished man of the world, a man with a hundred characters, most clever and cunning. Before his *sangfroid* you sit up and gasp. Yet that is its very weakness. Brilliant, dazzling, yet often impossible, almost absurd. If Lupin were less brilliant, perhaps, he would have a greater popular hold. He is not convincing. Lay aside any desire other than to be entertained, however, and LeBlanc is a genius, truly Gallic. You must grant his premises; then you will find him logical.

I must point to the kaleidoscopic protean acts of Lupin in *The Hollow Needle*, where LeBlanc introduces the English Mr. Holmlock Shears in competition with Arsène Lupin—as Mr. Sherlock Holmes had once taken M. Lecoq to task.

Of all Lupin I like best *The Teeth of the Tiger*. There's a plot! Not only have we the protean Lupin but a woman—and such a woman! Fallen in love with a girl—he becomes convinced she is guilty. Dramatic dilemma! He has sworn to capture the criminal.

Nor can I pass unmindful of *The Mystery of the Yellow Room*, by Gaston Leroux. A crime is committed in a room with no conceivable exit for escape. But the murderer *does* escape. Chesterton has called it the best detective tale of our time. Chesterton's own "Father Brown" is worthy of high place in any list.

Among the British my mind's eye falls on William Le Queux and *The Double Shadow*. But I can not sever my attention from E. Phillips Oppenheim and his host of mystery tales, nor adequately express my admiration for them. I have yet to find one of Oppenheim's characters who did not talk and act precisely as he does in life in his particular atmosphere. This is delineation of rare excellence. I know no one else living who can do it. And to think, his book shelf must be five yards wide, by now!

I recall one outstanding character, "Detective Quest." Not only was *The Black Box* enjoyable as a book but as a picture—starring Herbert Rawlinson, whom I later had seen playing "Craig Kennedy" in a serial after Arnold Daly had played the part in *The Exploits of Elaine*.

In the Arsène Lupin school I would place Louis Joseph Vance and his rapid-fire "Lone Wolf." Not *à propos* of this or anything at all but just because it occurs to me, I cannot help recalling *The Mysterious Card* by Cleveland Moffet.

In the conventional detective story the interest is made to focus on *who did it*, and the climax of apprehending *him*. Austin Freeman maintained that the real point was, *How was the discovery made?* In his stories of "Professor John Thorndyke" and his "Watson," the reader is taken into the author's confidence, sees the crime and all the evidence.

As a rule these stories are in two parts—the case up to the crime and immediately after it—and then his Watson tells what Thorndyke did. The reader knows everything; the detective nothing. Of the Thorndyke stories I pick *The Red Thumb Mark*.

Another old friend of mine is Thomas W. Hanshew's "Cleek," master crook and vanishing cracksman—"Cleek, the man of forty faces." One very excellent story is "The Mystery of the Steel Room," where Cleek turns into the master detective. Another, equally good, is the "Rope of Fear," another snake story.

With Lupin, The Lone Wolf, and Cleek we are introduced to another angle of the detective story—the master criminal. He arises from the revolt against the cocksure detective, much as the revolt against Aristides arose because Athenians were tired of hearing him always called "The Just."

Sax Rohmer has created in the grotesque and bizarre "Dr. Fu Manchu" one of the most fascinating characters of our times. Here also the detective gets the worst of it. For sheer grotesque terror, I commend "The Adventure of the Toadstools."

Somehow, at times I am in the mood when apes and aborigines, snakes and poisonous plants seem to have just the right "psych" for mystery. I hark back to "red-mouthed shadows rushing past." It is then that I am sure that sound pictures must be right and that I shall soon see some of my old favorites to which I owe so much, reproduced properly on the screen. The only thing that is not censurable is good clean melodrama—which is about the only thing that is ever really censored! Who are standing on their heads, "who's looney now"?

Foremost among the revolters against the cocksure detective is the creation of E.W. Hornung, brother-in-law of Conan Doyle—"Raffles," the amateur cracksman and gentleman burglar. The audacity of Raffles and Bunny has placed the tales of their exploits among the current crime classics.

Here in America I assume we are all still familiar with a peculiarly native character, "Get-Rich-Quick Wallingford" by George Randolph Chester whose friendship I greatly enjoyed. Two other American contemporaries I feel should be noted. One is Frank L. Packard's "Jimmie Dale"—the "Grey Seal," a sort of philanthropic crook; another of the dual personality type. The other is Burton Egbert Stevenson's *The Mystery of the Boule Cabinet*, both splendid mystery stories and of high literary merit.

Many years ago I read *The Circular Staircase* of Mary Roberts Rinehart with extreme interest. I reread it not long ago with equal enjoyment and would place it high on the list. Mrs. Rinehart's detective tales are splendid stories, but no outstanding detective character in them captures the public. This seems to be true of all the women writers of detective fiction.

Once I made that remark before. I went further and said that no writer, man or woman, had ever created a girl detective whose name had captured the public. The flood of letters that came to me was like a swarm of locusts. But by the Broadway or *Ile de France* test, I was right; I believe I would be right by the Main Street or Fall River Line test, Hollywood or Orange Blossom Special test, or whatever have you? I am defying the lightning of letters for a reason.

I might go on through contemporary fiction finding many stories of a very high level. But to go on further would be like a catalogue of ships—or a roster of the crime-book-a-month leagues or something.

Once I thought this was an age of science, and that, consequently, the mechanism of detective stories had undergone a considerable change since the time of Poe and Gaboriau; in fact, that a modern detective story, if it at all aimed at popular favor, should be based on scientific lines. Later on, I departed from that idea. But I wonder which is right? What does the reader of detective stories really like and believe to be the great detective stories?

Reading great detective stories with one eye on the date shows a gradual and marked evolution in construction since Poe.

What does the reader today think is the best 1930 Model Detective Story? What does the ultimate consumer think is the great detective story—and why? I invite his expression of opinion.

Whither are we drifting?

Writer's Digest, August 1930

How Writers Make Good

RECENTLY I READ IN SOME LITERARY NOTES a reference to my own experiences as a "struggling author." It ran something as follows: "Arthur B. Reeve sold his first story to *Cosmopolitan* and sprang into instant success after years of just getting by with serious articles in newspapers and minor magazines."

Like much of our snappy inside information today, nothing could be much further from the truth. I sold my first story for exactly seven dollars and a half and had the experience of having my first "Craig Kennedy" story turned down by Bob Davis. In fact, the story became a commuter. I was literally kicked upstairs into the *Cosmopolitan* with it. This same "Craig Kennedy" feature has been published, well, I should say, including reprints, foreign editions and so on, until well over three and one-half million copies of my books have been sold. Another publisher's blurb artist once figured out that with magazine, newspaper syndicate, book, motion picture and play circulation, but excluding the radio, these same stories have had a circulation far in excess of the population of the earth.

Now, what's wrong with the picture? Of course, the obvious first answer is duplication of circulation, but that's not what I started to tell you about.

Because one or two authors such as E. Phillips Oppenheim have managed to strike editorial fancy at the very start of their careers, a popular idea has grown up that if one is going to make a name in the literary world, one's first story is accepted by return mail, one's first check runs into the thousands, and one is instantly hailed as the genius of the age.

Authors whose bank accounts run into six figures laugh with a touch of grim humor at this illusion. It is much more possible that their first hundred stories were returned with curt printed rejection slips, and that their first remuneration paid for little more than the paper, typing and postage.

The author who has not yet arrived can, however, very well ask: "At what point in his development does the struggling writer become a financial success, as a rule?"

Paste this in your hat. Only a very fine hairline separates the struggling writer and the successful author in countless cases. To identify this line, to describe it, to analyze it, is not an easy task. But, drawing from my own experience, I can attempt to picture the various conditions that prevail on this borderline between futile strivings and actual accomplishment.

Two things have to be considered. They are the mind of the writer and his familiarity with the publishing business.

Now, first as to the mind of the writer. Let us assume you are on the bottom rungs of the literary ladder. You write a few stories, articles, fillers for newspapers or pulp fiction magazines. You earn anywhere from fifty dollars to one thousand dollars a year, wasting an enormous amount of time in unproductive effort.

Sometimes you feel that the whole business of writing is rotten and that manuscripts are chosen by editors on the toss of a coin. Other times you feel that you yourself lack that vital spark which writers presumably must have to attain success.

You work in turn at articles, fillers, novels, stories, short or novelette length, pictures, plays; writing humor, mystery and detective material, romance, adventure, social satire, psychological characterization, what-not. Everything seems to fall flat. Yet an occasional check spurs your ambition. Sometime—this year—next year—perhaps twenty years hence, you may attain success. In the meantime you are a lone traveler on an uncharted sea—fighting blindly against obstacles you cannot visualize.

Bear this in mind. Man is essentially blind to his own form, mental or physical. It is seldom that writers can recognize their own abilities in relation to market demands. I might say that it is almost impossible for any one but an extremely cold-blooded intellectual with a background of publishing experience to see his own work as others see it.

Some years ago a middle-aged friend of mine showed me seventeen manuscripts, three of which had been published. He said, "Arthur, I'm giving it up! The very manuscripts I think are poor are accepted by editors, while the ones I feel are really good come back to me with rejection slips. I have no literary judgment."

It turned out that my friend had a style that was especially suited for success stories and when, as a last resort, he wrote seven success articles and sold them for three times the amount he was accustomed to receive, he settled down to this one type of writing and made good.

Therefore the first step a writer must take to win success is to determine his own special talents and form. That settled, comes the second step. This second step, though not difficult, is certainly tedious. It is familiarization with the publishing business and with various phases of the copyright laws.

Once I wrote a story which I called "The Radio Detective." Frankly I did not when I wrote it and certainly do not now consider this story better than many I have written; not even better than many I see by authors who cannot be receiving more than two cents a word for their work. In fact, the original story sold for not much more than that price in *Boys' Life*.

Now mark the importance of marketing knowledge. I retained all rights except those needed by *Boys' Life* to publish the story. They bought first American serial rights. Once it had appeared I brought the story out in book form with my publishers, Harper & Brothers. Twice now I had collected on this story. Then there was the newspaper (second serial rights) syndication. Payment a third time. Next Universal Films bought the motion-picture rights. Payment a fourth time. I was paid a fifth time for adapting the story for the screen. As the story was changed and lengthened in screen serialization I was asked to re-novelize the elaborated story. Sixth payment, for syndicating in newspapers the lengthened story. Finally came the cheap popular edition of this last novelization by Grosset & Dunlap. By the time I had footed up the seventh payment on that story it was netting me around fifteen dollars a word—and I still own the talking picture, television and radio rights.

All together we may assume that the difference between two cents a word and fifteen dollars a word lies not alone in writing ability but in practical marketing experience and knowledge of potential exploitation.

It is frequently said, and with reason, that there is *one* novel in every man or woman. That *one* novel might make the man or woman rich for life—if the author understands the secret of the capitalization of the written word.

The Fascination of the Ghost Story
(Introduction to *The Best Ghost Stories*, Modern Library, 1930)

WHAT IS THE FASCINATION WE FEEL FOR THE MYSTERY OF THE GHOST STORY?

Is it of the same nature as the fascination which we feel for the mystery of the detective story?

Of the latter fascination, the late Paul Armstrong used to say that it was because we are all as full of crime as Sing Sing—only we don't dare.

Thus, may I ask, are we not fascinated by the ghost story because, no matter what may be the scientific or skeptical bent of our minds, in our inmost souls, secretly perhaps, we are as full of superstition as an obeah man—only we don't let it loose?

Who shall say that he is able to fling off lightly the inheritance of countless ages of superstition? Is there not a streak of superstition in us all? We laugh at the voodoo worshiper—then create our own hoodooes, our pet obsessions.

It has been said that man is incurably religious, that if all religions were blotted out, man would create a new religion.

Man is incurably fascinated by the mysterious. If all the ghost stories of the ages were blotted out, man would invent new ones.

For, do we not all stand in awe of that which we cannot explain, of that which, if it be not in our own experience, is certainly recorded in the experience of others, of that of which we know and can know nothing?

Skeptical though one may be of the occult, he must needs be interested in things that others believe to be objective—that certainly are subjectively very real to them.

The ghost story is not born of science, nor even of super-science, whatever that may be. It is not of science at all. It is of another sphere, despite all that the psychic researchers have tried to demonstrate.

There are in life two sorts of people who, for want of a better classification, I may call the psychic and the non-psychic. If I ask the psychic to close his eyes and I say to him, "Horse," he immediately visualizes a horse. The other, non-psychic, does not. I rather incline to believe that it is the former class who see ghosts, or rather some of them. The latter do not—though they share interest in them.

The artists are of the visualizing class and, in our more modern times, it is the psychics who think in motion pictures, or at least in a succession of still pictures.

However we explain the ghostly and supernatural, whether we give it objective or merely subjective reality, neither explanation prevents the non-psychic from being intensely interested in the visions of the psychic.

Thus I am convinced that if we were all quite honest with ourselves, whether we believe in or do not believe in ghosts, at least we are all deeply interested in them. There is in this interest something that makes all the world akin.

Who does not feel a suppressed start at the creaking of furniture in the dark of night? Who has not felt a shiver of goose flesh, controlled only by an effort of will? Who, in the dark, has not had the feeling of some *thing* behind him—and, in spite of his conscious reasoning, turned to look?

If there be any who has not, it may be that to him ghost stories have no fascination. Let him at least, however, be honest.

To every human being mystery appeals, be it that of the crime cases on which a large part of yellow journalism is founded, or be it in the cases of Dupin, of Le Coq, of Sherlock Holmes, of Arsene Lupin, of Craig Kennedy, or a host of others of our fiction mystery characters. The appeal is in the mystery.

The detective's case is solved at the end, however. But even at the end of a ghost story, the underlying mystery remains. In the ghost story, we have the very quintessence of mystery.

Authors, publishers, editors, dramatists, writers of motion pictures tell us that never before has there been such an intense and wide interest in mystery stories as there is to-day. That in itself explains the interest in the super-mystery story of the ghost and ghostly doings.

Another element of mystery lies in such stories. Deeper and further back, is the supreme mystery of life—after death—what?

"Impossible," scorns the non-psychic as he listens to some ghost story.

To which, doggedly replies the mind of the opposite type, "Not so. I believe *because* it is impossible."

The uncanny, the unhealthy—as in the master of such writing, Poe—fascinates. Whether we will or no, the imp of the perverse lures us on.

That is why we read with enthralled interest these excursions into the eerie unknown, perhaps reading on till the mystic hour of midnight increases the creepy pleasure.

One might write a volume of analysis and appreciation of this aptly balanced anthology of ghost stories assembled here after years of reading and study by Mr. J.L. French.

Foremost among the impressions that a casual reader will derive is the interesting fact, just as in detective mystery stories, so in ghost stories, styles change. Each age, each period has the ghost story peculiar to itself. To-day, there is a new style of ghost story gradually evolving.

Once stories were of fairies, fays, trolls, the "little people," of poltergiest and loup garou. Through various ages we have progressed to the ghost story of the eighteenth and nineteenth centuries until to-day, in the twentieth, we are seeing a modern style, which the new science is modifying materially.

High among the stories in this volume, one must recognize the masterful art of Algernon Blackwood's "The Woman's Ghost Story."

"I was interested in psychic things," says the woman as she starts to tell her story simply, with a sweep toward the climax that has the ring of the truth of fiction. Here perhaps we have the modern style of ghost story at its best.

Times change as well as styles. "The Man Who Went Too Far" is of intense interest as an attempt to bring into our own times an interpretation of the symbolism underlying Greek mythology, applied to England of some years ago.

To see Pan meant death. Hence in this story there is a philosophy of Pan-theism—no "me," no "you," no "it." It is a mystical story, with a storm scene in which is painted a picture that reminds one strongly of "The Fall of the House of Usher"—with the frankly added words, "On him were marks of hoofs of a monstrous goat that had leaped on him"— uncompromising mysticism.

Happy is the Kipling selection, "The Phantom 'Rickshaw," if only for that obiter dictum of ghost-presence as Kipling explains about the rift in the brain: "—and a little bit of the Dark World came through and pressed him to death!"

Then there are the racial styles in ghost stories. The volume takes us from the "Banshees and Other Death Warnings" of Ireland to a strange example of Jewish mysticism in "The Silent Woman." Mr. French has been very wide in his choice, giving us these as well as many examples from the literature of England and France. Finally, he has compiled from the newspapers, as typically American, many ghost stories of New York and other parts of the country.

Strange that one should find humor in a subject so weird. Yet we find it. Take, for instance, De Foe's old narrative, "The Apparition of Mrs. Veal." It is a hoax, nothing more. Of our own times is Ellis Parker Butler's "Dey Ain't No Ghosts," showing an example of the modern Negro's racial heritage.

In our literature and on the stage, the very idea of a Darky and a graveyard is mirth-provoking. Mr. Butler extracts some pithy philosophy from his Darky boy: "I ain't skeered ob ghosts whut am, c'ase dey ain't no ghosts, but I jes' feel kinder oneasy 'bout de ghosts whut ain't!"

Humor is succeeded by pathos. In "The Interval" we find a sympathetic twist to the ghost story—an actual desire to meet the dead.

It is not, however, to be compared for interest to the story of sheer terror, as in Bulwer-Lytton's "The Haunted and the Haunters," with the flight of the servant in terror, the cowering of the dog against the wall, the death of the dog, its neck actually broken by the terror, and all that go to make an experience in a haunted house what it should be.

Thus, at last, we come to two of the stories that attempt to give a scientific explanation, another phase of the modern style of ghost story.

One of these, perhaps hardly modern as far as mere years are concerned, is this same story of Bulwer, "The Haunted and the Haunters." Besides being a rattling good old-fashioned tale of horror, it attempts a new-fashioned scientific explanation. It is enough to read and re-read it.

It is, however, the lamented Ambrose Bierce who has gone furthest in the science and the philosophy of the matter, and in a very short story, too, splendidly titled "The Damned Thing."

> "Incredible!" exclaims the coroner at the inquest.
> "That is nothing to you, sir," replies the newspaper man who relates the experience, and in these words expresses the true feeling about ghostly fiction, "that is nothing to you, if I also swear that it is true!"

But furthest of all in his scientific explanation—not scientifically explaining away, but in explaining the way—goes Bierce as he outlines a theory. From the diary of the murdered man he picks out the following which we may treasure as a gem:

> "I am not mad. There are colors that we cannot see. And—God help me!—the Damned Thing is of such a color!"

This fascination of the ghost story—have I made it clear?

As I write, nearing midnight, the bookcase behind me cracks. I start and turn. Nothing. There is a creak of a board in the hallway.

I know it is the cool night wind—the uneven contraction of materials expanded in the heat of the day.

Yet—do I go into the darkness outside otherwise than alert?

It is this evolution of our sense of ghost terror—ages of it—that fascinates us.

Can we, with a few generations of modernism behind us, throw it off with all our science? And, if we did, should we not then succeed only in abolishing the old-fashioned ghost story and creating a new, scientific ghost story?

Scientific? Yes. But more—something that has existed since the beginnings of intelligence in the human race.

Perhaps, you critic, you say that the true ghost story originated in the age of shadowy candle light and pine knot with their grotesqueries on the walls and in the unpenetrated darkness, that the electric bulb and the radiator have dispelled that very thing on which, for ages, the ghost story has been built.

What? No ghost stories? Would you take away our supernatural fiction by your paltry scientific explanation?

Still will we gather about the story teller—then lie awake o' nights, seeing mocking figures, arms akimbo, defying all your science to crush the ghost story.

Letter From Arthur B. Reeve to Leo Margulies

615 Greenwood Ave., Trenton, N.J.
February 27, 1935

Dear Leo:

I imagine you wonder what has become of Craig Kennedy.

Well. I'm still in bed after a collapse the night after the Hauptmann trial ended. Just getting to sit up and write a few letters in bed. Today the Doc informs me I <u>may</u> go to New York by next Tuesday.

It was like this. I had already fought off Flemington flu the night of your famous party, had fought it off with aspirin, citrus fruit juices and egg nogs. Anne Hurst of our staff had been forced home. Red Gallagher was in bed. I was the sturdy oak.

Well, a couple of weeks later I got a rather bad case of laryngitis. Still the iron man I figured I didn't need a voice. I wasn't broadcasting. I thought I licked that, too.

The last Sunday night before the trial ended I was caught in the middle of the night with an acute attack of cardiac asthma. Couldn't get my breath. Like steel bands around my chest. Face blue. Covered cold sweat. Gasping for air <u>to live</u>. They called a doctor and a priest about two in the morning. Priest gave me extreme unction. Doctor hypo of morphine and atropine. Then it was a battle of two worlds.

I came back. Doctor said bed for a week. Monday morning he came about ten. I felt the iron man again. The moment he shut the door I was up, shaving, and drove 25 miles to Flemington in time to hear most of [Hauptmann attorney, Edward J. Reilly's] summation and file my story. (The Doc was the same who was keeping [Hauptmann trail justice] Judge Trenchard in shape, by the way.)

Well, I got away with it. Next day went again--[prosecutor David T. Wilentz] summation and my story. Another attack, worse that night. As I lay there under opiate I just couldn't stand thought of missing final day, judge's charge, and possible verdict. In the morning I got up again. We had a great scoop plan on. I was needed. Old newspaper man in me came back like a war correspondent.

Got away with that. All day. My last story, a valedictory. Stuck around half the night, waiting verdict. Meanwhile Red Gallagher and Frank Toughill and myself snipped a telephone wire than [sic] ran down outside my window in court. Drew in the live ends. Our wire upstairs, anyway. Clipped in. We had a direct wire from inside the court room to the city desk in

Philadelphia! Bunched up under eagle eyes of state troopers and deputy sheriffs, after court doors locked when jury came in, Red and I whispered running story of verdict to Toughill under table. Slammed AP fake report extras Life Imprisonment, scooped all the other papers AP, News with indoor wireless, everybody, one of big unprincipled scoops of modern news.

Then I collapsed. Been in bed ever since. But what a time! I feel as if I had brought CRAIG KENNEDY back with a bang. Never missed a day, seven days a week story, broke the Hearst ownership of the defense, then this scoop. Leo, that was living! It was worth it and all that followed.

Maybe I was recognized by Literary Digest, Cosmopolitan and all that. But now with all these doctor's bills, nurses, damned creditors and so on I have got to make money.

How comes the CRAIG KENNEDY magazine idea? I think I've brought Craig back with a bang. Made plenty of friends down there too. Surely there must be something doing with the Craig Kennedy idea. I may go in the gutter but Craig isn't going in the gutter. No more. I believe there's a big chance. I believe you're the one who knows best how, also.

Write me a long letter. I am just dying to hear from my friends. They probably don't know yet what happened. None of it in the papers except results. Just drop a line.

My regards and you know I mean it.

Sincerely,

[signature]

ARTHUR B. REEVE

II

ART GALLERY

Holiday

COSMOPOLITAN

Contributors to this Number:
Robert W. Chambers
Charles Dana Gibson
Gen. Nelson A. Miles
George Randolph Chester
Charles Edward Russell
Ellis Parker Butler
Kin Hubbard
George Fitch
Wallace Irwin
Alfred Henry Lewis
Arthur B Reeve
Bailey Millard
David Graham Phillips
Edwin Markham

15 Cents

January 1911   Cover by Harrison Fisher

The issue with Reeve's second published Craig Kennedy story, "The Silent Bullet"; and the first issue with Reeve's name on the cover. *Cosmopolitan* published 82 Kennedy stories from 1910 to 1918. Reeve's name often appeared on the cover, but the visage of Craig Kennedy—never! *Cosmopolitan* published a variety of fiction but the covers always featured an attractive young woman.

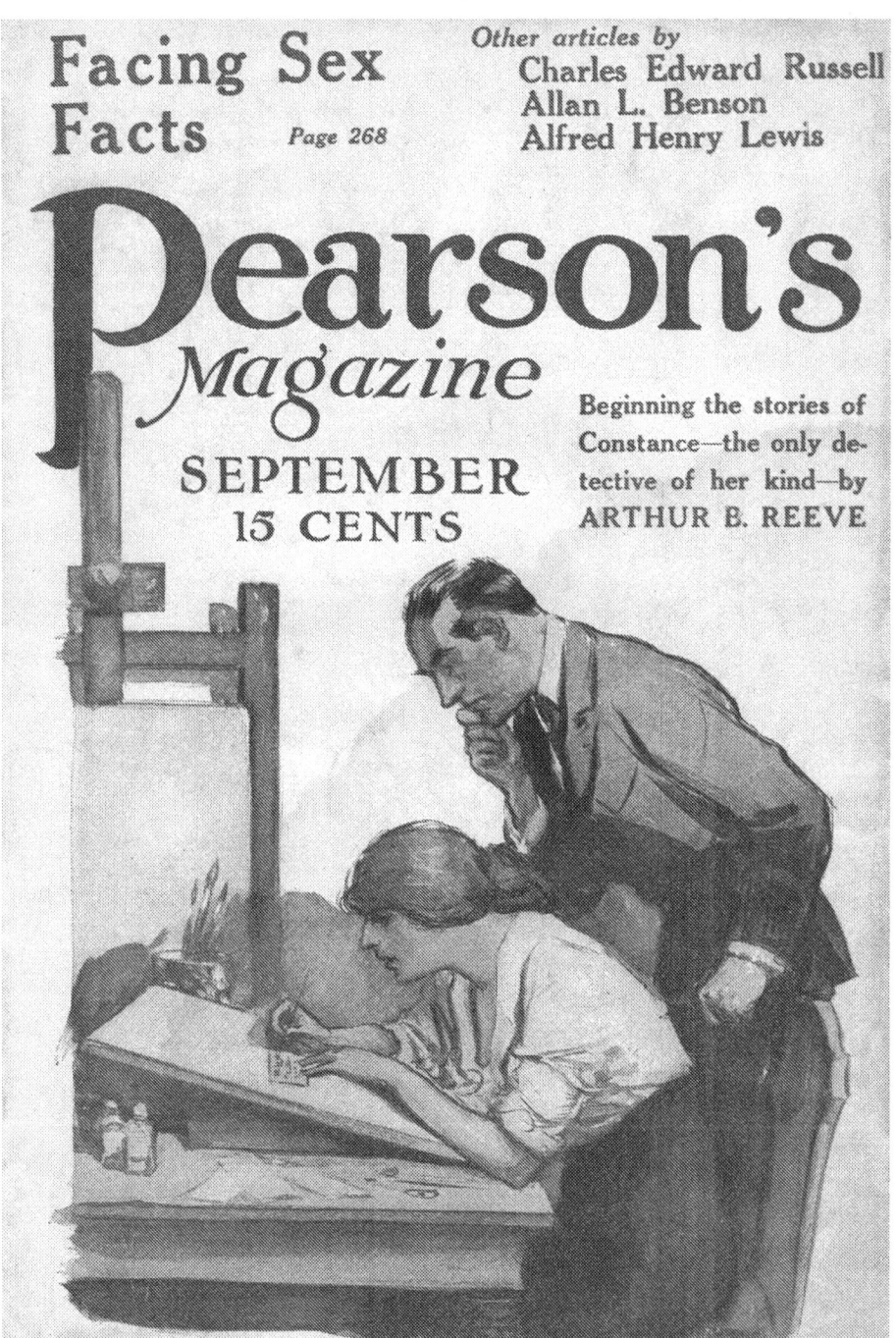

September 1913

Reeve never shied away from female protagonists. In addition to Constance Dunlap, he had another detective, Clare Kendall, and, of course, his film serial heroine, Elaine Dodge.

October 1913   Cover by C.D. William

With every cover illustration featuring a woman, there was added incentive for a woman detective, in this case, Constance Dunlap, with her second adventure.

February 1914   Cover by Ruth Eastman

Reeve's short novel here, "The Abduction Club," was eventually merged with
another story, "The Ear in the Wall," for book publication under the latter title.
And Craig Kennedy was renamed Guy Garrick.

MAY 1914
PRICE 15 CENTS
THE
RED BOOK
MAGAZINE

The first of
a new series
of detective
stories by
ARTHUR
B. REEVE

Rupert Hughes
Elinor Glyn
Kennett Harris
L.J.Beeston
Ida M.Evans
Freeman Tilden
Ellis Parker Butler
Cyrus Townsend Brady
Albert Payson Terhune
George Randolph Chester
and 7 others

Cover by Henry Hutt

This issue introduced Guy Garrick, like Craig Kennedy, a scientific detetctive.

At last she spoke, in soft, low, purring tones. "I see you engaged in a transaction that will bring you great wealth," she murmured slowly, as if some unseen force, not herself, were impelling the words from her lips.

The Red Book Magazine, September 1914   Illustration by George Brehm

Guy Garrick gets his fortune told by a charming charlatan in this illustration from "The Clairvoyant Trust." This will not work out as well as she thinks.

Cosmopolitan, February 1915   Illustration by Will Foster

Craig Kennedy, himself, listening to the argument of his trusty confidant, newsman Walter Jameson. The illustration, from "The X-Ray Detective," is typical of Will Foster's refined depictions of the Kennedy milieu: nicely-dressed people and not much action.

THE SYRACUSE HERALD SUNDAY MORNING, MARCH 14, 1915.

THE NOVEL EXPERIENCES OF GUY GARRICK, DETECTIVE

THE CAVE OF ALADDIN
By ARTHUR B. REEVE

There, in the smooth stone wall, yawned a black hole.

FALKLAND ISLANDS FORM DISMAL TREELESS LAND

Dreary English Possession Was Near Scene of Great Naval Battle Recently.

DYING ON BATTLEFIELD

Reds Dying on a Feather Bed, Writes an Irish Soldier.

The Syracuse Herald, March 14, 1915

There was a time when the daily paper included popular fiction, this one a reprint from the June 1914 *Red Book Magazine*. This syndicated piece (story and illustration) would have appeared in a number of papers across the country.

"Carton—Miss Ashton, this is Kennedy," Craig protested into his vocaphone. "Don't take that cab! Wait! I'll explain!"

American Sunday Monthly Magazine, December 5, 1915   Illustration by Armand Both

An illustration from the serialized *The Ear in the Wall*. To modern eyes, Kennedy's "vocaphone" looks more like a school project than super-science, slightly more sophisticated than the nearby cutlery.

July 16, 1918   Cover by John A. Coughlin

The title of this serial could not have been a reference to the *Elaine* films that
Reeve co-authored. Those silent serials were a great success.

September 17, 1918   Cover by John A. Coughlin

Craig Kennedy, scientific detective, was more than a man of gadgetry. He also embraced the "soft science" of psychology, as the name of the above serial implies. Using the analytical tools of Freud, damage to the subsconcious could be identified and repaired.

The Ogden Standard-Examiner (Utah), October 16, 1921   Illustration by J.A. May

Reeve disappeared from the magazines for several years. Instead, his fiction could be found syndicated in newspapers, such as this short novel, serialized over two months. Much of this material was never reprinted elsewhere.

Cover by F.E. Schoonover

Craig Kennedy appeared in six straight issues of *Everybody's* beginning with this one.

Cover by Hap Hadley

Reeve, indeed, was coming to *Mystery Magazine*—in the following issue. For newsstand browsers who might reasonably, if naively, have thought the Reeves supplied a story titled "Coming," it was a case of false advertizing. Such announcements placed on the front cover was uncommon—justifiably so.

February 15, 1924

A British reprint of a story that appeared in the October 1923 *Everybody's*. And that's "Fine Stories" not "True Stories."

This flimsy saddle-stitched magazine eventually turned into a pulp. Here, Reeve shares the byline with his wife, Margaret Wilson Reeve, as he did in a previous story for the magazine. Mrs. Reeve dabbled in writing, submitting the occasional story to womens' magazines.

August 30, 1924   Cover by Angus MacDonall

Reeve proved his adaptability with a series of stories that began in this issue of *The Country Gentleman*, a 10-½ x 14-inch saddle-stitched magazine, all challenging Craig Kennedy with crimes having an agricultural theme.

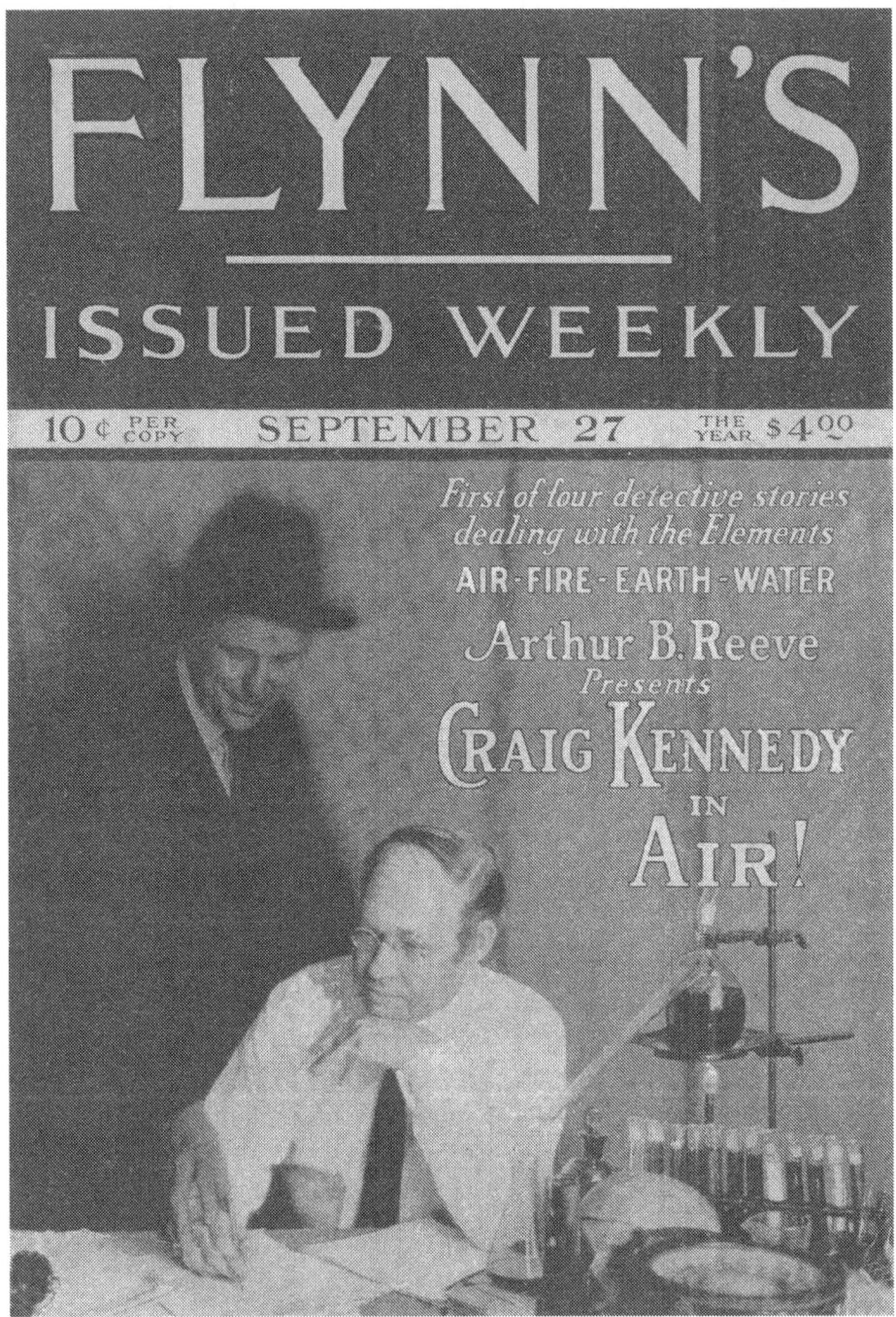

September 27, 1924

The author's hand guided by the spirit of his creation. This issue inaugurated a series of Craig Kennedy stories eventually collected in the book *The Fourteen Points*.

December 13, 1924

"Go north, formerly young man!" Craig Kennedy stayed young and perfect while his creator struggled to remain relevant.

1926

The two-color cover from a novelization of the film serial, probably a newspaper supplement or a handout at theatres. Reeve loved to boast of the number of times he'd sold this same story, *The Radio Detective*, in different forms. Reeve's name suffers a common misspelling here.

September 22, 1928

Is there a difference between a detective and a scientist? this cover seems to ask. This was Reeve's first appearance in *DFW* after the title change from *Flynn's*.

October 6, 1928

"Mr. Kennedy! When Mr. Houdini does it, it's *entertaining*!"

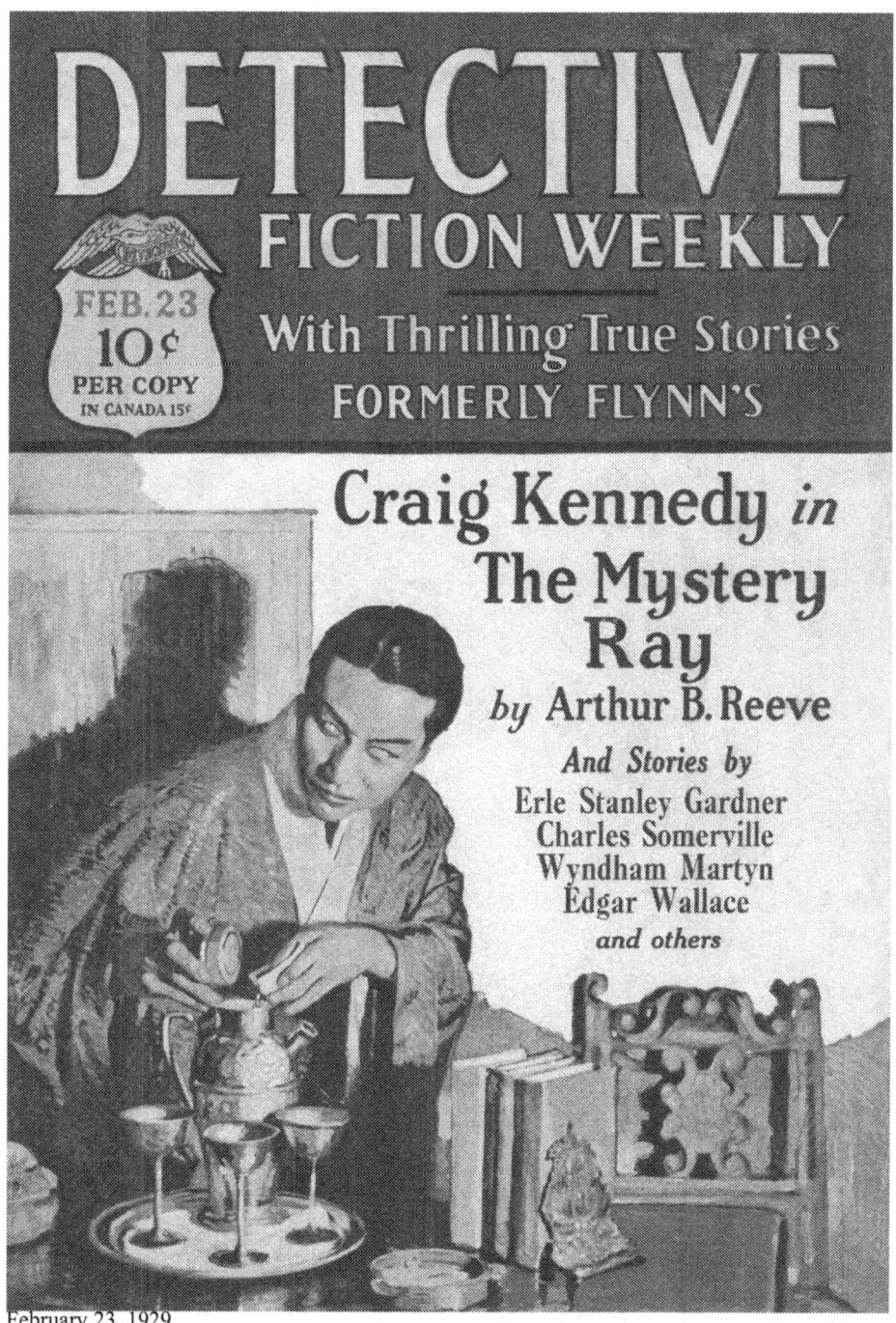

February 23, 1929

Tough to resist a story with this inducement: "Curious Words Scribbled by a Gibbering Idiot Give Craig Kennedy the Clew to a Sinister Plot." This was the first installment of a three-part serial.

Radio Digest Illustrated, October 1929   Cover by Roy Best

This issue inaugurated a six-part Craig Kennedy serial. The "Gigolo" turns out to be the name of a boat that sinks with a lovely girl aboard.

The Illustrated Detective Magazine, December 1929

Some members of the public weren't quite sure whether the ubiquitous Craig Kennedy was real or not. Features like this didn't help. Reeve became accustomed to being addressed as "Mr. Kennedy."

January 1930   Cover by Jno Ruger

This new magazine was made-to-order for Reeve. Indeed, he's most responsible for establishing the concept of the scientific detective. The issue also reprinted a story by Edwin Balmer & William B. MacHarg of Luther Trant, a scientific detective who preceded Craig Kennedy by two years.

Cover by Jno Ruger

Reeve retained the title of "Editorial Commissioner" when the name of *Scientific Detective* changed to *Amazing Detective Tales*. That and other changes didn't save the magazine. It folded after five issues apiece under each title.

Writer's Digest, August 1930

This ad appeared in the issue with Reeve's article "How Writers Make Good," his only known writers' mag piece. The reference to "500 stories" is an exaggeration unless books, film scripts, newspaper articles, etc., are counted. Reeve was, however, a very productive writer.

Hamilton Daily News (Ohio), January 24, 1931

With the "scientific detective" having fallen out of fashion, Reeve rejuvenated his career as a gangland expert, as radio host, journalist and fictioneer.

1931

Reeve's only non-fiction book, a history of the racketeering wrought by Prohibition. The book grew out of Reeve's nationally-broadcast radio show *Crime Prevention Program*, which ran on NBC from July 1930 to March 1931.

The page reproduces a newspaper feature:

MAGAZINE FEATURES   **Modesto News-Herald**   COMIC FEATURES

THE SEX RACKET   by Arthur B. Reeve

Another Amazing Episode of Craig Kennedy and the Gangsters

Illustration by Stookie Allen

September 12, 1931

Reeve's sixteen stories for newspaper syndication, *Craig Kennedy and the Gangsters*, a spinoff from the radio show, took the reader on a "guided tour" of the rackets. The mob boss of the series, Tony Magnifico, reappeared in gang stories Reeve provided the pulps.

April 1932   Cover by Howard Parkhurst

Craig Kennedy was not only a great detective, he was a great skeptic. In his career he thwarted a variety of fakes and frauds, such as this would-be fortune teller.

September 1932   Cover by Howard Parkhurst

The editor's blurb for the novel reads: "From the underworld of Paris comes a problem and a criminal to test the keen brain of the Master—Craig Kennedy."

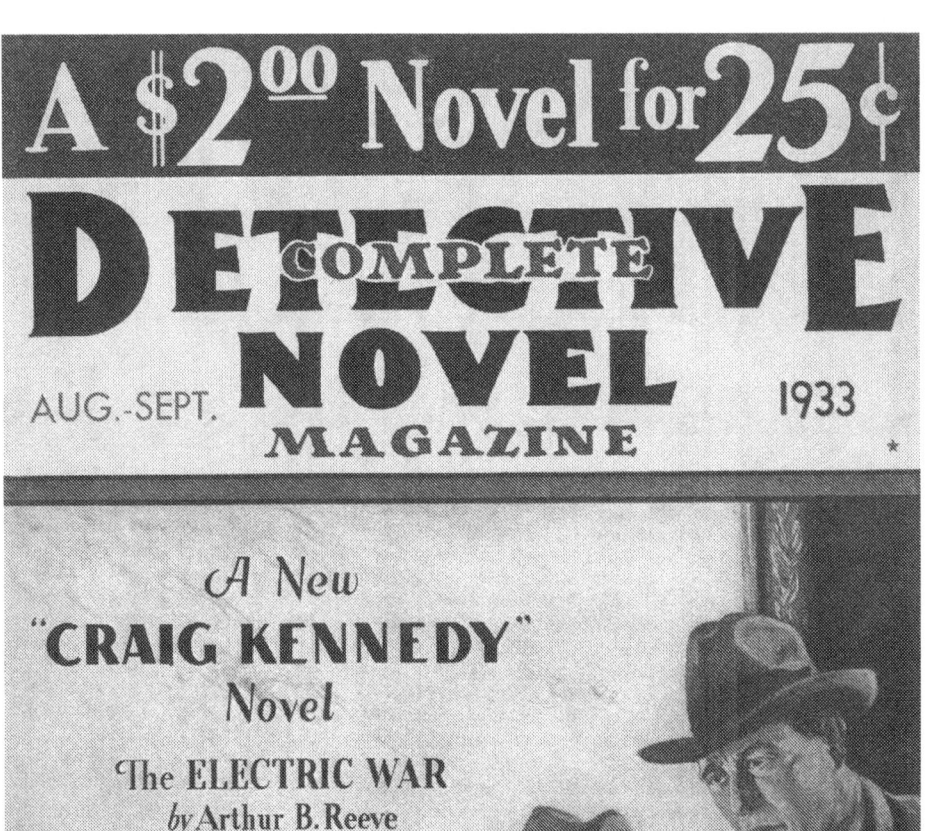

Cover by Howard Parkhurst

Reeve had a nice run of ten appearances in this pulp, including several novel-length Craig Kennedy stories. *The Electric War* revived arch-villain, The Clutching Hand, from Reeve's first film, *The Triumph of Elaine* (1914).

October 1933   Cover by William Reusswig

Reeve's only appearance in a Popular Publications pulp. He rose to the occasion
with a tale of devil worshippers and nude corpses.

GAWD HATES A RAT!

by

ARTHUR B. REEVE

Van Kirk was on his feet instantly as the door banged and the lock in it grated. In the hall he encountered two men. One

Creator of
CRAIG KENNEDY

112

Gang World, December 1933

Reeve could go from the cover of *Dime Detective* to the back pages of this cheap gang pulp almost overnight.

January 1934

"The Inca Dagger" was a novelette-length reworking of Reeve's first true novel, *The Gold of the Gods* (1915), which centered on a "Peruvian dagger." The pulp story emphasized action over the scientific marvels of the novel.

WORLD MAN HUNTERS

The RETURN
OF CRAIG
KENNEDY
in
Murder Around the Corner
by
ARTHUR B. REEVE

A dead man on the street—a girl in flight—Craig Kennedy "on the trail"—a combination that will hold your
interest and give you "the inside" on the new rackets of
a great city and the methods Kennedy employs to combat
them

6

World Man Hunters, January 1934

The triumphant return of a character who hadn't gone anywhere. As should
now be clear from the bottom blurb, Kennedy's racket-busting potential has
completely replaced his "scientific detective" label.

Reeve appeared in all three issues of this short-lived pulp with stories renewing
the battle between Craig Kennedy and the gangsters.

Reeve may have been recruited to help save this failing magazine, which lasted only one more issue. His story here pitted Guy Garrick against—who else?—the gangsters.

Murder *at* Night

By the acid vat, Kennedy struggled desperately with his adversary

Featuring the Scientific Detective and Master of Deduction Whose Exploits Have Thrilled Millions, in an Action-Packed Yarn of Diabolical Crime!

A Craig Kennedy Mystery
By ARTHUR B. REEVE
Author of "The Scientific Cracksman," "The Silent Bullet," etc.

DEATH stalked the night. Intangible, invisible, its gaunt hand seemed to hang pendant over the squat buildings which formed the principal plant of the Mifflin Dye Company. Rogers, the watchman, who had kept the vigil through a thousand nights, shivered unaccountably as a vagrant cloud swept across the face of the moon and plunged the earth into complete darkness.

He sat now in a small chair at the entrance to the shed known as Unit

51

Thrilling Detective, August 1934

Reeve's only sale to *Thrilling Detective*. Note that the "Author of" credit harkens back to Reeve's first two Craig Kennedy stories, as if he hadn't done anything in the near quarter-century since. Editor Leo Margulies apparently hadn't noticed the fall from grace of the "scientific detective."

September 1934   Cover by Lyman Anderson

Compare this cover to the *Cosmopolitan* cover which leads this section for a hint
at how far Reeve's stock had fallen by this time. Not that we'd mind seeing a
Harrison Fisher girl wielding a Tommy gun . . .

January 1935   Cover by Rafael De Soto

An old-time detective helps establish a new pulp. The stories were unsold manuscripts that uncredited co-author, Ashley T. Locke, expanded to novelette length. Reeve was nearing the end but his name still held star power.

May 1935   Cover by Margaret Brundage

Reeve's Craig Kennedy, consummate scientist-debunker, was a mismatch for
the pure fantasy of the greatest *Weird Tales* stories. Editor Farnsworth Wright
was attempting to attract detective-story readers into the fold. Regular readers
were not enthusiastic.

III

REEVE:
IN PRINT AND
PERFORMANCE

A1: Magazines - Fiction

Magazine titles are listed in **_Bold Italic_**s; story titles, in **Bold**. Explanatory notes related to the entire magazine run precede the issue listings; notes related to a single issue or subset of the run appear below the relevant issues. See **B1: Books** and **B3: The Craig Kennedy Stories** for more information on the reprinting of the stories in book form. :: Most of Reeve's stories featured detective Craig Kennedy. Exceptions, where known, are noted. :: Most of the stories run 10-15 pages. Longer stories are noted. :: All listings are American magazines, though certainly Reeve stories were occasionally reprinted in foreign publications. Known English reprints are listed in **A2**.

Adventure
1914
> February   **The Abduction Club**
> (Short novel. Features Craig Kennedy with Clare Kendall in a supporting role. Merged with the *American Sunday Monthly Magazine* serial *The Ear in the Wall* for book publication with *The Ear in the Wall* as the final title, and Craig Kennedy changed to Guy Garrick.)
> December   **The Stolen War Secret**
> (Short novel.)

Alfred Hitchcock's Mystery Magazine
> 2003 September   **The Bacteriological Detective**
> (*Cosmopolitan*, February 1911)

Amazing Detective Tales
1930
> June   **The Diamond Maker**
> (*Cosmopolitan*, May 1911)
> July   **The White Slave**
> (*Cosmopolitan*, June 1912)
> August   **The Scientific Cracksman**
> ("The Case of Helen Bond," *Cosmopolitan*, December 1910)
> September   **The Body That Wouldn't Burn**
> ("Spontaneous Combustion," *Cosmopolitan*, July 1911)
> October   **The Man Who Was Dead**
> ("The Artificial Paradise," *Cosmopolitan*, October 1911)
> [November   **The Money Master**]
> (This story, which may have been a reprint of "The Master Counterfeiter," *Cosmopolitan*, February 1912, was advertized, but *Amazing Detective* folded with the October issue.)

Argosy, The
    1907 June   **The Cat That Didn't Come Back**
        (Reeve's first-known fiction in a professional publication.)

Argosy All-Story Weekly
    1925 May 23   **Revenge**

Argosy
    1932 December 3   **Murder on the Mike**

Best Detective Magazine
    1929 December   **The Sinister Shadow**
        (*Detective Story Magazine*, August 27, 1918)
    1931 April   **Craig Kennedy's Greatest Mystery**
        (*Detective Story Magazine*, July 12, 1924)

Black Book Detective Magazine
    1934 January   **The Inca Dagger**
        (A 45-page reworking of Reeve's first true novel, *The Gold of the Gods* [1915].)

Boys' Life
(Reeve's appearance here was part of an effort to expand *BL* from an internal publication of the Boy Scouts to a national magazine.)
    1923 Oct - Dec   **Craig Kennedy, Radio Detective**
          (3-part serial.)
    1924
        January   **Deep Sea Treasure**
        February   **A Son of the North Woods**
        March   **The Polar Flight of the ZR-10**
        May   **The Honor System**
        July   **The Bon Homme Richard Returns**
        September   **The Ghost Chase**
        Nov - Dec   **The Voice in the Dark**
          (2-part serial. Chapters subtitled "An Adventure Which Befell Ken Adams on the Way to the Jamboree" and "Conclusion of Ken Adams' Adventure on the Jamboree Trip.")
    unknown   **The Robot Mystery**
        (Anthologized in *The Boy Scouts Year-Book of Ghost and Mystery Stories* [D. Appleton-Century, 1933]. The book collected *Boys' Life* stories from 1924-30.)

Burroughs Bulletin, The
    1974 #33   **Tarzan the Mighty**
        (Reprint of a 1928 newspaper serial which novelized a film serial.)

Clues

1929

1st November	**The Mystery in the Museum**

(Issue includes non-fiction piece, "Mr. Reeve Speaks of Theodore Roosevelt and Craig Kennedy.")

2nd November	**The Mystery of the Phantom Voice**
1st December	**The House of a Hundred Murders**
2nd December	**The Mystery of the Vault**
1930 1st January	**The Mystery in the Mire**

Complete Detective Novel Magazine

1932

April	**The Kidnap Club**

(Lead novel. Not the same as "The Abduction Club," *Adventure*, February 1914. Published simultaneously with the book edition of *The Kidnap Club*.)

May	**Death in the Cards**
June	**The Junior League Murder**
July	**Murder Under the Southern Cross**
August	**Murder Never Dies**
September	**Murder in Green**

(Lead novel.)

December	**Murder in the Tourist Camp**
1933 August/September	**The Electric War**

(Lead novel. Revised and reprinted in book form as *The Clutching Hand*.)

1934 January	**Murder in the Rumpus Room**

(Features "Scarley Scott: Soul Detective.")

1935 January/February	**The Royal Racket**

(Features "Clare Kendall: Girl Detective." Not the same as the *Craig Kennedy and the Gangsters* newspaper short having the same title.)

Complete Underworld Novelettes

1934 August	**Guy Garrick, P.D.**

Cosmopolitan

(The core of Reeve's fame and legacy. The majority were reprinted in the *Craig Kennedy Stories* collection, and the remainder in *The Panama Plot*, with the exception that the last four [May-Aug 1918] appear not to have been reprinted. Most stories were illustrated by Will Foster.)

1910 December   **The Case of Helen Bond**

(The first published story of Craig Kennedy, Scientific Detective.)

1911

January	**The Silent Bullet**
February	**The Bacteriological Detective**
March	**The Deadly Tube**
April	**The Seismograph Adventure**

Cosmopolitan (continued)

1911 (cont.)

May	**The Diamond Maker**

(The editor's introductions to the stories start labeling Craig Kennedy the "scientific detective" with this issue.)

June	**The Azure Ring**
July	**Spontaneous Combustion**
August	**The Terror in the Air**
September	**The Black Hand**
October	**The Artificial Paradise**
November	**The Steel Door**
December	**The Sand-Hog**

1912

January	**The Bacillus of Death**
February	**The Master Counterfeiter**
March	**The Firebug**
April	**The Yeggman**
May	**The Poisoned Pen**
June	**The White Slave**
July	**The Forger**
August	**The Unofficial Spy**
September	**The Smuggler**
October	**The Invisible Ray**
[November	Reeve cover credit, but no story.]

1913

April	**The Green Curse**
May	**The Sybarite**
June	**The Phantom Circuit**
July	**The Elixir of Life**
August	**The Dream Doctor**
September	**The Death House**
October	**The Submarine Mystery**
November	**The Bomb-Maker**
December	**The Ghouls**

1914

January	**The Air-Pirate**
February	**The Billionaire Baby**
March	**The Radium Robber**
April	**The Eugenic Bride**
May	**The Dead-Line**
June	**The Curio Shop**
July	**The Germ Letter**
August	**The Wireless Wire-tappers**
September	**The Family Skeleton**
October	**The Devil-worshipers**
November	**Happy Dust**

Cosmopolitan (cont.)

1914 (cont.)

| December | The Murder Syndicate |

1915

January	The Diamond-Queen
February	The X-Ray Detective
March	The Tango Thief
April	The Supertoxin
May	The Sixth Sense
June	The Absolute Zero
July	The Sleep-Maker
August	The Evil Eye
September	The House of Death
October	The Demon Engine
November	The Social Gangster
December	The Voodoo Mystery

1916

January	The Treasure-Train
March	The Truth-Detector
May	The Soul-Analysis
June	The Mystic Poisoner
July	The Phantom Destroyer
August	The Beauty-Mask
September	The Love-Meter
October	The Vital Principle
November	The Submarine Mine
December	The Rubber Dagger

1917

January	The Gun-runner
February	The Sunken Treasure
April	The Love-Philter
May	The Panama Plot
June	The Black Diamond
July	The Bitter Water
August	The Nitrate King
October	The Coca King
November	The Phantom Parasite

1918

January	The Door of Dread
February	The Black Cross
April	The Psychic Scar
May	The Star-Shell
June	The Film Murder
July	The Treason Trust
August	The Love-Game

Country Gentleman, The

(Stories reprinted in *Craig Kennedy on the Farm*.)

1924

August 30	**Frozen Paper**
October 25	**The Hypocrites**
December 13	**The Barn Burner**

1925

January 31	**The Gas Tramp**
March 14	**Woman's Wiles**
April 4	**The Long Arm**
May 16	**Land Poor**
August 1	**Dead Beets**
November	**The Harvest Home**

Detective Fiction Weekly

1928

September 28	**Blood Will Tell**
October 6	**Radiant Doom**
December 22	**Craig Kennedy's Christmas Case**

1929

Feb 23 - March 9	**The Mystery Ray**
(3-part serial.)	
March 16	**The Beauty Wrecker**
August 31	**Poisoned Music**
September 7	**The Crime Student**

Detective Story Magazine

1918

July 16 - August 6	**Craig Kennedy and the Film Tragedy**

(4-part serial. Reprinted in book form as *The Film Mystery*.)

August 27	**The Sinister Shadow**
Sept 17 - Oct 8	**The Soul Scar**

(4-part serial. Reprinted in book form as *The Soul Scar*.)

1924 July 12	**Craig Kennedy's Greatest Mystery**

1928

July 7	**Craig Kennedy Gets His Girl**
July 28	**Kennedy Gets the Dope**
August 11	**Craig Kennedy and the Model**
August 25	**Craig Kennedy and the Ghost**
October 13	**The Dead Line**
October 27	**Craig Kennedy Splits Hairs**

Dime Detective Magazine

1933 October 1	**The Golden Grave**

(Novelette. Issue includes Reeve profile, "The Scientific Detective.")

Everybody's Magazine

(Stories illustrated by Harold Anderson.)

1923

September	**Thicker Than Water**
October	**Dead Men Tell Tales**
November	**The Radio Wraith**
December	**The Hawk**

1924

January	**The Jazz Addict**
February	**Counterfeit Beauty**

Flynn's

(Reprinted as *The Fourteen Points*, i.e. the four elements, plus the four compass points, plus the six senses.)

1924

September 27	**Craig Kennedy and the Elements: Air**
October 11	**Craig Kennedy and the Elements: Fire**
October 25	**Craig Kennedy and the Elements: Earth**
November 8	**Craig Kennedy and the Elements: Water**
December 13	**Craig Kennedy and the Compass: North**
December 20	**Craig Kennedy and the Compass: East**
December 27	**Craig Kennedy and the Compass: South**

1925

January 3	**Craig Kennedy and the Compass: West**
[January 24	Reeve photo on cover, but no story in issue.]
January 31	**Craig Kennedy and the 'Six' Senses: Sight**
February 7	**Craig Kennedy and the 'Six' Senses: Smell**
February 14	**Craig Kennedy and the 'Six' Senses: Taste**
February 21	**Craig Kennedy and the 'Six' Senses: Touch**
February 28	**Craig Kennedy and the 'Six' Senses: Hearing**
March 7	**Craig Kennedy and the 'Six' Senses: The 'Sixth' Sense**

(The sixth sense was "common sense," not clairvoyance.)

Gang World

1933 December	**Gawd Hates a Rat!**

(Features Kirk Van Kirk.)

Hearst's Magazine

(Essentially part of the *Cosmopolitan* run. Reeve, presumably, was "borrowed" to boost the revitalized magazine. "The Campaign Grafter" was reprinted in Volume 2 of the *Craig Kennedy Stories*. The other three are in Volume 3.)

1912

November	**The Campaign Grafter**
December	**The Kleptomaniac**

Hearst's Magazine (cont.)
   1913
      January   **The Opium Joint**
      February   **The Vampire**

High School Recorder
(A publication of Boys' High School, Brooklyn.)
   1898 December   **Interscholastic Sonnets**

Illustrated Detective Magazine, The
[Reprints in conjunction with "Craig Kennedy's Illustrated Detective News."]
   1929 December   **The Silent Bullet**
           (*Cosmopolitan*, January 1911)
   1930
      January   **The Steel Door**
           (*Cosmopolitan*, November 1911)
      February   **The Black Hand**
           (*Cosmopolitan*, September 1911)
      March   unknown

Kelly's Magazine
(*Kelly's* was a pulp, rebinding unsold issues of *Complete Detective Novel Magazine* and *Wild West Stories and Complete Novel Magazine*. The Reeve story originally appeared in *CDNM*, December 1932.)
      1932   **Murder in the Tourist Camp**

Mystery Magazine
   1923
      [October 15   Cover announcement, but no story.]
      November 1   **I'll Win! I'll Win!**
           (Co-authored with Mrs. Arthur B. Reeve, Margaret W. Reeve.)
   1924 Feb 15 - March 1   **By the Breadth of a Hair**
           (2-part serial. Co-authored with Margaret W. Reeve.)
   1926 January 15   **In the Rush Hour**
           (Features Mary Mannix, a doctor/detective.)

Nassau Literary Magazine, The
(A Princeton University magazine.)
   1901 May   **The Golf Dream**
           (First use of a character named Craig Kennedy—he's an athlete, not a detective.)

Pearson's Magazine

(Stories from Sept 1913 through August 1914 feature Constance Dunlap, and were reprinted in Volume 12 of the *Craig Kennedy Stories*.)

1913

September	**The Forgers**
October	**The Embezzlers**
November	**The Gun Runners**
December	**The Eavesdroppers**

1914

January	**The Gamblers**
February	**The Clairvoyants**
March	**The Plungers**
April	**The Abductors**
May	**The Shoplifters**
June	**The Blackmailers**
July	**The Dope Fiends**
August	**The Fugitives**
September	**The Crimeometer**

(Features Clare Kendall. Advertized as a "new series," but there was apparently no followup.)

Popular Detective

(According to a 1975 letter from Leo Margulies, former chief editor of the Thrilling chain, to researcher J. Randolph Cox, these were unsold Craig Kennedy short stories rewritten into 20 to 25-page novelettes by Ashley T. Locke, a mystery pulp author and occasional contributor to Thrilling pulps. The first four novelettes were reprinted as *Enter Craig Kennedy*.)

1934

November	**Craig Kennedy Returns**
December	**Enter Craig Kennedy**

1935

January	**Craig Kennedy Walks with Death**
February	**Craig Kennedy Strikes Back!**
April	**Craig Kennedy's Strangest Case**
May	**Craig Kennedy Intervenes**
June	**The Navy Murder Case**

Popular Magazine, The

(All stories are approximately 50-60 pages.)

1912

May 1	**The Green-goods King**
July 1	**The Treasure Vault**
1913 April 1 - 15	**The Death Thought**

(2-part serial.)

Popular Magazine, The (cont.)
1914
> Jan 1 - 15   **The Scientific Gunman: An Adventure with**
>   **Craig Kennedy, Scientific Detective**
> (2-part serial. Revised and published in book form as *Guy Garrick*. Character names change, including, most obviously, Craig Kennedy to Guy Garrick.)
>
> May 1 - 15   **The Terrorists**
> (2-part serial.)

Radio Digest Illustrated
> 1929 Oct - 1930 March   **The Gigolo Mystery**
> (6-part serial.)

Red Book Magazine
(All issues feature Guy Garrick. Illustrated by George Brehm.)
1914
> May   **The Sleep Maker**
> (Incorporated into the novel *Guy Garrick*, which was primarily taken from "The Scientific Gunman," *The Popular Magazine*, January 1 & 15, 1914.)
>
> June   **In the Cave of Aladdin**
> July   **The Soldier of Fortune**
> August   **Playing for High Stakes**
> September   **The Clairvoyant Trust**
> November   **The House of a Thousand Murders**

Scientific Detective Monthly
1930
> January   **The Mystery of the Bulawayo Diamond**
> February   **The Bacteriological Detective**
>   (*Cosmopolitan*, February 1911)
> March   **The Seismograph Adventure**
>   (*Cosmopolitan*, April 1911)
> April   **The Terror in the Air**
>   (*Cosmopolitan*, August 1911)
> May   **The Azure Ring**
>   (*Cosmopolitan*, June 1911)

Thrilling Detective
(See the note following the *Popular Detective* entries. At about 5000 words, this was probably not one of the group rewritten by Ashley T. Locke.)
> 1934 August   **Murder at Night**

Underworld, The

    1928

        May   **The Embezzler**

        ("The Embezzlers," *Pearson's Magazine*, October 1913)

        June   **The Gun Runners**

        (*Pearson's Magazine*, November 1913)

Underworld Detective, The

    1934 September   **Trailing a Killer**

        (Lead character: Samuel Baggart.)

Weird Tales

    1935 May   **The Death Cry**

        (Novelette.)

World Man Hunters

(Reeve is in all three issues of this brief run, and was advertized for the fourth, but the magazine folded.)

    1934

        January   **Murder Around the Corner**

        (Advertized as "Return of Craig Kennedy.")

        February   **Doped**

        March   **The Murders Over the Weekend**

Tally of Magazine Fiction Appearances

The following list tallies Reeve's fiction appearances in American magazines during his lifetime. Only professional sales are included, i.e. his school publications are excluded. Reprints are included. Magazines are classified by pulp (p) and other (o). It's not our intent to describe detailed distinctions between magazines, but simply to give a rough idea as to where Reeve found his success, divided by high and low markets. Pulps, as a rule, were cheaper all-fiction magazines printed on pulp paper; whereas slicks, the majority of "other," were printed on quality paper and included a mix of fiction and nonfiction. The notable category-tweener is *Pearson's* which, during Reeve's tenure, included a fiction/nonfiction mix, but was printed on pulp paper in pulp format.

Type	Magazine	Stories	Serial parts included
p	*Adventure*	2	2
p	*Amazing Detective Tales*	5	5
p	*Argosy, The*	1	1
p	*Argosy All-Story*	1	1
p	*Argosy*	1	1
p	*Best Detective Magazine*	2	2
p	*Black Book Detective Magazine*	1	1
o	*Boys' Life*	9	12
p	*Clues*	5	5
p	*Complete Detective Novel Magazine*	10	10
p	*Complete Underworld Novelettes*	1	1
o	*Cosmopolitan*	82	82
o	*Country Gentleman*	9	9
p	*Detective Fiction Weekly*	7	9
p	*Detective Story Magazine*	10	16
p	*Dime Detective Magazine*	1	1
o	*Everybody's Magazine*	6	6
p	*Flynn's*	14	14
p	*Gang World*	1	1
o	*Hearst's Magazine*	4	4
p	*Illustrated Detective Magazine*	4	4
p	*Kelly's Magazine*	1	1
p	*Mystery Magazine*	3	4
p	*Pearson's Magazine*	13	13
p	*Popular Detective*	7	7
p	*Popular Magazine, The*	5	8
o	*Radio Digest Illustrated*	1	6
o	*Red Book Magazine*	6	6
p	*Scientific Detective Monthly*	5	5
p	*Thrilling Detective*	1	1

Type	Magazine	Stories	Serial parts included
p	*Underworld, The*	2	2
p	*Underworld Detective, The*	1	1
p	*Weird Tales*	1	1
p	*World Man Hunters*	3	3
	Total	225	245
	Pulp	108	120
	Other	117	125

Sales to Street & Smith

The Street & Smith Archives at Syracuse University contain records for most of Reeve's sales to S&S, a unique opportunity, in the absence of Reeve's own business records, to view his arrangements with a publisher. Two of Reeve's *Detective Story* shorts were reprinted in *Best Detective*, but payment and other details were not available.

Pay date	Pub date	Pub title	Word cnt	Paid	2007 val	Rate
The Popular Magazine						
12/15/11	05/01/12	**The Green-goods King**	30,000	$800	$17,186	2.7¢
03/01/12	07/01/12	**The Treasure Vault**	30,000	800	17,016	2.7
07/19/12	04/01-04/15/13	**The Death Thought**	33,600	800	17,016	2.4
	(2-part serial.)					
02/28/13	01/01-01/15/14	**The Scientific Gunman**	34,200	800	16,848	2.3
	(2-part serial.)					
12/19/13	05/01-05/15/14	**The Terrorists**	38,400	800	16,848	2.1
	(2-part serial.)					
Detective Story Magazine						
04/26/18	07/16-08/06/18	**CK and the Film Tragedy**	44,000	750	10,355	1.9
	(4-part serial. Reeve's original title: "The Film Mystery.")					
06/21/18	08/27/18	**The Sinister Shadow**	9,000	125	1,726	1.4
07/12/18	09/17-10/08/18	**The Soul Scar**	44,000	750	10,355	1.9
	(4-part serial. Original title: "The Soul Star.")					
04/18/24	07/12/24	**CK's Greatest Mystery**	7,800	150	1,829	1.9
	(Original title: "The Orchid.")					
03/30/28	07/07/28	**CK Gets His Girl**	7,200	225	2,743	3.1
	(Original title: "The Elixir of Fate.")					
04/06/28	07/28/28	**Kennedy Gets the Dope**	7,200	225	2,743	3.1
04/27/28	08/11/28	**CK and the Model**	6,600	210	2,560	3.2
	(Original title: "The Companionate Marriage [or Murder].")					
05/11/28	08/25/28	**CK and the Ghost**	7,400	225	2,743	3.0
	(Original title: "The Spirit Lover.")					
06/13/28	10/13/28	**The Dead Line**	6,000	195	2,378	3.3
07/27/28	10/27/28	**CK Splits Hairs**	7,500	234	2,853	3.1
	(Original title: "The Perfect Crime.")					

Pay date: Records indicate date on which payment to author was made.
Publication date: Date of issue with story.
Published title: Title in magazine, which occasionally differs from Reeve's original title. "CK" = Craig Kennedy.
Word count: Approx. word count of story based on (number of pages x 600). Actual average word count varies based on type size, page layout, number of illustrations, etc. Page counts were not known on a few of the stories or serial segments; extrapolations

were made from stories of similar vintage.

Paid: Records indicate amount paid to author.

2007 value: The value of the payments in 2007 dollars, derived from the Bureau of Labor Statistics inflation calculator. The calculator uses the average Consumer Price Index for each calendar year. Since the CPI was not calculated prior to 1913, values for 1911 and 1912 were estimated by assuming the pre-WWI annual inflation of 1%.

Rate: Word rate in cents calculated from (amount paid ÷ word count). Stories in *The Popular* were obviously paid on a flat fee; stories in *Detective Story* appear to have been paid by word-rate. Since word counts were estimated, numbers like 1.9 and 3.2 should be considered by whole number amounts, 2¢ and 3¢ a word, respectively.

Additional info

Rights purchased: For the first three Reeve stories in *The Popular*, S&S bought all serial rights while Reeve retained dramatic and book rights. For the final two stories in *The Popular*, Reeve's rights expanded to include motion pictures. For his first serial in *Detective Story* ("Film Tragedy"), the entry reads: "Magazine rights — this does not include newspaper rights, but author agrees not to use them till story is rewritten in longer form." For "The Sinister Shadow," S&S purchased "magazine rights"; for "The Soul Scar," "American magazine rights." Starting with "Craig Kennedy's Greatest Mystery," S&S purchases American serial rights.

Payment: Starting with "Craig Kennedy's Greatest Mystery," payment is made to the Craig Kennedy Service Corp., 429 W. 42nd St.

A2: Magazines - Fiction - United Kingdom

Reeve was likely reprinted much more extensively in foreign markets, especially England, than this small sampling of known appearances represents.

Detective Magazine, The
1924 February 15   **Dead Men Tell Tales**
    (*Everybody's*, October 1923)

Hush
1930
    September   **The Love Potion**
    (Probably "The Love-Philter," *Cosmopolitan*, April 1917)
    October   **The Bitter Water**
    (*Cosmopolitan*, July 1917)
    December   **The Psychic Scar**
    (*Cosmopolitan*, April 1918)
1931 February   **The Door of Dread**
    (*Cosmopolitan*, January 1918)

Nash's Magazine
(According to Sam Moskowitz, *Nash's* reprinted much fiction from *Cosmopolitan*. In the Craig Kennedy stories, Kennedy's nationality was changed to British and the settings moved to England.)
1911
    May   **The Story of the Deadly Tube**
    ("The Deadly Tube," *Cosmopolitan*, March 1911)
    June   **The Seismograph Adventure**
    (*Cosmopolitan*, April 1911)
    July   **The Story of the Diamond Maker**
    ("The Diamond Maker," *Cosmopolitan*, May 1911)
    August   **The Azure Ring**
    (*Cosmopolitan*, June 1911)
    September   **A Case of Spontaneous Combustion**
    ("Spontaneous Combustion," *Cosmopolitan*, July 1911)
    October   **The Terror in the Air**
    (*Cosmopolitan*, August 1911)
    November   **The Black Hand**
    (*Cosmopolitan*, September 1911)
    December   **The Artificial Paradise**
    (*Cosmopolitan*, October 1911)
1912
    January   **The Steel Door**
    (*Cosmopolitan*, November 1911)

Nash's Magazine (continued)

    1912 (cont.)

        February   **The Tunnel Mystery**
            ("The Sand-Hog," *Cosmopolitan*, December 1911)

        March   **The Bacillus of Death**
            (*Cosmopolitan*, January 1912)

        April   **The Master Counterfeiter**
            (*Cosmopolitan*, February 1912)

        May   **The Firefiend**
            ("The Firebug," *Cosmopolitan*, March 1912)

        June   **The Cracksman**
            ("The Yeggman," *Cosmopolitan*, April 1912)

        July   **The Poisoned Pen**
            (*Cosmopolitan*, May 1912)

        August   **The White Slave**
            (*Cosmopolitan*, June 1912)

        September   **The Forger**
            (*Cosmopolitan*, July 1912)

        October   **The Unofficial Spy**
            (*Cosmopolitan*, August 1912)

        December   **Craig Kennedy and the Invisible Ray**
            ("The Invisible Ray," *Cosmopolitan*, October 1912)

Nash's Pall Mall Magazine

    1916

        January   **The Devil-worshippers**
            (*Cosmopolitan*, October 1914)

        March   **The X-Ray Detective**
            (*Cosmopolitan*, February 1915)

        May   **The Absolute Zero**
            (*Cosmopolitan*, June 1915)

        August   **The Soul-Analysis**
            (*Cosmopolitan*, May 1916)

    1917

        May   **The Truth-Detector**
            (*Cosmopolitan*, March 1916)

        June   **The Rubber Dagger**
            (*Cosmopolitan*, December 1916)

        August   **The Love-Philter**
            (*Cosmopolitan*, April 1917)

A3: Magazines - Nonfiction

This is unlikely to be a complete listing since new Reeve citations continue to surface from time to time. It does, however, demonstrate the wide range of subject matter in Reeve's journalistic endeavors.

American Review of Reviews
1908 February	**Why Not a "Red Cross" for the Army of Industry?**
1911 February	**The Potash Industry and the American Farmer**

Bibliotheca Sacra
1905 Vol. 62, No. 247	**Is Evolution Calvinistic?**

Charities and the Commons
1907 February 2	**The Death Roll of Industry**

Clues
1929 1st November	**Mr. Reeve Speaks of Theodore Roosevelt and Craig Kennedy**

Editor, The
1914 June 6	**A Letter from Arthur B. Reeve**

Everybody's Magazine
1907 February	**Our Industrial Juggernaut**

Flynn's
1924 December 6	**Spreading the Net**

Forum, The
1919 July	**When the Criminal Takes to Science and Its Effect on the Fictionist**

Hampton's Broadway Magazine
1908 November 18	**Newest Man-Killing Devices and the Warless Age**

(Predicts weapons of war, 40 years hence.)

Hampton's Magazine
1909 January	**Men and Monkeys—Primates**

Harper's Weekly
1913
January 4	**The High Cost of Dying**
July 4	**The Infallible Finger-print**

High School Recorder
(A publication of Boy's High School, Brooklyn. Reeve joined the staff for his senior year of 1998-99, editing "societies" with another student and contributing other content.)

Illustrated Detective Magazine, The
1929 December	**Craig Kennedy's Illustrated Detective News,** v1#1
1930	
January	**Craig Kennedy's Illustrated Detective News,** v1#2
February	**Craig Kennedy's Illustrated Detective News,** v1#3
March	**Craig Kennedy's Illustrated Detective News,** v1#4

Independent, The
1906 November 22	**Football Safe and Sane**
1907	
August 29	**The Standard of Decent Living**
December 5	**What's the Matter With Football?**
1913 July 10	**In Defense of the Detective Story**

Live Wire, The
1908	
March	**Towering Buildings That Grab Gales From the Skies, Snatch Electricity From the Earth, and in Many Other Ways "Butt In"**
September	**"Frightened to Death"**

McClure's Magazine
(All entries are part of the "Detective Burns' Great Cases" series. Articles were by William J. Burns, "as told to" various authors. Burns was a former Secret Service agent who ran the William J. Burns International Detective Agency. These are the four pieces authored by Reeve.)
1912 October	**The Mystery of the Double Eagles**
1913	
February	**The Mysterious Counterfeiter**
March	**The Conspirators**
May	**The Customs Spy**

Munsey's
1909	
May	**The Great Revivalists**
November	**Our New College Presidents**
1910 January	**Imprisonment for Debt**

Nassau Literary Magazine, The
(A Princeton publication.)
1902 October	**Rudyard Kipling**

Our Own Times
(Reeve edited this annual.)
    1906-10

Outing Magazine
    1909 September   **Three Hundred Years on the Hudson**
    1910
        February   **Humble Origin of the Royal Game of Golf**
        April   **Beginnings of Our Great Games** (Baseball and Cricket)
        May   **Beginnings of Our Great Games** (Tennis and Lacrosse)
        June   **Beginnings of Our Great Games** (Football and Polo)
        October   **The World's Greatest Athletic Organization**
        December   **What America Spends for Sport**

Outlook Magazine
    1907
        March 2   **Is Workman's Compensation Practicable?**
        June 15   **Seeing New York in a Horse-Car**

Princeton University Yearbook
(Titles and dates of Reeve's contributions are currently unknown.)

Princetonian
(Titles and dates of Reeve's contributions are currently unknown.)

Public Opinion
(Reeve's first job in journalism. He was assistant editor and contributed articles from 1903-06.)
    1906 (approx.)   **How Can Football Be Saved? Walter Camp**
                           Discusses Question
            (Reprinted in *The Washington Post*, January 14, 1906.)

Railroad Man's Magazine
    1908 October   **Man Who First Said Hands Up**
    1909 November   **Harriman, the Master Builder**
            (Edward Henry Harriman, a wealthy railroad executive, died September 9,
            1909. Reeve's article was featured on the cover.)

Reader Magazine
    1905 October   **Sociology of Sunshine**

Scientific Detective Monthly
    1930 January   **What Are the Great Detective Stories and Why?**
                (The Table of Contents uses the above title; the title with the article is "It Takes
                Arthur B. Reeve To Tell What Are the Great Detective Stories *and* Why?")

Scrap Book, The

1907

August	**Modern Methuselahs**
September	**The Humor of Yellow Photography**
October	**What the Stork Has Done in 6000 Years**
December	**Gambling's Golden Age Has Gone**

1908

February	**Theosophy—The Religion of the Occult**
March	**Woman and the Ballot**
April	**Law—A Business Career**
May	**Men-Monkeys Who Built Our Babels**
July	**Tricks of the Talesmen**

(Article on the lies told to avoid jury duty.)

August	**Back to Nature**
September	**Fitting the Right Man into the Right Place**
October	**Remarkable Records of Thrift**

1909

January	**1908—A Year of Absurdities**
March	**High-Powered Senses**
April	**Brand New Superstitions**
May	**Convicted—Albert T. Patrick's Cry for "Liberty or Death"**
June	**Dictating What Woman Shall Wear**
August	**Working Your Way Through College**
November	**Zip! Off on a Joy-ride**

1910

January	**Halley's Homing Comet**
March	**Why Not "Own Your Own Home"?**
April	**Our Lost State Capitals**
November	**Our Most Dignified Office**
December	**Cipher Secrets Revealed**

1911

January	**The Curious History of 1910**
February	**End of the Peabody Fund**
May	**Now the 17-Year Locust**
June	**Freak Legislation Enacted in Earnest**
July	**The Short Ballot for Our Civic Ills**
August	**Extracting the Loan-Shark's Teeth**
November	**Beware the Affinity!**

Success, The Human Magazine

1925 December	**Who Says There's No Santa Claus?**

Survey

1909 December 4	**Capital and Labor Agree on Workmen's Compensation**

Thrills
1927 June   **Halley's Homing Comet**
          (*The Scrap Book*, January 1910)

Travel
1910 June   **Making Christians in Foreign Lands**

World To-Day
1907 April   **New York's New Water System**
1909 September   **What the Sage Fortune is Doing**

World's Work Magazine
1906 December   **The Romance of Tunnel Building**
1907 October   **A New Kind of Insurance**
1908 February   **The Prevention of Poverty**
1913 March   **Five Rattling Detective Adventures**
          (Subtitled "The New Method of Detectives Who Have Turned Scientists—
          How Crooks Are Made to Catch Themselves.")
1920
     November   **New and Old South Sea Bubbles: Ponzi and Some
                               of His Predecessors**
     December   **Old and New South Sea Bubbles: Some Historic
                               Swindles of Two Centuries**

Writer's Digest
1930 August   **How Writers Make Good**

B1: Books - United States

This listing is believed to be complete.

1912

The Silent Bullet   Dodd, Mead

(Subtitled *The Adventures of Craig Kennedy, Scientific Detective*. Republished as *Craig Kennedy Stories: Volume 1*, with no subtitle.)

1913

The Poisoned Pen   Dodd, Mead

(Republished as *Craig Kennedy Stories: Volume 2*. From the *New York Times* review, April 6, 1913: ". . . for all his array of batteries and dictagraphs it is really Mr. Reeve's very lively imagination which keeps one anxious to know what extraodinary thing is going to happen next, forbidding any pause until the tale is finished. Only those few very superior and pitiable people who cannot enjoy detective stories will fail to be interested and entertained by *The Poisoned Pen*.")

1914

The Death House   Winthrop

(The Winthrop editions were paperbound. No information on complete contents. "The Death House" was a short story in *Cosmopolitan*, September 1913.)

The Dream Doctor   Hearst's International Library

(Republished as *Craig Kennedy Stories: Volume 3*.)

Guy Garrick   Hearst's International Library

(Republished as *Craig Kennedy Stories: Volume 11*.)

The Phantom Circuit   Winthrop

(*Cosmopolitan*, June 1913)

The Yeggman   Winthrop

(*Cosmopolitan*, April 1912)

1915

The Exploits of Elaine   Hearst's International Library

(Republished as *Craig Kennedy Stories: Volume 9*.)

The Gold of the Gods   Hearst's International Library

(Republished as *Craig Kennedy Stories: Volume 8*.)

The War Terror   Hearst's International Library

(Republished as *Craig Kennedy Stories: Volume 4*.)

1916

Constance Dunlap, Woman Detective   Hearst's International Library

(Republished as *Craig Kennedy Stories: Volume 12*.)

1916 (continued)

The Ear in the Wall   Hearst's International Library
> (Republished as *Craig Kennedy Stories: Volume 7.*)

The Romance of Elaine   Hearst's International Library
> (Republished as *Craig Kennedy Stories: Volume 10.*)

The Social Gangster   Hearst's International Library
> (Republished as *Craig Kennedy Stories: Volume 4.*)

1917

The Adventuress   Harper & Brothers
> (Serialized in newspapers starting May 1917.)

The Treasure Train   Harper & Brothers
> (Republished as *Craig Kennedy Stories: Volume 6.*)

1918

The Panama Plot   Harper & Brothers
> **The Panama Plot**
>> (*Cosmopolitan*, May 1917)
>
> **The Love Philter**
>> (*Cosmopolitan*, April 1917)
>
> **The Black Diamond**
>> (*Cosmopolitan*, June 1917)
>
> **The Bitter Water**
>> (*Cosmopolitan*, July 1917)
>
> **The Nitrate King**
>> (*Cosmopolitan*, August 1917)
>
> **The Green Death**
>> (Probably "The Coca King," *Cosmopolitan*, October 1917)
>
> **The Phantom Parasite**
>> (*Cosmopolitan*, November 1917)
>
> **The Door of Dread**
>> (*Cosmopolitan*, January 1918)
>
> **The Black Cross**
>> (*Cosmopolitan*, February 1918)
>
> **The Psychic Scar**
>> (*Cosmopolitan*, April 1918)

Craig Kennedy Stories   Harper & Brothers
> (See **B3** for chapter listings and sources of the stories in this set.)
> Vol 1: **The Silent Bullet**
> Vol 2: **The Poisoned Pen**
> Vol 3: **The Dream Doctor**
> Vol 4: **The War Terror**
> Vol 5: **The Social Gangster**
> Vol 6: **The Treasure Train**

1918 (cont.)

Craig Kennedy Stories (cont.)
Vol 7: **The Ear in the Wall**
Vol 8: **The Gold of the Gods**
Vol 9: **The Exploits of Elaine**
Vol 10: **The Romance of Elaine**
Vol 11: **Guy Garrick**
Vol 12: **Constance Dunlap**

1919

The Master Mystery   Grosset & Dunlap
(Novelization of film. Co-authored with John W. Grey.)
The Soul Scar   Harper & Brothers
(Reprints serial from *Detective Story Magazine*, September 17 to October 8, 1918.)

1921

The Film Mystery   Harper & Brothers
(Reprints *Craig Kennedy and the Film Tragedy*, a serial from *Detective Story Magazine*, July 16 to August 6, 1918.)
The Mystery Mind   Grosset & Dunlap
(Novelization of film.)

1923

Craig Kennedy Listens In   Harper & Brothers
(Includes "The Wireless Phantom," "Buried Alive!," "The Brass Key," "The Boulevard of Bunk," "The Soul Merchant," and "Buccaneers of Booze." Selected from the "Romance-Mystery Novelettes" serialized in newsprint in 1922-23. The copyright attributions are to King Feature Syndicate and Harper & Brothers.)

1924

Atavar, the Dream Dancer   Harper & Brothers
(A Craig Kennedy novel. No previous publication known.)

1925

The Boy Scout's Craig Kennedy   Harper & Brothers
(Reprints stories from *Boys' Life*. Includes "The Polar Flight of the ZR-10," "A Son of the North Woods," "The Radio Detective," "Deep-Sea Treasure," "The Honor System," and "The Cruise of the Sea Scouts." "Radio Detective" is a retitling of "Craig Kennedy, Radio Detective"; "Cruise" is a retitling of "The Bon Homme Richard Returns." Stories feature Craig Kennedy and his nephew, Ken Adams. Introduction by Chief Scout Executive, James E. West.)
Craig Kennedy on the Farm   Harper & Brothers
(Reprints stories from *The Country Gentleman*.)

1925 (cont.)

The Fourteen Points   Harper & Brothers

(Reprints stories from *Flynn's* magazine. Includes 8-page introduction by Munsey editor, Robert H. Davis; with a photo of Reeve taken by Davis.)

1926

Pandora   Harper & Brothers

(No previous publication known.)

The Radio Detective   Grosset & Dunlap

(Novelization of film serial.)

1930

The Best Ghost Stories   Modern Library

(Reeve contributed the introduction, "The Fascination of the Ghost Story.")

1931

The Golden Age of Crime   The Mohawk Press

(A history of the rise of racketeering during Prohibition.)

1932

The Kidnap Club   The Macaulay Company

(Reprints Reeve's first novel from *Complete Detective Novel Magazine*, April 1932.)

1934

The Clutching Hand   The Reilly & Lee Company

(Revised version of "The Electric War," *Complete Detective Novel Magazine*, August/September 1933. From the *New York Times* review, April 29, 1934: "In this book we find Kennedy and his faithful satellite, Walter Jameson, at grips with their old enemy, the Clutching Hand, who is aided and abetted by a choice assortment of minor villains. The Clutching Hand, sometimes known as the Crime Master, is trying to get possession of a secret that will place the whole world in his power, and Kennedy is determined that he shall not have it.")

1935

Enter Craig Kennedy   The Macaulay Company

(Reprints the first four Reeve/Locke stories from *Popular Detective*. From the *New York Times* review, November 3, 1935: "Automata with the brains of men, cadavers that walk about and obey the orders conveyed to them, invisible creatures endowed with superhuman strength . . . If you like wildly impossible yarns dealing with things that science has not yet discovered . . . you need seek no further.")

The Iron Ghost

("Craig Kennedy Returns," *Popular Detective*, November 1934.)

1935 (cont.)

Enter Craig Kennedy (cont.)

The Devil's Brew

("Enter Craig Kennedy," *Popular Detective*, December 1934.)

Kennedy Walks with Death

("Craig Kennedy Walks with Death," *Popular Detective*, January 1935.)

Kennedy Strikes Back!

("Craig Kennedy Strikes Back!" *Popular Detective*, February 1935.)

1936

The Stars Scream Murder   D. Appleton-Century Company

(A title in "The Tired Business Man's Library." From the *New York Times* review, March 29, 1936: "Craig Kennedy . . . has gone in for astrology. When the charred body of rich old Maria Daskam is found in the ruins of her fire-swept tower at Hampton Hall, a quick reading of her horoscope convinces him at once that this is no accident. The stars scream murder, he declares. . . .")

Chicago Daily Tribune, May 4, 1918

The Panama Plot

Being a Review in Rime of Arthur B. Reeve's Novel of That Title

By J.P. McEvoy

Arthur B. Reeve,
With intent to deceive,
Has concocted a book very few could achieve.
Such puerile and futile
Inane and inutile
Invertibrate goo
Is the gift of but few.
And while there are those who may read and adore 'em,
The Panama Plot and the rest of the quorum,
I rise to remark that the pons assinorum
Of sapient sleuths who are super scientific
And pesky prolific
With isms and ologies, schisms and ics
Is Kennedy (Craig) and the rest of his dicks.

Take the Panama Plot
(For you may—I will not)
Somebody it seems wants to blow up the locks
(That would block and canal
And would simply raisehal)
And some one is using an aeroplane, too,
But the question is who?
Rah! Rah! there's the rub,
Let's discover the dub,
Says Kennedy's pal, the most arrant of asses
(For sleuths select pals from the goophiest classes)
And Kennedy's umbra, or side kick, or pardner
Is baffled by Craig, who's a friend of Ring Lardner.

Oh Kennedy's pal is a gooph,
Oof! Oof!
I long to do things to his roof,
Oof! Oof!
Oh, squirrels who inhabit arboreal huts
And seek for your sustenance succulent nuts,
Oh hasten to harvest this king of all mutts,
This immature amateur assinine blop,
The guy is a large nucataneous crop,
And his master Craig Kennedy
If, that's what we pay for,
A white paper shortage
Is something to pray for,
Something to hanker and hunger and lay for.
Forsooth,
Gawstrewth!
Accouchments resulting in such an idear
As the Panama Plot it were clubby to queer,
And Arthur when gravid again with a plot
Of flaccid flapdoodle like this one, do not
Inflict it on us, have a heart, if you please,
And save us from all such impossible cheese.
And a boon you'll achieve
    Oh believe us,
For Arthur B. Reeve
    You bereave us.

B2: Books - United Kingdom

1912

    The Black Hand   Eveleigh Nash
        (A retitling of *The Silent Bullet*, Dodd, Mead, 1912.)

1915

    The Exploits of Elaine   Hodder & Stoughton

1916

    Constance Dunlap, Woman Detective   Hodder & Stoughton
    Craig Kennedy, Detective   Simpkin & Co.
        (A retitling of *The War Terror*, Hearst's, 1915.)
    The Dream Doctor   Hodder & Stoughton
    The Gold of the Gods   Hodder & Stoughton
    Guy Garrick   Hodder & Stoughton
    The Poisoned Pen   Hodder & Stoughton
    The Romance of Elaine   Hodder & Stoughton
    The Triumph of Elaine   Hodder & Stoughton

1917

    The Diamond Queen   Hodder & Stoughton
        (A retitling of *The Social Gangster*, Hearst's, 1916.)
    The Ear in the Wall   Hodder & Stoughton

1918

    The Adventuress   W. Collins Sons & Co.

1920

    The Panama Plot   W. Collins Sons & Co.
    The Treasure Train   W. Collins Sons & Co.

1922

    The Film Mystery   Hodder & Stoughton

1924

    Craig Kennedy Listens In   Hodder & Stoughton

B3: Books - The 12-Vol "Craig Kennedy Stories"

This 1918 matched set, published by Harper & Brothers, has been accorded its own section since it by far the most common form Reeve's stories are found in. This is in marked contrast to the other Reeve books issued in the author's lifetime, all of which are relatively scarce, particularly in dustwrapper. The 12-volume set incorporated some of those single-volume collections, albeit in maroon cover with gold-lettered spines and no dustwrapper. (It also incorporated their copyright dates.) The set sold widely through magazine ads in 1919. Even today (2007), individual copies of the original set are easily obtained for $3-5 a copy. Contemporary publishers have reprinted selected volumes, making them even more common. By making Reeve as ubiquitous in bookshops as Charles Dickens or Mark Twain, the set must have contributed to keeping Reeve's name alive. However, it probably helped to freeze his long-term legacy at works written by 1918, since magazine and book appearances past that time are so much scarcer. :: The below listing attempts to document the magazine and book origins of each volume as far as practicable. It is not as cut-and-dry as one might prefer. In the early volumes, magazine stories correspond to book chapters. But in most cases, the stories were rewritten to stitch them together in pseudo-novel format, often in varying order from their magazine publication dates. Sometimes, the magazine story starts in the middle of a chapter; in many cases, magazine stories were split into multiple chapters. Some of the volumes—e.g. *The Gold of the Gods*— were book originals; chapters have been listed for these as well, because of Reeve's tendency to recycle titles. The last two volumes, *Guy Garrick* and *Constance Dunlap*, do *not* feature Craig Kennedy as a character.

Volume 1: The Silent Bullet
chapter—starting page

0 1 **Craig Kennedy's Theories**
(*Cosmopolitan*, December 1910. The first 500 words of "The Case of Helen Bond.")

1 5 **The Silent Bullet**
(*Cosmopolitan*, January 1911)

2 34 **The Scientific Cracksman**
(*Cosmopolitan*, December 1910. The remainder of "The Case of Helen Bond.")

3 65 **The Bacteriological Detective**
(*Cosmopolitan*, February 1911)

4 93 **The Deadly Tube**
(*Cosmopolitan*, March 1911)

5 122 **The Seismograph Adventure**
(*Cosmopolitan*, April 1911)

6 157 **The Diamond Maker**
(*Cosmopolitan*, May 1911)

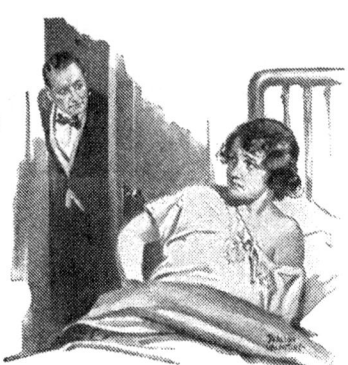
Adventure, August 3, 1919

In 1919, ads for the 12-volume set were commonplace in *Adventure*, *Argosy*, *Blue Book*, *People's*, etc.

Volume 1: The Silent Bullet (continued)

Volume 2: The Poisoned Pen

Volume 3: The Dream Doctor

(With this volume, individual stories are split into two chapters.)

Volume 3: The Dream Doctor (cont.)

Volume 4: The War Terror

(With this volume, magazine stories are now split into three chapters.)

Volume 4: The War Terror (cont.)

Volume 5: The Social Gangster

Volume 7: The Ear in the Wall (cont.)

Volume 8: The Gold of the Gods

(Reeve's first true novel—i.e. not cobbled together from short stories.)

Volume 11: Guy Garrick

(A rewriting of the 2-part serial, *The Scientific Gunman, The Popular Magazine*, January 1 & 15, 1914. Craig Kennedy has been changed to Guy Garrick, and other characters change name, as well. The magazine version has 15 chapters, as opposed to 25 here. "The Sleep Maker," *Red Book Magazine*, May 1914, was incorporated into the text with character names changed.)

Volume 12: Constance Dunlap

Volume 12: Constance Dunlap (cont.)

C1: Newspapers - Fiction

Commonly, in Reeve's day, bestselling authors appeared in newspapers, typically with works reprinted from other media, but sometimes with originals. The majority of the works were syndicated and thus appeared in a wide variety of newspapers across North America. The below listings, taken from accessible sources, are far from complete, and indeed a comprehensive record of Reeve's newspaper appearances would be won at great price. However, this limited listing suggests how widespread Reeve's name and works were, and also the availability of secondary markets for a successful author. Dates listed refer to the specific newspaper cited; dates of the same items in other papers frequently vary. Where we had multiple examples, we used the most complete record as the exemplar for the series.

1912

The Adventures of Craig Kennedy, Scientific Detective
The Washington Post

(The order of these stories, with the first two switched from their published order in *Cosmopolitan*, and the title change from "The Case of Helen Bond" to "The Scientific Cracksman," suggests a reprint of Reeve's first book collection, *The Silent Bullet*, rather than the *Cosmopolitan* stories.)

September 8   **The Mystery of the Silent Bullet**
("The Silent Bullet," *Cosmopolitan*, January 1911)

September 15   **The Scientific Cracksman**
("The Case of Helen Bond," *Cosmopolitan*, December 1910)

September 22   **The Bacteriological Criminal**
("The Bacteriological Detective," *Cosmopolitan*, February 1911)

September 29   **The Mystery of the Deadly Tube**
("The Deadly Tube," *Cosmopolitan*, March 1911)

October 6   **The Record of the Seismograph**
("The Seismograph Adventure," *Cosmopolitan*, April 1911)

October 13   **The Crime of the Diamond Maker**
("The Diamond Maker," *Cosmopolitan*, May 1911)

October 20   **The Woorali Double Poison Mystery**
("The Azure Ring," *Cosmopolitan*, June 1911)

October 27   **The Mystery of "Spontaneous Combustion"**
("Spontaneous Combustion," *Cosmopolitan*, July 1911)

November 3   **The Gyroscope Aeroplane Adventure**
("The Terror in the Air," *Cosmopolitan*, August 1911)

November 10   **The Black Hand Kidnappers and a Dictograph**
("The Black Hand," *Cosmopolitan*, September 1911)

November 17   **The Mescal Bean Mystery**
("The Artificial Paradise," *Cosmopolitan*, September 1911)

November 24   **The Problem of the Steel Door**
("The Steel Door," *Cosmopolitan*, November 1911)

1912 (continued)
The Adventures of Craig Kennedy
The Sandusky Register

October 8   **The Bacteriological Detective**
(Since this paper retains Reeve's original title, it's likely that *The Washington Post* reprints were retitled by the newspaper.)

1913

The Adventures of Clare Kendall: Woman Detective
The Washington Post

May 11   **A Skirmish With the Occult**
(First of the series.)
June 8   **The Pearl Doctor**
July 13   **The House of Cards**
August 24   **The Temple of Beauty**
November 9   **The Mystery of the Stolen da Vinci**
(All stories in the Semi-Monthly Magazine Section. Advertized as "the first great woman detective of fiction." Illustrated by Arthur Litle [May, June, July], W.L. Jacobs [August], and Robert A. Graef [November]. Listings in the *Chicago Daily Tribune* confirm all titles and dates. Note that Clare Kendall resurfaced as a character in the February 1914 *Adventure* novelette, The Abduction Club," and the September 1914 *Pearson's Magazine* as part of a "new series" which apparently didn't continue. The next known appearance of Clare came in the Jan/Feb 1935 issue of *Complete Detective Novel Magazine.*)

1913-14

The New Adventures of Craig Kennedy, Scientific Detective
The Washington Post

(These stories, and the order they're reprinted in, follow the composition of Reeve's second book collection, *The Poisoned Pen*.)
August 3   **Solving the Mystery of the Poisoned Pen**
("The Poisoned Pen," *Cosmopolitan*, May 1912)
August 10   **The Case of the Murdered Maid**
("The Yeggman," *Cosmopolitan*, April 1912)
August 17   **The Germ of Death**
("The Bacillus of Death," *Cosmopolitan*, January 1912)
August 24   **Mystery of the Firebug**
("The Firebug," *Cosmopolitan*, March 1912)
August 31   **The Confidence King**
("The Master Counterfeiter," *Cosmopolitan*, February 1912)
September 7   **The Sand-hog**
(*Cosmopolitan*, December 1911)
September 14   **The Clairvoyant**
("The White Slave," *Cosmopolitan*, June 1912)

1913-14 (cont.)
The New Adventures of Craig Kennedy, Scientific Detective (cont.)

September 21	**The Forger**	

(*Cosmopolitan*, July 1912)

September 28   **The Unofficial Spy**
    (*Cosmopolitan*, August 1912)
October 5   **The Smuggler**
    (*Cosmopolitan*, September 1912)
October 12   **The Invisible Ray**
    (*Cosmopolitan*, October 1912)
February 8   **The Case of the Campaign Grafter**
    ("The Campaign Grafter," *Hearst's Magazine*, October 1912)

The New Adventures of Craig Kennedy
The Evening Bulletin (Philadelphia)
December 13   **The Invisible Ray**

1914-15

The Exploits of Elaine
The New York American
December 27   1. **The Clutching Hand**
January 3   2. **The Twilight Sleep**
January 10   3. **The Vanishing Jewels**
January 17   4. **The Frozen Safe**
January 24   5. **The Poisoned Room**
January 31   6. **"The Vampire"**
February 7   7. **The Double Trap**
February 14   8. **The Hidden Voice**
February 21   9. **The Death Ray**
February 28   10. **The Life Current**
March 7   11. **The Hour of Three**
March 14   12. **The Blood Crystals**
March 21   13. **The Devil Worshippers**
March 28   14. **The Reckoning**
April 4   15. **The Serpent Sign**
April 11   16. **The Cryptic Ring**
April 18   17. **The Watching Eye**
April 25   18. **The Vengeance of Wu Fang**
May 2   19. **The Saving Circles**
May 9   20. **Spontaneous Combustion**
May 16   21. **The Ear in the Wall**
May 23   22. **The Opium Smugglers**
May 30   23. **The Tell-Tale Heart**
June 6   24. **Shadows of War**
June 13   25. **The Lost Torpedo**

1914-15 (cont.)

The Romance of Elaine

June 20	26.	**The Gray Friar**
June 27	27.	**The Vanishing Man**
July 4	28.	**The Submarine Harbor**
July 11	29.	**The Vanishing Man**
July 18	30.	**The Wireless Detective**
July 25	31.	**The Death Cloud**
August 1	32.	**The Searchlight Gun**
August 8	33.	**The Life Chain**
August 15	34.	**The Flash**
August 22	35.	**The Disappearing Helmets**

The Triumph of Elaine

August 29	36.	**The Final Chapter**

(Serialized in Hearst newpapers. Illustrated with photos from the films. Note that there are discrepancies between the chapter listings in the two *Elaine* volumes in the *Craig Kennedy Stories* and the listings here: 31 chapters in the *CKS* versus 36 here; the first 18 chapters are titled the same in both places; the five chapter titles for 19-23 account for the difference, although some, like "Spontaneous Combustion," appear elsewhere in the Reeve canon; chapter 24 resumes the parallel with the *CKS* with the exception that "The Vanishing Man" is used twice here, the second likely an erroneous replacement for "The Conspirators"; and the last chapter has been promoted to the title of the serial. :: *The Exploits of Elaine* started in one paper [*The Evening Telegram*, probably Elyria, Ohio] as late as March 9, 1917. Chapter 1 in the *Telegram* is prefaced with a rewritten version of the opening chapters of the first published CK story, "The Case of Helen Bond," the "Craig Kennedy's Theories" chapter in the collection, *The Silent Bullet*. The book version of *The Exploits of Elaine* doesn't include this preface.)

1915

The Novel Experiences of Guy Garrick, Detective

The Syracuse Herald

March 14	**The Cave of Aladdin**

The Boston Daily Globe

(Reprints all six Guy Garrick stories from *Red Book Magazine*, in different order.)

April 18	**The Clairvoyant Trust**
April 25	**The Cave of Aladdin**
May 2	**The Soldier of Fortune**
May 9	**The House of a Thousand Murders**
May 16	**Playing for High Stakes**
May 23	**The Sleep Maker**

1915 (cont.)

The Further Achievements of Craig Kennedy, Scientific Detective

The Boston Daily Globe

September 26   **The Dream Doctor**
  (*Cosmopolitan*, August 1913)
October 3   **The Sybarite**
  (*Cosmopolitan*, May 1913)
October 10   **The Phantom Curcuit**
  (*Cosmopolitan*, June 1913)
October 17   **The Green Curse**
  (*Cosmopolitan*, April 1913)
October 24   **The Elixir of Life**
  (*Cosmopolitan*, July 1913)
October 31   **The Opium Joint**
  (*Hearst's Magazine*, January 1913)
November 7   **The Vampire**
  (*Hearst's Magazine*, February 1913)
November 14   **The Submarine Mystery**
  (*Cosmopolitan*, October 1913)
November 21   **The Ghouls**
  (*Cosmopolitan*, December 1913)

1915-16

The Ear in the Wall

American Sunday Monthly Magazine

October 3   **Part 1**
November 7   **Part 2**
December 5   **Part 3**
January 2   **Part 4**
February 6   **Part 5**
March 5   **Part 6**
April 7   **Part 7**

(The *ASMM* was a supplement carried by the Hearst newspapers. Illustrated by Armand Both. Merged with the *Adventure* magazine story, "The Abduction Club" for book publication as *The Ear in the Wall*.)

1916-17

Craig Kennedy and the War Terror

The Boston Daily Globe

(These stories appear to come from Reeve's book collection, *The War Terror*, taking some chapter names for the stories rather than the *Cosmopolitan* titles.)

December 31   **The Murder Syndicate**
January 7   **The Air Pirate**
January 14   **The Radio Detective**

1916-17 (cont.)

Craig Kennedy and the War Terror (cont.)

January 21	**The Curio Shop**
January 28	**The Radium Robber**
February 11	**The Germ Letter**
February 18	**The Devil Worshipers**
February 25	**The Lie Detector**
March 4	**The Electrolytic Murder**
March 11	**The Eugenic Bride**
March 18	**The Billionaire Baby**

1917

The Adventuress

The Janesville Daily Gazette

(The May 19 issue advertized a new four-page fiction section to be included with the Sunday *Chicago Examiner*. The ad announced the serialization of *The Adventuress*, featuring Craig Kennedy, with the claim: "It was bought exclusively for this paper at the highest price ever paid this author for a novel.")

1918

The Hidden Hand

The Lincoln Sunday Star (Nebraska)

January 6	**Episode 1: The Gauntlet of Death, 2: Counterfeit Faces**
January 13	**Episode 3: The Island of Dread, 4: The False Locket**
January 20	**Episode 5: The Air Lock**
January 27	**Episode 6: The Flower of Death**
February 3	**Episode 7: The Fire Trap**
February 10	**Episode 8: The Slide for Life**
February 17	**Episode 9: Jets of Flame**
February 24	**Episode 10: Cog of Death**
March 3	**Episode 11: Trapped By Treachery**
March 10	**Episode 12: The Eyes in the Wall**
March 17	**Episode 13: The Jaws of the Tiger**
March 24	**Episode 14: The Unmasking**
March 31	**Episode 15: The Girl of the Prophecy**

(Chapter by chapter synopses of the 1917 film. These titles match up with the film titles. The titles of Episodes 1 & 2 are absent from this particulat newspaper and have been added from the film listing.)

Craig Kennedy Detective Stories

The Boston Daily Globe

(Stories match the title and order of the book collection, *The Treasure Train*.)

March 31	**The Treasure Train**
April 7	**The Truth Detector**

1918 (cont.)

Craig Kennedy Detective Stories (cont.)

April 14	**The Soul-Analysis**
April 21	**The Mystic Poisoner**
April 28	**The Phantom Destroyer**
May 5	**The Beauty Mask**
May 12	**The Love Meter**
May 19	**The Vital Principle**
May 26	**The Rubber Dagger**
June 2	**The Submarine Mine**
June 9	**The Gun Runner**
June 16	**The Sunken Treasure**

1921

The Mystery Mind

Trenton Evening Times
March -June (approx.)
(Serialized novelization of 1920 film, by Reeve and John W. Grey.)

The Black Menace

The Ogden Standard-Examiner (Utah)

September 25	**I: The Black Menace**
	II: The Green Death
	III: The Double Cross
October 2	**III (cont.)**
	IV *unknown*
	V: The Mansion of Mystery
October 9	**V (cont.)**
	VI: The Deadly Bacilli/The Germ Letter
	VII: The Armored Man
	VIII: The Tear Bullet
	IX: The Chorus Man
October 16	**IX (cont.)**
	X: The Kidnapping
	XI: The Forged Note
	XII: The Star Shell
October 23	**XII (cont.)**
	XIII: The Infernal Machine
	XIV: The Pool of Flame
	XV: The False Clue
October 30	**XVI: The Raid**
	XVII: The Gray Cruiser
	XVIII: The Smoke Screen
	XIX: The Nerve Doctor
	XX: The Gorgon

1921 (cont.)
The Black Menace (cont.)

("A Craig Kennedy Story." This short novel ran every Sunday on two-page spreads, illustrated by J.A May. The chapter titles were drawn from several sources, thus the duplicate title for Chapter VI.)

1922
Craig Kennedy stories
The News-Sentinel (Fort Wayne)

February 26	**The Silent Bullet**
April 16	**The Diamond Maker**
May 14	**The Black Hand**
November 18	**The Billionaire Baby**
November 25	**The Family Skeleton**
December 23	**The Love Meter**

(In the Sunday Magazine Section. All reprints from *Cosmopolitan*.)

Mysterious Messages
Chicago Herald and Examiner

(Serialized in 30 daily installments starting May 21 in the American Pictorial section of the *New York American*. Identical ads for the first installment starting two days hence, seen in the Saturday, April 15, 1922 issues of *The Olean Evening Times* and the *Syracuse Herald*, describe the story as Reeve's "Greatest New Love Serial Story." The story was part-contest, with daily prizes of $5 awarded to everyone who decoded the message included with each installment. A sample coded message was included in the ad:

THGINOTDEREDRUMEBLLIWEHS

The final installment was to feature the best 500-word reader-submitted solution to the story, with prizes of $2500, $1500, and $1000 paid to the top three finishers.)

On Wings of Wireless
The Decatur Review (Illinois)

June 5	**Chapter I: The Radio Dance**
June 6	**Chapter II: The Sea Vamp**
June 7	**Chapter III: The Mystery Craft**
June 8	**Chapter IV: The Inner Circle**
June 9	**Chapter V: Music in the Air**
June 10	**Chapter VI: The Wireless Dictagraph**
June 12	**Chapter VII: Interference**
June 13	**Chapter VIII: Alternating Affections**
June 14	**Chapter IX: The Direction Finder**
June 15	**Chapter X: Broadcasting**
June 16	**Chapter XI: The Noises of Space**
June 17	**Chapter XII: I'll Tell the World!**

1922 (cont.)
On Wings of Wireless (cont.)

(Features Guy Garrick. Described in ads as "A gripping radio mystery story. . . . The plot hinges on the wireless telephone—a sinister agency for evil and the means by which a baffling mystery is solved. Radio, Reeve, mystery, suspense, originality and punch." "A mystery story as marvelous as radio itself. It is the story of super-criminals who seize upon the radio as a tool in their colossal crimes." Amusingly, though the serial was widely syndicated, many local papers advertized the story as having been written exclusively for them.)

1922-23

Romance-Mystery Novelettes of Craig Kennedy
Chester Times (Pennsylvania)

December 4-9	1.	*The Wireless Phantom*
December 11-16	2.	**The Coroner's Cocktail**
December 18-23	3.	**Blood Will Tell**
December 25-30	4.	**The Poison Kiss**
January 1-6	5.	**The Beauty Parlor**
January 8-13	6.	**Dealers in Dreams**
January 15-20	7.	*The Brass Key*
January 22-27	8.	**The Love Cult**
Jan 29 - Feb 3	9.	*Buried Alive*
February 5-10	10.	**The Mystery of the Museum**
February 12-17	11.	*The Soul Merchant*
February 19-24	12.	*The Boulevard of Bunk*
Feb 26 - Mar 3	13.	**The Phantom Finger**
March 5-10	14.	**The Divorce Mill**
March 12-17	15.	*Buccaneers of Booze*
March 19-24	16.	**The Dope Devil**
March 26-31	17.	**Heart Balm**
April 2-7	18.	**The Love Addict**
April 9-14	19.	**The Paper Pushers**
April 16-21	20.	**The "New" Crime**

(A selection of these stories was collected in *Craig Kennedy Listens In*—indcated by **italics** above. Our *Chester Times* listing was the most complete we found of this syndicated series, but was missing any installments from novelette no. 1. It's assumed to be "The Wireless Phantom" since that is the only unaccounted for story in *Craig Kennedy Listens In*. The novelettes were divided into nine chapters through the first half of the series, then dropped to eight. Each novelette was left unfinished with the *Chester Times* awarding $50 to the closest reader solution. Readers had a week to submit entries; Reeve's ending was published several weeks later.)

1925

Atavar

The Hartford Courant
> (Serialization of Reeve's 1924 novel.)

July 27	**Chapter 1: Desire/Prologue**
July 28	unknown
July 29	**The Gilded Lily**
July 30	**Chapter VII: Facts**
July 31	**Chapter IX: Clues**
August 1	**A Treasure Ship**
August 3	**A Nocturnal Visitor**
August 4	**Chapter XV: Astarte Closes**
August 5	**Chapter XVII: Mystery**
August 6	**Chapter XIX: Pursuit**
August 7	unknown
August 8	unknown

Craig Kennedy and the Fourteen Points

The Los Angeles Times
> (Serialization of Reeve's *Flynn's* stories which were collected in book form as *The Fourteen Points*.)

August 9	**North**
August 16	**South**
August 23	**East**
August 30	**West**
September 6	**Air**
September 13	**Water**
September 20	**Earth**
September 27	**Fire**
October 4	**Smell**
October 11	**Sight**
October 18	**Taste**
October 25	**Touch**
November 1	**Hearing**
November 8	**The Sixth Sense**

1926

The Radio Detective

The Charleston Gazette

September 26	Conclusion

> (Serialized in conjunction with the local showing of the movie.)

1929

Tarzan the Mighty

(Serialized novelization of a Universal film serial.)

The Havre Daily News (Montana)

February 12	**Chapter X: The Imposter, XI: The Stolen Heritage**

Morning News (Florence, South Carolina)

March 1	**Chapter III: Black John Plots**
March 10	**Chapter X: The Imposter, XI: The Stolen Heritage**

1931-32

Craig Kennedy and the Gangsters

Modesto News-Herald

(The first eleven stories were numbered. All stories had the overriding title *Craig Kennedy and the Gangsters*, except for "Gypping the Gypper" and "The Warning." All stories were illustrated. Stookie Allen illustrated "Sex Racket," "Gypper," and "Warning." Artist signatures were illegible on the rest.)

July 4	1.	**The Murder Contract**
July 11	2.	**Checked Off!**
July 18	3.	**The Royal Racket**
July 25	4.	**The Arsenal**
August 1	5.	**Muscling In**
August 8	6.	**The Fixer**
August 15	7.	**Racket Law**
August 22	8.	**Double Zero**
August 29	9.	**Marked Money** (Misnumbered "eighth.")
September 5	10.	**The Gun Broker**
September 12	11.	**The Sex Racket**
September 19	*nn.*	**A Hundred Grand**
September 26	*nn.*	**The Pay-Off**
October 3	*nn.*	**Gypping the Gypper**
October 10	*nn.*	**Money Racket**
October 17	*nn.*	**The Warning**

The Syracuse Herald, April 15, 1922

C2: Newspapers - Nonfiction

All items here are bylined by Reeve, unless otherwise indicated. The majority are syndicated, and would have appeared potentially in many cities, so the cited newspaper is significant primarily to establish the date of the piece. It also hints at Reeve's reach, which is certainly understated by this listing. :: Reeve told Mort Weisinger ("Pseudonym Sidelights," *The Author & Journalist*, August 1935) that he wrote many newspaper articles under the initials T.D.M., meaning Too Damn Much. We'll assume, at least, that he wrote many articles pseudonymously, even if "T.D.M." was a gag—an easy assumption since none of the pseudonymous pieces have been identified. :: Reeve's crime reporting is certainly underrepresented here. In a 1932 interview, he described his experience as a special writer for New York and Philadelphia dailies: "In the last 15 years I have been assigned to all of the important cases. The Hall-Mills case right here in New Jersey was one of them. There was the Starr Faithfull case, too. The Benjamin Collings murder took place right in front of my home at Setauket, L.I. . . ."

1900

The Sun

May 6   title unknown

(Probably a letter, identified by a reader-reply in the May 20 edition, which refers to Reeve's comments defending "the time-honored Calvinistic doctrine of predestination." See also Reeve's article for the theological journal, *Bibliotheca Sacra*.)

1905

The Atlanta Constitution

June 25   **First Saint of United States Soon To Be Canonized at Rome**

1906

The Washington Post

January 14   title unknown

(Reprint of "How Can Football Be Saved? Walter Camp Discusses Question," *Public Opinion*.)

1907

The Hartford Courant

June 17   **The Horse Cars of New York**

(Probably a reprint of "Seeing New York in a Horse-Car," *Outlook Magazine*, June 15, 1907.)

1908

The Washington Times Magazine
September 27   **Hands Up!**
("Man Who First Said Hands Up," *Railroad Man's Magazine*, October 1908)

1910

The New York Times
July 3   **Sunday Ice: Is Law Forbidding It Being**
Too Rigorously Enforced?
(Letter from Reeve protests law banning the selling of ice on Sunday as discriminatory to the poor.)

1912

unknown
October
(Reeve covered the first trial of Lt. Charles Becker, a police officer accused of murder.)

The Hartford Courant
November 30   **The Toxin of Christmas: Little Shop Girl's Struggle**
With Late Christmas Buyers

1916

The Washington Post
April 2   **New Kind of Insanity in the Peck Tragedy**
(Reeve's credentials listed as "Famous Criminologist and Writer of Scientific Detective Stories.")

1919

Trenton Evening Times
December 4   **"Craig Kennedy" Reconstructs Billy Dansey Kidnaping Case**
(Second article in series.)
December 5   **"Kennedy" Scouts Accident Theory**
December 6   **Keep Up Search, "Kennedy's" Plea**
(Reeve analyzed evidence in case of missing Hammonton, New Jersey boy, who was either kidnapped or murdered. A followup story in the *Times*, not written by Reeve, reported on Reeve's receipt of a letter purporting to clear up the mystery: "Reeve Gets Tip Billy Dansey is Alive on Coast," December 20.)

1922

San Antonio Evening News
> February 8   **Most Dangerous Game Is Woman: Craig Kennedy's
>   Mentor Discusses Case**

The Washington Post
> February 9   **Trails in Taylor Mystery**
> (Reeve wrote a series of syndicated articles on the famous murder case of Paramount film director, William Desmond Taylor, who was shot to death on February 1, 1922. Reeve did no original reporting, but merely provided commentary and speculation on published information.)

Sunday State Journal (Lincoln, Nebraska)
> April 9   **What Happened During This Policeman's 50 Years**
> (Developments in crime detection from the point of view of a 50-year veteran of the NYPD.)

San Antonio Evening News
> September 20   **Keen Intellect Needed To Solve Two Killings
>   Says Detective Writer**
> September 22   **Underworld Blackmail Theory Is Presented in Double
>   Killing Case**
> (The "Hall-Mills" case in Brunswick, New Jersey, which concerned the mysterious murders of a minister and a female choir leader.)

1924

Austin Statesman
> October 26   **Women Are More Honest Than Men But—**
> (Full-page interview with Reeve; author not listed. Subtitled: "When They Commit a Crime It Is a Capital One. They Are More Expert Evaders of the Truth. When Their Emotions Get the Upper Hand They Break All Traces. They Seldom Make a Comeback to Honesty. They can Fool a District Attorney Easier Than a Man Can." Illustrated with a photo of Reeve and a line drawing.)

1925

The Oakland Tribune
> August 2   **Those Girls of Today!**
> (Reeve is one of three writers who contributed articles on the morality of modern women. The other two were Will Irwin and Ida M. Tarbell.)

Chicago Daily Tribune
> October 3   **Confessions**
> (Letter from Reeve responding to the question of what book he would have liked to have written other than his own.)

1926

(This pair is the same piece, bylined by Gene Cohn in the *Daily Independent*. It's a brief interview wherein Reeve expounds on "mystery." Illustrated with a portrait of Reeve.)

Iowa City Press-Citizen

    January 20   **Craig Kennedy Says Mystery Stories Best**

The Helena Daily Independent

    March 4   **We're All Detectives Under the Skin, Says Craig Kennedy**

1928-29

Masterpieces of Mystery

The Atlanta Constitution

        (Reeve is listed as editor of this short-story series, and provides introductory comments.)

June 10	1. **The Murders in the Rue Morgue** - Edgar Allan Poe
June 17	2. *unknown*
June 24	3. **The Sign of the Four** - Arthur Conan Doyle
July 1	4. **Outcasts of Paris** - Eugene Francois Vidoco
July 8	5. **Zadig** - Voltaire
July 15	6. **The Adventure of the Hansom Cab** - R.L. Stevenson
July 22	7. **Inspector Bucket** - Charles Dickens
July 29	8. **Sergeant Cuff** - Wilkie Collins
Aug 5	9. **The Stories of Three Burglars** - Frank R. Stockton
Aug 12	10. **The Horla** - Guy de Maupassant
Aug 19	11. **The Biter Bit** - Wilkie Collins
Aug 26	12. **The Doomdorf Mystery** - Melville Davisson Post
Sept 2	13. **A Scandal in Bohemia** - Arthur Conan Doyle
Sept 9	14. **The Purloined Letter** - Edgar Allan Poe
Sept 16	15. **The Safety Match** - Anton Chekhov
Sept 23	16. **Some Scotland Yard Cases** - Robert Anderson
Sept 30	17. **Gentlemen and Players** - E.W. Hornung
Oct 7	18. **The Riddle of the Rope of Fear** - M.E. & T.W. Hanshew
Oct 14	19. **The Sign of the Shadow** - Maurice LeBlanc
Oct 21	20. **The Murder at the Jex Farm** - Oswald Crawford
Oct 28	21. **The Border** - Henry C. Rowland
Nov 4	22. **The Man Who Was Lost** - Jacques Futrelle
Nov 11	23. **The Mystery of the Steel Disk** - Broughton Brandenburg
Nov 18	24. **The Mystery of Seven Minutes** - Louis Joseph Vance
Nov 25	25. **The Lost Room** - Fitz-James O'Brien
Dec 2	26. **The Woman in the Case** - Arthur Train
Dec 9	27. **The Yellow Cat** - Wilbur Daniel Steele
Dec 16	28. **The Oblong Box** - Edgar Allan Poe
Dec 23	29. **A Suspicious Character** - William Hamilton Osborne
Dec 30	30. **The Mystery of the Steel Room** - Thomas W. Hanshew
Jan 6	31. **The Great K. & A. Train Robbery** - Paul Leicester Ford

1928-29 (continued)

Masterpieces of Mystery (cont.)

Jan 13	32.	**The Mystery at 89th St., New York** - George S. McWatters
Jan 20	33.	**The Adventure of the Toadstools** - Sax Rohmer
Jan 27	34.	**The Fenchurch Street Mystery** - Baroness Orczy
Feb 3	35.	**The Case of Mrs. Magnus** - Burton E. Stevenson
Feb 10	36.	**Cowardice Court** - George B. McCutcheon
Feb 17	37.	**Cheap** - Marjorie L.C. Pickathall
Feb 24	38.	**The Great Valdez Sapphire** - anonymous
March 3	39.	**The Episode of the Black Casquette** - Joseph Ernest
March 10	40.	**The Listener** - Algernon Blackwood
March 17	41.	**The Mysterious Card** - Cleveland Moffett
March 24	42.	**A Study in Scarlet** - Arthur Conan Doyle
March 31	44.	**The Lost Duchess** - anonymous
April 7	45.	**The Pipe** - anonymous
April 14	46.	**The Hand on the Latch** - Mary Cholmondeley
	47.	*unknown*
April 21	48.	**The Beast With Five Fingers** - William F Harvey
April 28	49.	**The Mystery of Marie Roget** - Edgar Allan Poe
April 5	50.	**The Risen Dead** - Max Pemberton

The New York Times

September 25   **Challenges "Who's Who" Republican Poll**

(A letter to the editor. Reeve challenges the accuracy of the poll of voters in *Who's Who in America*.)

1931

Hamilton Daily News

January 24   **Who Will Shake the Gangster Grip?**

The Oakland Tribune

February 1   **Who Will Break Gangster's Grip?**

(Full-page illustrated article "as told to Carol Bird." Subtitled: "Noted Writer of Fiction Crime Stories Deplores the Setting Up of a New World Dynasty Ruled By the Racketeer.")

The New York Herald-Tribune Sunday Magazine

March 22   **What Price Crime?**

(Reprinted in a Crime Crusade Foundation brochure. Report that racketeering costs the country $3-5 billion a year.)

The Oakland Tribune

March 29   **18 Billion a Year for Crime**

(Reeve describes a police lineup in this piece on the cost of crime.)

1931 (cont.)

The Hartford Courant

September 17   **Crime Analyst Scouts Pirate Theory In Collings Mystery**

September 18   **Collings Family Life May Hold Solution, Reeve Says**

September 19   **Collings Murder Indicates Premeditation, Reeve Says**

The Atlanta Constitution

September 20   **Crime Expert Says Story of Mrs. Collings Strange**

(Benjamin Collings was murdered on his yacht, and his body washed ashore near Reeve's Long Island residence. An editorial in the September 19 *Courant* commented on Reeve's theories.)

1934

The Los Angeles Times

December 16   **Reeve Sees Crime Foes**

(Syndicated article on the new Department of Justice headquarters in D.C. Includes an interview with Bureau of Investigation director, J. Edgar Hoover.)

New York Evening Post

unknown   **The New Deal Against Crime**

(Described as "your new series" in a December 12, 1934 letter to Reeve by Critchell Rimington, Vice President of publisher John Day Company.)

1935

January-February

(As correspondent for a Philadelphia newspaper, Reeve traveled to Flemington, New Jersey, every day to cover the trial of Bruno Hauptmann for the kidnapping of the Lindbergh baby.)

C3: Newspapers - Comic Strips

This listing documents the two Reeve-authored comic strip series. Both feature Craig Kennedy, with occasional mentions of reporter-sidekick, Walter Jameson. All listings are from the *Syracuse Herald*, though the 1926 strip, at least, ran in a variety of papers.

1926

(This strip ran Monday through Saturday on the comic strip page, alongside *Moon Mullins*, *The Bungle Family*, *Mutt and Jeff*, and others. Total: 156 strips. Sundays are indicated by a gap in the listing. Each strip carried the title of the arc, e.g. "Craig Kennedy in The Studio Mystery." The McNaught Syndicate, Inc., NY, is indicated in the strips. The artist was H.J. Flemming, who later surfaced as DC comics artist, Homer Fleming, from 1936-45.)

The Studio Mystery

June 7	Artist and Model
June 8	Two Peaches!
June 9	The Broken Lens!
June 10	The Bird Has Flown!
June 11	Alma's Dilemma
June 12	Jealousy
June 14	Cold-Blooded Business
June 15	Passing the Buck
June 16	A Jump Ahead of the Police
June 17	The Good Samaritan
June 18	The Shock
June 19	A Woman Scorned

The Green Curse

June 21	*no title*
June 22	Priceless Loot
June 23	A Shadow of the Nether World
June 24	A Weird Experience
June 25	Spirited Away!
June 26	A Quick Getaway!
June 28	The Up-to-Date Ghost
June 29	A Note of Mystery
June 30	Deep Stuff
July 1	Setting the Trap
July 2	A New Angle
July 3	The Optophone
July 5	*unknown*
July 6	The Police Bomb
July 7	Like Rats in a Trap!
July 8	Gassed!

The Green Curse (continued)

July 9	Overcome
July 10	Who's Guilty?
July 12	Shackled!

The White Hand

July 13	*unknown*
July 14	A New Detective Stunt
July 15	In the Haunt of Crime
July 16	Setting the Trap
July 17	Tricky Work
July 19	A New Threat!
July 20	At Headquarters
July 21	Listening In
July 22	Midnight
July 23	The Bargain
July 24	Hands Up!
July 26	Daddy!

The Beauty Shop

July 27	The Sybarite
July 28	Poor Little Dead Butterfly
July 29	The Shadow of Tragedy
July 30	"It's a Corpse Light!"
July 31	New Clews
August 2	Scandal
August 3	The Rayograph
August 4	The Shock
August 5	The Heart Station
August 6	The Tell-Tale Heart
August 7	Confession!

Dead Men Tell Tales

August 9	Amnesia!
August 10	The Hypnotic Third Degree
August 11	A Voice in the Dark
August 12	"You Shall Not Pass"
August 13	The Interrupted Elopement
August 14	The Wagstaff Millions
August 16	The Poor Little Rich Girl
August 17	Wheels Within Wheels
August 18	Smoking Them Out
August 19	Wandering Minds
August 20	Eavesdropping
August 21	Is There a New Will?
August 23	Bound and Gagged

Dead Men Tell Tales (cont.)

August 24	Suspicion
August 25	A House of Hypnotism
August 26	Sealed Lips!
August 27	The Dead Returns!
August 28	All's Wells!

The Mystery of the Gray Flapper

August 30	*no title*
August 31	Lost—An Heiress
September 1	Gone Away
September 2	Not a Trace!
September 3	The Gray Flapper
September 4	The First Clew!
September 6	*unknown*
September 7	The Plot Thickens
September 8	Under the Spell
September 9	Complications
September 10	The Last Step!
September 11	The Beauty Slayer

The Dream Murder

September 13	Automatic Murder
September 14	Deserted Mates
September 15	A Beautiful Enigma
September 16	Bohemia!
September 17	She-Deviltry
September 18	Another Gun!
September 20	Another Angle
September 21	More or Less Incriminating
September 22	Rough Stuff
September 23	Whose Gun?
September 24	Just One More Step!
September 25	Cornered!
September 27	Hoarded Gold!
September 28	The Ghost Walks
September 29	The Subterranean Clew
September 30	Watched!
October 1	A Quarrel
October 2	Spying
October 4	A Stranger
October 5	Another Victim
October 6	A Nice Job!
October 7	The Truth Drug
October 8	Dora Talks at Last!
October 9	Dust!

The Second-Hand Girl

October 11	Counterfeiters
October 12	Drowned in the Air!
October 13	The Suicide Note
October 14	The Iron Door!
October 15	Degeneration
October 16	*unknown*
October 18	Caught!
October 19	In a Hole
October 20	Facing Fate!
October 21	No Escape!
October 22	Death Relaxes Its Grip!
October 23	Conviction

The Hi-Jackers

October 25	The Mysterious Leak
October 26	Bad Business
October 27	Vanishing Hooch!
October 28	"Revenooers!"
October 29	Doublecrossed!
October 30	Battling Bootleggers
November 1	The Wrong Boat!
November 2	Lost—A Rum Runner
November 3	Passing the Buck
November 4	Getting the Goods
November 5	Buccaneers of Booze
November 6	The Squealers

The "Perfect Crime"

November 8	Foul Play!
November 9	The Other Husband
November 10	Jealousy
November 11	The Hang-Over
November 12	The Alibi Breaks Down
November 13	Calling a Bluff
November 15	He Who Hesitates—
November 16	Taking a Chance
November 17	Pay—and Shadow!
November 18	Paid—In Full?
November 19	Ready for the Crash!
November 20	Held for Murder!

Kidnaped!

November 22	The Alarm
November 23	The Hunch
November 24	Padlocked Lips!
November 25	*no strip*

Kidnaped! (cont.)

November 26	Loose Talk
November 27	Second Sight
November 29	Frightfulness?
November 30	The Threat!
December 1	Monkey Business
December 2	The Monkey Gets the Goods!
December 3	They're Off!
December 4	Who Carried Off Ruth?
December 6	Partners in Crime

1929

(This series ran a puzzle-mystery in six daily strips from Monday through Saturday. Each strip bore the title of the story arc. The four arcs are believed to be the complete listing. Each strip had four panels with a descriptive paragraph below each. Accompanying each Saturday's strip was a sidebar by Reeve describing his conclusion to the mystery. The artist was Will B. Johnstone, cartoonist, painter, musical comedy playwright [with his brothers], and future Marx Brothers scenarist. Ads indicated the strip was written exclusively for the *Syracuse Herald*, although such claims often prove exaggerated. The strips ran on the front page of the *Herald*, with the exception that the concluding strip of the last three arcs ran on a feature page inside. Copyright by the Craig Kennedy Service Corp.)

April 15-20	**The Rothstone Murder**
	(Based on the officially unsolved murder of notorious New York gambler and mob kingpin, Arnold Rothstein, on November 4, 1928.)
April 22-27	**The Belwell Murder**
April 29 - May 4	**The Murder of Love Nest Inn**
May 6-11	**The Ballroom Murder**

July 15, 1926

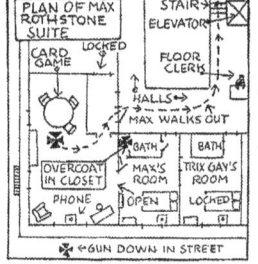

April 15, 1929

D: Stage

It would be nice to report that Craig Kennedy, "the American Sherlock Holmes," made the same successful transition to the stage as his British counterpart. It was tried. In June 1911, actor James K. Hackett announced his intention to appear in a play based on Reeve's *Cosmopolitan* stories. In September 1913 and February 1914, the upcoming play received mention in stage news columns. In March 1915, it finally got underway. A brief article in the *Times* (April 29, 1915) named the play and its players. Title: *The Man in Request*. Producer: James K. Hackett. Director, writer: Brandon Tynan. Cast: Norman Trevor (Craig Kennedy), Katherine La Salle, Walter Thomas and William Eville. By the time it opened in New England at the end of May, it had been rechristened *The Bannock Mystery*. It received a poor review in Hartford (see next page), and closed down after playing Detroit at the end of June. Hackett intended to restart it and eventually bring it to New York City, but that never happened. :: In the Drama section of the Sunday *New York Times*, July 18, 1926, an extensive cataloging of upcoming works for the stage included this listing: "A play based on the Craig Kennedy stories of Arthur B. Reeve, by De Witt Newing, with Frank Wilcox, Mr. Newing's business partner, starred." There's no evidence this latter venture ever got off the ground.

The Hartford Courant, May 25, 1915

BANNOCK MYSTERY IS VERY CRUDE

Hackett Production Needs Renovation

ACTORS DID ABOUT ALL THEY COULD

Rather Sad Exhibition At Parsons Theater

"My heart is rent in twain," cried the heroine of "The Bannock Mystery," somewhere near the end of the fourth act in the first performance of that play at the Parsons Theater last evening. The line rang true, for, after what she had gone through, it would have been a stout heart, indeed, that stood the strain by the time 11:45 o'clock arrived. Whatever "The Bannock Mystery" may become after it has been cut to pieces and remade and the characters learn their lines, at least as well as the prompter, whose voice became last evening almost part of the performance, no one can say. But in the form that it was given last evening we are strongly inclined to believe that few critics would deny it, the proud position of being classed among the three or four worst plays ever presented.

It would be a hopeless and a thankless task to try to unravel on paper the plot that made up the story of crime and its detection at the hands of the "scientific" detective, Craig Kennedy, as cast into dramatic form by Brandon Tynan from the story of Arthur B. Reeves [sic]. It is doubtful if many in the rather small audience managed to decide what it was all about.

The last cast was made up of actors and actresses of varying degrees of capability and otherwise, but the failure of one to get his cue and another to say correctly his lines worked tremondous havoc in the first act and the three other acts suffered from the same cause. But, even in melodrama, "the play's the thing" and what must be done to "The Bannock Mystery" to make it worth while is probably the greatest mystery in the whole business. All the pseudo-scientific tricks with which the detective of the stories confounds the criminals were employed, but on the stage they appeared far more "pseudo" than on the printed page. What will happen to the play between last night and tonight, when it will be seen again, we cannot say, but almost any changes will be to its improving.

The leeading players were Norman Trevor, Joseph Brennan, Walter Thomas, George Mack, Katherine Lasalle and Grace Reals. They did what they could. James K. Hackett, who was present, produced the play. So capable an actor as Mr. Hackett has long been acknowledged to, he may be able to make a good play out of "The Bannock Mystery." He has a man's job ahead of him.

E: Radio

Given Reeve's propensity for branching out into different media, one would expect him to have better penetrated the world of radio. His ownership of a famous character, his catalog of short works, and radio's need for dramatic content would seem to have made the perfect synthesis. However, we're not aware that *Craig Kennedy* ever spoke over the airwaves. Reeve's main contribution to radio was *Crime Prevention Program*, which Reeve co-wrote (with NBC continuity man, Finis Farr) and hosted, addressed to the rampant crime brought on by Prohibition. The 30-minute show presented a short drama featuring detective Thurlow Wade, and an expert guest who spoke on crime prevention (see next page). The nationally-broadcast show ran on NBC's WJZ network on Monday evenings at 8:30 EDT from July 14, 1930 into October. Then it jumped to the WEAF network, another NBC affiliate, running at 10:00 Friday evenings. In March 1931 the show went off the air. Other miscellaneous Reeve radio appearances are as follows:

Mystery readings
(The details, all from daily radio listings, are sparse.)

> 1925 WOR-Newark
>> October 17, 8:00 - 8:15 p.m.   **Mystery's Own Story**
>> November 14, 9:30 - 9:45 p.m.   **Mystery**
>> December 18, 2:45 - 3:00 p.m.   story

Heywood Broun show guest appearances

> 1932 WEAF
>> November 12, 6:45 - 7:00 p.m.   speaker
>> November 19, 7:00 - 7:15 p.m.   speaker
>> November 26, 6:45 - 7:00 p.m.   speaker
>> December 3, 7:00 - 7:15 p.m.   speaker
>>> (These listings, four consecutive Saturdays, indicate that Reeve was guest on the famous newspaperman's show.)

• • •

We know of one instance where a Craig Kennedy story was adapted for radio, thanks to the research of Victor A. Berch, Karl Schadow and Steve Lewis (see Bibliography):

Murder Clinic
(This series on WOR, from June 21, 1942 to October 27, 1943, presented 30-minute dramatizations of vintage detective stories.)

> 1943 August 22   **The Absolute Zero**
>> (*Cosmopolitan*, June 1915. Most shows appear to be lost, and there is currently no known recording of "The Absolute Zero.")

Guest Speakers on *Crime Prevention Program*

In March 1931, Reeve attempted to launch a national organization called the Crime Crusade Foundation, which built on his efforts with *Crime Prevention Program*. The Foundation's letter stationary printed the below list of the guest speakers from the 1930-31 radio show down the left side. Specific dates, where known, have been added.

Edward P. Mulrooney	Police Commissioner of NYC (July 14)
John O'Brien	Chief Inspector, Police Dept., NYC
John J. Sullivan	Assistant-Chief Inspector, Police Dept., NYC
John J. Hennessey	Deputy-Chief Inspector, Police Dept., NYC
Capt. John H. Ayers	Charge of Missing Persons Bureau, Police Dept. NYC
Inspector Louis Costuma	Bureau of Crime Prevention, Police Dept., NYC
Dr. Sylvester R. Leahy	Psychiatrist
Grover A. Whalen	Former Police Commissioner of NYC
Lady Margaret Armstrong	Head of Catholic Big Sisters (September 22)
Mrs. Sidney Borg	Head of the Jewish Big Sisters
George MacDonald	President of Big Brothers and Big Sisters Federation
Philip Leboutillier	President, Retail Drygoods Association
Barron Collier	Treasurer, Boy Scouts Foundation of Greater NY
Judge William E. McGeehan	Supreme Court, NY State
Prof. Raymond Moley	Columbia University
Howard W. Ameli	US Attorney, Eastern District, Brooklyn
Matthew Woll	Vice Pres. American Federation of Labor
Silas M. Newton	Oil and Gas Operator, NY and Dallas (March 20)
Miss Jane Hoey	Ass't Director Welfare Council, City of New York
B.J. McGinn	Vice Pres. American Surety Company
Thomas C.T. Crain	District Atty., County of New York, NYC
Judge Daniel F. Cohalen	Supreme Court, State of NY
William Edwin Hall	President Boys Club Federation of America
James E. West	Chief Scout Executive Boy Scouts of America
George F. Worthington	Counsel Committee of Fourteen
Sam A. Lewisohn	Chairman, Prison Investigation Committee
W.R. George	Founder George Junior Republics
Dr. J. Campbell White	Natl. Commission for Crime Prevention through Moral And Religious Education
James E. Baum	American Bankers Association
Paul J. McCauley	Ass't Atty. General, NY State in Charge of Bureau Of Securities
James A. Beha	Former Superintendent of Insurance NY State, General Manager & Counsel, National Bureau of Casualty & Surety Underwriters
William Lewis Butcher	Once of NY State Crime Commission (August 4)

F: Film

Most of the below details were obtained from the Internet Movie Database (imdb.com). Unless noted otherwise, Reeve was the official scenarist. In many cases, Reeve supplied the story while others wrote the screenplay. Film-writing credits in those days, however, were not always fairly or accurately attributed. The script could be completely rewritten with the credit remaining with the original author; or, and this would be a potential problem with Reeve, a famous-name author might sell his name to a project while having little or nothing to do with developing the script.

The Exploits of Elaine (1914)
Studio: Pathé
Directors: Louis J. Gasnier, George B.
    Seitz, Leopold Wharton
Format: 14-part serial
Scenarist: Charles William Goddard
Stars: Pearl White (Elaine Dodge),
    Arnold Daly (Craig Kennedy)
Other characters: , Walter Jameson,
    Wu Fang, The Clutching Hand
Release date: December 29, 1914
Notes: Named to the National Film
    Registry, Library of Congress

The New Exploits of Elaine (1915)
Studio: Pathé
Directors: Louis J. Gasnier, Leopold
    Wharton, Theodore Wharton
Format: 10-part serial
Stars: Pearl White (Elaine Dodge),
    Arnold Daly (Craig Kennedy)
Release date: April 5, 1915

The Romance of Elaine (1915)
Studio: Pathé
Directors: George B. Seitz, Leopold
    Wharton, Theodore Wharton
Format: 12-part serial
Stars: Pearl White (Elaine Dodge),
    Arnold Daly (Craig Kennedy),
    Lionel Barrymore (Mr. X)
Other stars: Warner Oland
Other characters: Walter Jameson
Release date: June 14, 1915

The Indianapolis Star, November 28, 1917

The Hidden Hand (1917)

Studio: Pathé
Format: 15-part serial
Co-scenarist: Charles A. Logue
Star: Doris Kenyon
Release date: November 25, 1917

The House of Hate (1918)

Studio: Pathé
Director: George B. Seitz
Format: 20-part serial
Co-scenarist: Charles A. Logue
Star: Pearl White (Pearl Grant)
Release date: March 10, 1918

The Master Mystery (1919)

Studio: Octagon Films, Inc.
Directors: Harry Grossman, Burton L. King
Format: 15-part serial
Co-scenarist: Charles A. Logue
Star: Harry Houdini (Quentin Locke)
Other characters: Q, the Automaton
Release date: March 1, 1919 (East); May 1, 1919 (West)

The Master Mystery
(French poster)

The Carter Case (1919)

Studio: Oliver Films
Directors: William F. Haddock, Donald MacKenzie
Format: 15-part serial
Co-scenarist: John W. Grey
Stars: Herbert Rawlinson (Craig Kennedy)
Other characters: William Pike (Walter Jameson)
Release date: March 17, 1919

The Tiger's Trail (1919)

Studio: Pathé
Directors: Robert Ellis, Louis J. Gasnier, Paul Hurst
Format: 15-part serial
Co-scenarists: Charles A. Logue, Frank Leon Smith
Star: Ruth Roland (Belle Boyd), Harry Moody (Tiger Face)
Release date: April 20, 1919
Notes: This serial was originally advertized as *The Long Arm*, an urban melodrama written by Reeve. Frank Leon Smith claimed credit for rewriting it as *The Tiger's Trail*, a western featuring Hindu tiger worshippers.

The Grim Game (1919)
Studio: Famous Players-Lasky
Director: Irvin Willat
Format: feature
Co-scenarist: John W. Grey
Star: Harry Houdini (Harvey Hanford)
Release date: August 25, 1919

The $1,000,000 Reward (1920)
Studio: Grossman Pictures
Directors: Harry Grossman, George Lessey
Format: 15-part serial
Co-scenarist: John W. Grey
Star: Lillian Walker
Release date: January 1920

Terror Island (1920)
Studio: Famous Players-Lasky
Director: James Cruze
Format: feature
Co-scenarist: John W. Grey
Star: Harry Houdini (Harry Harper)
Release date: April 1920

The Mystery Mind (1920)
Studio: Supreme Pictures
Directors: Will S. Davis, Fred Sittenham
Format: 15-part serial
Co-scenarist: John W. Grey
Star: J. Robert Pauline (Dr. Robert Dupont)
Release date: September 6, 1920

The Radio Detective (1926)
Studio: Universal
Directors: William James Craft, William A. Crinley
Format: 10-part serial
Star: Jack Daugherty (Eastern Evans), Jack Mower (Craig Kennedy)
Other characters: the Boy Scouts
Release date: April 26, 1926

The Return of the Riddle Rider (1927)
    Studio: Universal
    Director: Robert F. Hill
    Format: 10-part serial
    Co-scenarist: Fred McConnell
    Star: William Desmond
    Release date: March 8, 1927

The Mysterious Airman (1928)
    Studio: Weiss Brothers
    Director: Harry Revier
    Format: 10-part serial
    Star: Walter Miller (Jack Baker)
    Release date: June 1, 1928

Unmasked (1929)
    Studio: Weiss Brothers
    Director: Edgar Lewis
    Format: feature
    Scenarists: Edward Clark, Bert Ennis (dialogue), Albert Cowles (scenario)
    Star: Robert Warwick (Craig Kennedy)
    Release date: December 15, 1929; December 2, 1931 (re-release)
    Notes: First Craig Kennedy feature film; first Reeve talkie.

Finger Prints (1931)
    Studio: Universal
    Director: Ray Taylor
    Format: 10-part serial
    Scenarist: Basil Dickey
    Star: Kenneth Harlan (Gary Gordon)
    Release date: March 3, 1931

The Clutching Hand (1936)
    Studio: Weiss Serials
    Director: Albert Herman
    Format: 15-part serial
    Co-scenarists: Leon D'Usseau, Dallas M. Fitzgerald
    Star: Jack Mulhall (Craig Kennedy), Rex Lease (Walter Jameson)
    Other characters: Mae Busch (Mrs. Gironda), Yakima Canutt (Number Eight)
    Release date: April 18, 1936

The San Antonio Evening News, August 15, 1919

AMUSEMENTS
At the Royal

As the scientific detective, Craig Kennedy, which Herbert Rawlinson portrays in the serial film, "The Carter Case," showing at the Royal, he fights a continuous battle royal, in which his brains and ingenuity are no less displayed than his superb muscular prowess. Calling for the exercise of every intellectual as well as physical endowment the part is particularly suited to the star.

"Craig Kennedy has fascinated me," says Mr. Rawlinson, "ever since I read the first of the stories. I was laid up at the time with a broken leg. Complications had set in and the doctors threatened amputation. I was blue! Then a friend brought me a volume of Arthur B. Reeve's stories and I started to kid myself into seeing myself as the great detective scientist. Well, it must be true that visualizing yourself hard enough in any part will get you that part. For here I am!

"You see, chemistry and physics have been my hobby since school days. And Oliver Films, Inc., fitted up a little laboratory next to my dressing room in the studio for me to fuss with in off moments. Here I tried out Kennedy's experiments before doing them in the camera. There was lots of excitement when I got going at them.

"Then, too, Kennedy is such an all-around chap that I was kept jumping to keep up with him. I punched the bag and skinned the cat, swung clubs and boxed to keep in trim for the real fights which Kennedy, the sleuth, never dodges. My little gym in the studio got much of my spare time.

"You see, I had to keep fit or get licked. And seeing Kennedy get licked would just about start a riot among the thousands of his admirers."

The Royal bill also includes five acts of Pantages vaudeville and Alice Brady in "The World to Live In."

G: Television

In 1944, the Weiss Brothers, for whom Reeve wrote three films—*The Mysterious Airman* (1928), *Unmasked* (1929), *The Clutching Hand* (1936)—bought the rights to the Craig Kennedy stories. Adrian Weiss, son of founding brother Louis, took over the company in 1948 and began developing the company's properties for television. The syndicated series lasted one season and starred Donald Woods as Craig Kennedy and Lewis G. Wilson as Walter Jameson. Jack Mulhall, who played Craig Kennedy in *The Clutching Hand*, appeared in supporting parts. :: In 2006, VCI Entertainment issued a 2-disk DVD set with 13 of the 30-minute episodes (indicated in **boldface** below).

Craig Kennedy, Criminologist (1952)

episodes

1	**The Big Shakedown**
2	Dead Right
3	**The Case of Fleming Lewis**
4	**The False Claimant**
5	File 1313
6	**Formula for Murder**
7	I Hate Money
8	**The Amateur Ghost**
9	**1616 Hidden Lane Road**
10	**The Indian Giver**
11	The Kid Brother
12	**The Late Corpse**
13	**The Lonely Hearts Club**
14	**Murder Preferred**
15	**Murder on Stage 9**
16	**The Strange Destiny**
17	**Fugitive Money**
18	The Trap
19	The Mummy's Secret
20	The Secret Will
21	Murder on a Million
22	The Vanisher
23	There's Money In It
24	The Golden Dagger
25	Tall, Dark and Dead
26	The Mystery Bullet

CRAIG KENNEDY CRIMINOLOGIST

DONALD WOODS as "CRAIG KENNEDY"

LEWIS G. WILSON as "WALTER JAMESON"

IV

Bibliography

"The Actor Who Economized." *NYT*, Feb 8, 1914. Mentions an upcoming Craig Kennedy play, to be written by Brandon Tynan.

"*The Adventuress.*" *Boston Daily Globe*, Jan 5, 1918. Book review.

"*The Adventuress.*" *NYT*, Dec 9, 1917. Book review.

Amusements (column). *The San Antonio Evening News*, Aug 15, 1919. Interview with Herbert Rawlinson, the actor playing Craig Kennedy in the film, *The Carter Case*.

"Arthur B. Reeve." *The Writer*, June 1914. Brief biography.

"Arthur B. Reeve, Author, Dies at 55." *NYT*, Aug 10, 1936.

"Arthur B. Reeve Rites Wednesday." *Trenton Evening Times*, Aug 10, 1936.

"Arthur B. Reeve's House Sold." *NYT*, Dec 2, 1937. Sale of Northport, Long Island house belonging to Reeve.

"Arthur Maurice, Author, 73, Dead." *NYT*, Jun 1, 1946.

Ashley, Mike. "The Houdini Chain." *Postscripts* Number 6, Spring 2006; 80-89.

"Authors' Club Sale for Belgian Relief." *NYT*, May 13, 1915. Reeve listed as donating material for an Authors' Club of New York benefit.

"Authors Form Society to Fight Censorship." *The Washington Post*, May 1, 1927; 6. Reeve joined 40 other leading authors to form the Committee for the Suppression of Irresponsible Censorship.

"Bannock Mystery Is Very Crude." *The Hartford Courant*, May 25, 1915. Review of early performance of the Craig Kennedy play.

Barzun, Jacques and Wendall Hertig Taylor. *A Catalog of Crime*. Harper & Row, 1971; 548.

Berch, Victor A., Karl Schadow & Steve Lewis. *Murder Clinic: Radio's Golden Age of Detection*. 2006. Web page: http://www.mysteryfile.com/M_Clinic.html.

"Best Writers Join in Battle on Prohibition." *The Sheboygan Press*, Apr 29, 1929. Reeve listed with 212 writers who formed committee to join the Association Against the Prohibition Amendment.

"Bishop Dedicates New Hospital Unit." *NYT*, Jul 21, 1930. Reeve gave brief address at dedication of Long Island hospital.

Book Notes (column). *NYT*, Mar 17, 1932. Item in column announces Reeve's *The Kidnap Club*.

Books and Authors (column). *NYT*, Jun 6, 1915. Item quotes Reeve explaining background of science in Craig Kennedy stories.

——. Jan 30, 1921. Item describes Reeve being sworn in as foreman of the Federal Grand Jury in Brooklyn. Reference is made to a lengthy editorial in a "New York newspaper" expressing surprise that Reeve lived in the "Borough of Baby Carriages."

——. Feb 12, 1922. Item reports "nearly a million" copies of Reeve's books sold in the U.S. and Great Britain.

——. Jun 22, 1924. Item discusses Reeve's background.

——. Aug 23, 1925. Item describes Reeve's multiple sales of *The Radio Detective*.

——. Dec 27, 1925. Item reports on Reeve's Long Island real estate interests.

——. Jul 19, 1931. Item on John Day Company pamphleteering.

"Boston Student Has Signatures of Famous Men." *The Daily News* (Huntingdon, Penn.), Mar 26, 1930. Reeve wrote "With Kindest Regards of 'Craig Kennedy' himself" in famous signature book.

Butcher, Fanny. News and Notes of Books and of the Authors (column). *Chicago Daily Tribune*, Aug 10, 1918; 9. Item mentions Reeve's home in Northport, Long Island.

"Cape May." *NYT*, Aug 10, 1902. Reeve mentioned in social column as a "well-known Princeton man who has joined the large number of undergraduates of that university here."

"Chance and Norman Trevor." *NYT*, Feb 18, 1917. Profile of actor who played Craig Kennedy on stage.

Chronicle and Comment (column). *The Bookman*, April 1913. Brief biography.

"*The Clutching Hand*." *NYT*, Apr 29, 1934. Book review.

"Commencement Day at Old Nassau." *NYT*, Jun 11, 1903. Reeve mentioned as winning award for Political Economy.

Cook, Michael L. *Mystery, Detective, and Espionage Magazines*. Greenwood Press, 1983; 468-470.

"The Cosmopolitan of Ray Long." *Fortune*, March 1931; 49-50.

Cox, J. Randolph. "Arthur B. Reeve." In *Critical Survey of Mystery and Detective Fiction: Authors Pot-Z Index*. Pasadena, California; Englewood Cliffs, NJ: Salem Press, 1989; 1395-1400.

——. Letters to Leo Margulies, Jan 9, Feb 3, Apr 2, Jul 1, Jul 23, 1975. Leo Margulies Papers, Special Collections and University Archives, University of Oregon Libraries.

——. "A Reading of Reeve: Some Thoughts on the Creator of Craig Kennedy." *The Armchair Detective*, January 1978. Appended with extensive bibliography of book and periodical appearances.

"Craig Kennedy, Scientific Sleuth, Is Tracked Down." *The Olean Evening Times* (New York), Apr 20, 1923. Profile of Dr. Otto Schultze, inspiration for Craig Kennedy.

"Craig Kennedy Tales To Be Filmed." *The Hartford Courant*, Feb 29, 1920. Reports on contract between Reeve and Goldwyn Pictures to produce four Craig Kennedy films.

Crime Crusade Foundation. Two undated brochures, 1931. Archives of John Day Company, Inc., Box 52, Folder 18, Manuscripts Division, Department of Rare Books and Special Collections, Princeton University Library. 1) Contains "A Message from Arthur B. Reeve"; "What Price Crime?" by Reeve, reprinted from the Mar 22, 1931 *New York Herald-Tribune Sunday Magazine*; and "Program: Crime Crusade Foundation." 2) Contains "Crime Problems in the Oil Industry" by Silas M. Newton, printing an address given on *Crime Prevention Program*, Mar 20, 1931; "Announcement" by Reeve, printing a speech given on the same show.

"Crime Prevention Bill Over KGO." *The Oakland Tribune*, Jul 27, 1930. Lists cast members in Reeve's radio show, *Crime Prevention Program*.

"Crime's Gauntlet Flung Down to U.S. Criminologist Says." *The San Antonio Express*, Dec 27, 1930. Report on Reeve's address on the *Crime Prevention Program* radio show.

"Critchell Rimington Dies at 68; Publisher of Yachting Magazine." *NYT*, Feb 1, 1976.

Cushing, Charles Phelps. "Who Writes These Mystery Yarns?" *The Independent*, Apr 9, 1927. Photo-illustrated article. Includes discussion of Reeve and many other mystery writers including Arthur Conan Doyle, Carolyn Wells, G.K. Chesterton, E. Phillips Oppenheim, Sax Rohmer, etc.

Davis, Robert H. Introduction to *The Fourteen Points* by Arthur B. Reeve. Harper & Brothers, 1925; vii-xiii.

Delaney, John J. and James Edward Tobin. *Dictionary of Catholic Biography*. Doubleday, 1961; 979. Mentions Reeve's 1926 conversion to Catholicism.

"Detective Author Heads Grand Jury." *NYT*, Jan 6, 1921. Reeve was foreman of a Federal Grand Jury. His address was listed as 92 South Oxford Street, Brooklyn.

Dizer, Dr. John T. "The Birth and Boyhood of *Boys' Life*." On-line article at http://www. scoutingmagazine.org.

"Dr. Schultze Dead; Famed as Coroner." *NYT*, Jul 5, 1934. Reeve's close friendship with Otto H. Schultze, and the possibility that Schultze was the prototype for Craig Kennedy, is mentioned.

"*The Dream Doctor*." *NYT*, May 24, 1914. Book review.

Dunlap, Orrin E. Jr. "Reeve to Write" in *Listening In* (column), *NYT*, Jul 6, 1930. Reeve's authorship of upcoming radio detective series is announced.

Dunning, John. *The Encyclopedia of Old-Time Radio*. Oxford University Press, 1998.

"Dupin and Sherlock Holmes as Book Reviewers." *NYT*, Jan 23, 1921. A raft of mystery book reviews is written as a conversation between Sherlock Holmes, Auguste Dupin, and Craig Kennedy.

Educational Notes: Boys' High School (column). *The Brooklyn Daily Eagle*, Feb 23, 1896; 21. In his first freshman semester, Reeve was one of 22 boys (out of 1,094) to score over 90% on final exams.

——. Feb 28, 1897; 12. In his first sophomore semester, Reeve was one of 24 boys (out of 1,009) to score over 90% on final exams.

——. Jun 19, 1898; 49. Reeve was awarded a staff position on the *High School Recorder* for the upcoming fall. He shared responsibility for "societies" with another student.

——. Dec 25, 1898; 19. Reeve is mentioned twice. 1) He declaimed "The Blind Organist" at the Christmas exercises. 2) He contributed "a set of amusing 'Interscholastic Sonnets' " to the *High School Recorder*.

——. Jan 7, 1900; 38. During the Christmas holidays, Reeve attended a reunion of the class of February '99, and spoke about college.

"Eighty-Four Graduates." *The Brooklyn Daily Eagle*, Feb 11, 1899; 9. Reeve was one of 84 graduates of Boys' High School, Brooklyn, and one of 24 in the Academic course. As valedictorian he delivered the address, "American Characteristics."

"*Enter Craig Kennedy*." *NYT*, Nov 3, 1935. Book review.

The Evening World, Sep 6, 1930. Unnamed article is mentioned in *The Golden Age of Crime*; a lengthy quote describes Reeve's rebuff to gangsters eager to utilize his knowledge of crime.

"*The Film Mystery*." *NYT*, Mar 13, 1921. Book review.

Flynn, Joseph C.H. " 'Little Women' and Big Events." *NYT*, Dec 20, 1931. Letter from Assistant Attorney General of State of New York reminisces about press coverage, including reporter Reeve, of the first Charles Becker trial (October 1912).

"Foolish Figures." *The Helena Daily Independent*, Sep 11, 1925. Editorial questions recent Reeve criticism of the vast number of laws in the U.S.

Gentry, Curt. *J. Edgar Hoover: The Man and the Secrets*. W.W. Norton & Company, 1991.

"*The Gold of the Gods*." *NYT*, Jan 30, 1916; Book Review 39.

Grost, Michael E. "Arthur B. Reeve." In *A Guide to Classic Mystery and Detection*. Internet site: http://home.aol.com/MG4273/moffett.htm#Reeve.

"*Guy Garrick*." *NYT*, Nov 1, 1914. Book review.

"Harry K. Thaw Sued By Two Scenarists." *NYT*, Feb 26, 1928. Reeve and a co-scenarist sued Thaw, a movie producer, for failing to pay for eleven contracted scripts about ghosts and fake mediums.

Harwood, John. "Arthur B. Reeve and the American Sherlock Holmes." *The Armchair Detective*, October 1977.

——. "Arthur Benjamin Reeve." *Twentieth Century Crime and Mystery Writers*, John M. Reilly, editor. Second Edition. St. Martin's Press, 1985; 754-756.

Haycraft, Howard. *Murder For Pleasure: The Life and Times of the Detective Story*. Biblio and Tannen, 1974; 98-99, 329, 337-339.

Here and There (column). *The Indianapolis Star*, Jun 22, 1924. Brief biography.

Hubin, Allen J. *Crime Fiction IV: A Comprehensive Bibliography 1749-2000*. Volume III: Author Index N-Z. The Battered Silicon Dispatch Box, 2003; 1258.

"Huge Wire Service Set Up For Trial." *NYT*, Jan 2, 1935. Article describes extreme measures taken to wire the Flemington, New Jersey, courthouse where Bruno Richard Hauptmann was tried for kidnapping the Lindbergh baby. It also lists celebrity journalists expected to attend, including Reeve.

"Hypnotic Movies." *The Waterloo Times-Tribune*, Jun 12, 1921. Report on hypnotism comedies with J. Robert Pauline, written by Reeve.

"James K. Hackett to Produce a Play." *NYT*, Mar 28, 1915. Announcement of Craig Kennedy play.

The John Day Company. Author contract for *What Price Crime?*, Apr 1, 1931. Archives of John Day Company, Inc., Box 52, Folder 18, Manuscripts Division, Department of Rare Books and Special Collections, Princeton University Library.

Johnston, Elma Lawson. "Lays Increase in Crime to Prohibition." *Trenton Sunday Times Advertiser*, May 22, 1932. A major interview with Reeve that followed his move to Trenton.

Kaye, Joseph. *When I Was Twenty-One* (syndicated column). *Lime Springs Sun-Herald*, Aug 12, 1926. Reeve supplies brief bio.

"*The Kidnap Club*." *NYT*, Apr 24, 1932. Book review.

Lahue, Kalton C. *Continued Next Week: A History of the Moving Picture Serial*. University of Oklahoma Press, 1964.

Literati on the Coast (column). *The Washington Post*, Apr 25, 1920. Reports details of first Goldwyn Pictures Craig Kennedy film. Mentions Reeve's "many years of work with the Charity Organization Society of New York."

Long, Bruce. "Did Drug Gangsters Kill Taylor?" *Taylorology* 94, October 2000. Available at: http://www.silent-movies.com/Taylorology/.

Long, Ray. *20 Best Short Stories in Ray Long's 20 Years as an Editor*. Crown Publishers, 1932; vi.

"Managers Promise Many Plays." *NYT*, Jul 18, 1926. A Craig Kennedy play is included in catalog of announcements.

" 'The Man in Request' in Reheasal." *NYT*, Apr 29, 1915; 14. Item mentions the upcoming Craig Kennedy play.

"Many Republicans Aid Wilson Tribute." *NYT*, Jan 22, 1922. Reeve listed as contributor.

Margulies, Leo. Letter to J. Randolph Cox, Jan 28, 1975.

——. Letter to J. Randolph Cox, Mar 17, 1975.

McEvoy, J.P. "The Panama Plot: Being a Review in Rime of Arthur B. Reeve's Novel of That Title." *Chicago Daily Tribune*, May 4, 1918; 9.

"Miss Wilson To Be Bride." *Trenton Times*, Jan 30, 1906. Announced Reeve's wedding with brief background of wife and groom.

Moore, Louis. *The Fourteen Points* (review). *Literary Digest International Book Review*, Jun 1925; 471-472,474.

Moskowitz, Sam. *Science Fiction by Gaslight: A History and Anthology of Science Fiction in the Popular Magazines, 1891-1911*. The World Publishing Company, 1968.

——. *Strange Horizons: The Spectrum of Science Fiction*. Charles Scribner's Sons, 1976.

Mott, Frank Luther. *A History of American Magazines*. Volume II: 1850-1865. Cambridge: Harvard University Press, 1957. In particular, "The Country Gentleman"; 432-436.

——. *A History of American Magazines*. Volume IV: 1885-1905. Cambridge: Harvard University Press, 1957. In particular, Sketch 10 of the Supplement, "Cosmopolitan; Hearst's International"; 480-505.

——. *A History of American Magazines*. Volume V: Sketches of 21 Magazines 1905-1930. Cambridge: Harvard University Press, 1968. In particular, "Everybody's Magazine"; 85-86.

"Movie Director Dies in a Three-story Fall." *NYT*, Dec 7, 1925. Describes death of Sena Morena, a 29-year-old movie director who shared Reeve's Manhattan office. Whether suicide or accident remained in dispute.

"N.B.C. Lifts Crime Plots From Police." *The Syracuse Herald*, Aug 3, 1930. Behind the scenes details of Reeve's radio show, *Crime Prevention Program*.

"New Incorporations." *NYT*, Dec 21, 1918. Lists new charter of "Arthur B. Reeve and John W. Grey, Inc.," capitalization of $10,000. A.H. Small also listed.

——. Nov 11, 1932. Lists new charter in Trenton, NJ, of "Arthur B. Reeve, Inc," capitalized with 100 shares of common stock; nature of business as "motion pictures, plays, radio productions." Ellis L. Pearson, Trenton, also listed.

"News and Near News of Plays and the Players." *The Washington Post*, Oct 5, 1913. Reports on upcoming Craig Kennedy play.

"Notes of Social Activities in New York and Elsewhere." *NYT*, Sep 17, 1931. Reeve noted as "chairman of the committee" of the Englewood (New Jersey) Dahlia Society.

Obituary. *Publisher's Weekly*, Aug 15, 1936; 508.

"Official Favors Criticism." *NYT*, May 5, 1915. Reeve and Medical Examiner Otto H. Schultze listed among the speakers at Rotary Club of New York.

"Our Polar Expeditions." *The Brooklyn Daily Eagle*, Sep 25, 1897; 5. Reeve won second prize in the All Souls' Universalist Church essay contest on the title subject. Reeve was cited for entering the competition five times in succession, winning honorable mention twice. His address was listed as 273½ Skillman Avenue.

"*The Panama Plot.*" *NYT*, May 26, 1918. Book review.

"*Pandora.*" *Saturday Review of Literature*, Oct 1926; 261. Book review.

Parade (column). *The Literary Digest*, Aug 22, 1936; 38. Brief obituary.

Paragraph Glimpses of the Mimic World (column). *The Indianapolis Sunday Star*, May 30, 1915. Announces start of Craig Kennedy play tour.

The Passing Show (column). *The Syracuse Herald*, Jun 27, 1915. Item announcing the shelving of the Craig Kennedy play.

"Patchogue." *NYT*, Jul 28, 1895. Reeve listed as "among the arrivals."

Portrait. *The Independent*, Apr 9, 1927; 386.

——. *Illustrated London News*, Jun 27, 1953; 1095.

"Public Enemies Dwindle." *The Lincoln Star*, Dec 21, 1934. Editorial repeats Reeve's argument on the dwindling of the public enemies list in the previous three years.

A Reader's Notes (column). *The Indianapolis Star*, Jan 31, 1922. Brief item reports on Reeve connecting himself with a real detective agency in NYC to study the "new criminal."

"A Real Detective Story." *The Hartford Courant*, Sep 19, 1931. Editorial comments on Reeve's theories of the Benjamin Collings murder case.

Reeve, Arthur B. Letters to Arthur Bartlett Maurice, Jul 17, 1922, May 13, 1924. Archives of John Day Company, Inc., Box 1, Folder 84, Manuscripts Division, Department of Rare Books and Special Collections, Princeton University Library.

——. Letter to Critchell Rimington, Mar 25, 1931, on Crime Crusade Foundation letterhead. Archives of John Day Company, Inc., Box 52, Folder 18.

——. Outline of *What Price Crime?*, undated. Archives of John Day Company, Inc., Box 52, Folder 18.

——. Letters to Critchell Rimington, Jun 23, Jul 20, Jul 29, 1931, on Craig Kennedy Service Corporation letterhead. Archives of John Day Company, Inc., Box 52, Folder 18

——. Letter to Leo Margules, Feb 27, 1935. Leo Margulies Papers, Coll. 133, Folder 8, Box 9, Special Collections and University Archives, University of Oregon Libraries.

"Reeve Files as Bankrupt." *NYT*, Sep 14, 1928. Reeve listed assets of $600, liabilities of $39,271.

"Reeve Fire Called Arson." *NYT*, Apr 25, 1930. Kennel house on Reeve's Long Island estate destroyed, possibly in retaliation for denial of clam- and worm-digging rights on Reeve's property.

"Reeve Gets Tip Billy Dansey is Alive on Coast." *Trenton Evening Times*, Dec 20, 1919; 1. Report on Reeve receiving letter purporting to explain missing boy mystery. Syndicated national news story.

"Reeve Plaintiff in Suit Against Thaw." *The Charleston Daily Mail*, Feb 25, 1928.

"Reeve Rites Tomorrow." *NYT*, Aug 11, 1936.

"Reeve-Wilson Wedding Today." *Trenton Times*, Jan 31, 1906.

Rimington, Critchell. Letters to Reeve, Mar 30, May 12, May 19, Aug 11, Aug 15, Aug 29, Nov 24, 1931. Archives of John Day Company, Inc., Box 52, Folder 18, Manuscripts Division, Department of Rare Books and Special Collections, Princeton University Library.

———. Letters to Reeve, Dec 12, Dec 20, 1934. Archives of John Day Company, Inc., Box 107, Folder 33.

Sampson, Robert. *Yesterday's Faces: Volume 2: Strange Days*. Bowling Green University Popular Press, 1984; 23-46.

"Science's Weird Laboratory of Startling New Murder Stunts." *The Odgen Standard-Examiner* (Utah), Mar 30, 1930. Reeve profiled as one of many detective-story writers who visited New York's Museum of Peaceful Arts for ingenious plot ideas.

"The Scientific Detective." *Dime Detective Magazine*, Oct 1, 1933; 125-126.

"Scouts Mobilize Authors to Fight Dime Novels." *The Davenport Democrat and Leader*, Oct 21, 1923.

"746 Drivers Lose Licenses in State." *NYT*, Jul 15, 1927. Reeve listed as among 35 drivers who had their licenses revoked in the Manhattan district. Reeve's listed address is his Manhattan office.

Small Talk of the Stage and Its People (column). *Chicago Daily Tribune*, Sep 28, 1913. Mentions upcoming Craig Kennedy play.

"*The Soul Scar.*" *NYT*, Dec 21, 1919. Book review.

The Stage and Stage People (column). The Oakland Tribune, July 11, 1915. Item mentions James K. Hackett self-financing the Craig Kennedy play.

"*The Stars Scream Murder.*" *NYT*, Mar 29, 1936. Book review.

"The Story of Norman Trevor." *NYT*, Nov 11, 1917. Profile of actor who played Craig Kennedy on stage.

"Suffragists See Miss Davis at Work: Women's Political Union Delegation Calls on New Commissioner of Correction." *NYT*, Jan 6, 1914. "Mrs. Arthur B. Reeve" listed as one of the suffragists.

"Thaw Finally Wins a Verdict." *The Clearfield Progress* (Pennsylvania), Feb 12, 1930.

"Thaw Movie Suit Up in Winchester." *The Washington Post*, Mar 27, 1935. Continuation of legal fight between Harry K. Thaw and Reeve writing partner, John S. Lopez.

"Thaw Slapped By a Woman." *NYT*, Jun 16, 1927. Details of Harry Thaw's film plans.

"To Stage 'A Grain of Dust.' " *NYT*, Jun 27, 1911. Early mention of James K. Hackett's intentions for a Craig Kennedy play.

"Trenton Grads Do Much Writing." *Trenton Evening Times*, Oct 8, 1909. Reeve mentioned with Princeton graduates prominent in literary circles.

"An Up-to-date Detective: *The Poisoned Pen.*" *NYT*, Apr 6, 1913; Book Review 211.

Van Dover, J.K. "The Case of Craig Kennedy: Science in Pursuit of Crime." *Clues: A Journal of Detection*, Fall-Winter 1991; 115-29.

———. *You Know My Method: The Science of the Detective*. Chapter 8: Arthur B. Reeve. Bowling Green State University Popular Press, 1994; 159-189, 231-238.

Van Raalte, Joseph. *Bo-Broadway* (column). *The Chester Times* (Pennsylvania), Feb 5, 1931. Item about Reeve's strange mail.

Walsh, Richard J. Letter to Reeve, Aug 5, 1931. Archives of John Day Company, Inc., Box 52, Folder 18, Manuscripts Division, Department of Rare Books and Special Collections, Princeton University Library.

"*The War Terror.*" *NYT*, Apr 25, 1915. Book review.

"The Week at Long Island Resorts: Patchogue." *NYT*, Jul 28, 1895. Reeve mentioned in list of "arrivals" from New York and Brooklyn.

Weisinger, Mort. "Pseudonym Sidelights." *The Author & Journalist*, August 1935; 7.

Wells, Carolyn. *The Technique of the Mystery Story*. Chapter 6: The Scientific Detective of Fiction. The Home Correspondence School, 1913; 81-84.

Williams, Vera. "He Wrote 'The Perils of Pauline.'" *Independent Press-Telegram Southland Magazine* (Long Beach), Sep 9, 1956. Profile of silent-film writer, Basil Dickey, who claimed authorship of *The Exploits of Elaine* serial.

"With the Producers and Players." Column in *NYT*, Sep 27, 1927, includes comment about yachting scene from *The Radio Detective* being shot on Long Island.

"W.J. Flynn, Noted Detective, Dead." *NYT*, Oct 15, 1928.

Wright, Willard Huntington. "The Great Detective Stories." In *The Art of the Mystery Story: A Collection of Critical Essays*, Howard Haycraft, editor. Simon and Schuster, 1946; 48.

"Writer Pictures War of Today in Magazine of 1908." (Seattle, Associated Press) *Oshkosh Daily Northwestern*, Aug 5, 1940. Article recounts predictions for 1938 warfare made in Reeve's Nov 18, 1908 *Hampton's Broadway* article, "Newest Man-Killing Devices and the Warless Age."

Notes

1) There were other Arthur Reeves in the New York/New Jersey area, and at least one other Arthur B. Reeve, so newspaper listings were treated with caution.

2) In his February 27, 1935 letter to Leo Margulies, Reeve refers to recognition in *The Literary Digest*, but dates of such references are unknown.

Index

ALSO FROM OFF-TRAIL PUBLICATIONS

from **GHOULS** to
GANGSTERS

THE CAREER OF ARTHUR B. REEVE

VOLUME 1

Edited by John Locke

Volume 1 features short fiction from all phases of Reeve's career: slicks, pulps, and newspapers, all from the original publications. $20